T0349946

Praise for James Gould-Bourn

'Touching and often hilarious . . .
A truly joyful read'
Press & Journal

'A delightful story about fatherhood and childhood'
Owen King

James Gould-Bourn was born and raised in Manchester. He is an award-winning screenwriter and has previously worked for various landmine clearance NGOs in Africa and the Middle East. *Lost & Found* is his second novel.

Also by James Gould-Bourn

Keeping Mum

James Gould-Bourn

LOST & FOUND

ORION

An Orion paperback
First published in Great Britain in 2023 by Orion Fiction
an imprint of The Orion Publishing Group Ltd
Carmelite House, 50 Victoria Embankment
London EC4Y 0DZ

An Hachette UK Company

1 3 5 7 9 10 8 6 4 2

A CIP catalogue record for this book is
available from the British Library.

ISBN (Mass Market Paperback) 978 1 4091 9132 2
ISBN (eBook) 978 1 4091 9133 9
ISBN (Audio) 978 1 4091 9134 6

Typeset by Born Group
Printed and bound in Great Britain by Clays Ltd, Elcograf S.p.A.

MIX
Paper from
responsible sources
FSC® C104740

www.orionbooks.co.uk

For my wife, Vanessa Valentino

Prologue

'Good evening, my name is Kevin and you're through to the Listening Line.'

'Hi, Kevin, nice to meet you. I'm Ronnie and . . . Wait, should I give you my real name or a fake one?'

'Whatever you're most comfortable with. All of these calls are confidential.'

'OK. You can call me Ronnie then,' said Ronnie. 'It's not my real name though,' he added, suddenly losing his nerve.

'Not a problem at all. How are you feeling today, Ronnie?'

'Not great, to be honest.'

'I'm sorry to hear that. Would you like to tell me about it?'

'It's a bit embarrassing.'

'The Listening Line is a safe space. We don't judge anybody here.'

'Right. Well, that's good to know,' said Ronnie. 'I just . . . The thing is . . . the thing is that . . . well, how do I put this?'

The line went quiet for a few seconds.

'Hello?' said Kevin.

'I'm here. I was asking how I should put this.'

'Oh. I thought you were being rhetorical.'

'No, I really have no idea how to put this,' said Ronnie.

'Right. The thing is that I can't really tell you how to put it if I don't know what *it* is.'

'I've lost my shadow,' said Ronnie.

The line went quiet again.

'I'm sorry,' said Kevin. 'I didn't quite get that.'

'I said I've lost my shadow.'

'You've lost your shadow?' said Kevin.

Ronnie cleared his throat. 'That's correct,' he said. 'Or it's lost me. Either way, we've somehow become separated.'

Kevin didn't say anything for a moment. Ronnie was just about to ask if he was still there when Kevin started to laugh.

'Very funny, Mike,' said Kevin.

'Who's Mike?'

'Seriously, quit arsing about, I'm working here.'

'I think you're mistaking me for somebody else.'

Kevin stopped laughing. 'You're not Mike?'

'No, I'm Ronnie,' said Ronnie. 'That's not my real name though.'

'You mean this isn't a wind-up?'

'This isn't a wind-up,' said Ronnie. 'I wish it was.'

'Right,' said Kevin. 'Sorry. I thought . . . Sorry.' Ronnie could hear Kevin frantically leafing through a book of some description. 'Lost shadow, lost shadow . . .' he muttered. 'This sort of thing happen often then, does it?'

2

'No. Never. This is the first time.'

'Right. And when did you last see your shadow exactly?'

'I don't know,' said Ronnie. 'It's not really the sort of thing you pay much attention to, is it?'

'No, I suppose it isn't,' said Kevin. 'When you say it disappeared, did you actually *see* it disappear?'

'No, I just suddenly noticed that it wasn't there anymore.'

'Were you by any chance sitting in the dark at the time? Because you can't see shadows in the dark, can you?'

'I was at work.'

'And were the lights on?'

Ronnie sighed. 'Yes, the lights were on.'

'Right,' said Kevin, sounding a little deflated. Ronnie listened to the sound of more pages turning. 'It's a shame Carol isn't working today. She's really good with this sort of stuff.'

'You mean I'm not the first person to call about this?' said Ronnie, his voice infused with hope.

'Well, no, you *are* the first person to call about this, but, you know, Carol's been doing this for years, so she knows a lot more than I do. I just started recently. This is only my third week actually. I'm just working part time while I save up for uni.'

'What are you going to study?' asked Ronnie, feeling guilty for talking about himself so much, even though the telephone line was specifically set up so people could talk about themselves without feeling guilty. That was Ronnie in a nutshell.

'Engineering,' said Kevin. 'I wanted to study music, but my mum said there's no money in it.'

'I'm sure Barry Manilow would disagree.'

'Who?'

'Never mind,' said Ronnie. 'Is that what you want in life? To make money?'

'Not really. I just want to make music. I mean, money's nice to have, but I don't think it would make me happy.'

'Then you should do what *does* make you happy, whatever your mum thinks. You'll only regret it later if you don't.'

'Yeah. Yeah, you're right, I should,' said Kevin, a newfound sense of determination in his voice. 'Thanks, Ronnie.'

'No problem. Anything else I can assist you with today?' he joked.

Kevin laughed. 'Sorry, we were supposed to be talking about you,' he said. 'I'm a bit rubbish at this, aren't I?'

'Not at all. You're doing great.'

'I'll take your word for it.'

'Anyway, I better be off,' said Ronnie. 'This shadow isn't going to find itself.'

'Good luck,' said Kevin. 'Sorry I couldn't be more help. I hope it comes back soon.'

'I'm sure it will,' said Ronnie, trying to sound upbeat. 'I mean, how far can a shadow get on its own?'

Chapter One

The day Ronnie realised that his shadow was not where he'd left it – that is to say, attached to him – was an otherwise normal Wednesday. Not that it would have made any difference had it been a particularly abnormal Wednesday. Even if he'd woken up that morning to find that everything in his house had been stolen, including the bed in which he'd been sleeping, or he'd gone downstairs to find a Volkswagen Estate embedded in the wall of his living room with a semi-conscious badger slumped over the wheel, such scenarios would still seem comparatively normal if only for the fact that they were at least statistically possible, if not highly unlikely. Errant animals (if not specifically badgers) had been known to crash cars and nimble-fingered thieves had been known to steal the seemingly unstealable, but shadows were not known to abscond, evaporate, or whatever it was that Ronnie's shadow had done. It simply wasn't possible. And yet.

It all started with a snake, something that Bingham-on-Sea, like most towns in England, did not have a sizeable population of. Not wild ones anyway. There used to be a reptile house wedged between the joke shop and the games arcade on the seafront, but that had closed down years ago when the tourism dried up, much like the joke shop, the games arcade and most of the other small businesses in town.

Because of this, Ronnie was understandably alarmed to find what he thought was a cobra at work one day. He'd been hosing down the number 27 bus to Dibble Hill at the time, while his colleague, Carl, cleaned the inside. Ronnie was walking up and down the yard, giving the bus an even soaking, when suddenly something caught his eye. It was a shadow, projected onto the bus, of what looked like a snake reared up and swaying just inches from where he was standing.

Ronnie dropped the hose and stumbled backwards before tripping over a bucket and landing in the soapy suds he'd just upended onto the concrete. He looked around, his heart galloping, but the yard was distinctly void of wild animals, unless he counted Carl, who was busy picking his nose while simultaneously cleaning windows.

He stared at the spot where he'd just seen what he thought he'd seen, but all he saw now was the side of a bus. Ronnie smiled and shook his head.

'You're losing the plot,' he said to himself as he climbed back to his feet and grabbed the hose. It was only then that he understood what had startled him so much. It wasn't the shadow of a snake he'd seen but the shadow of the hose he'd been holding. This would not have been an easy mistake to make under normal circumstances. As Ronnie quickly realised, however, these were not normal circumstances because for reasons that were both mystifying and alarming, his shadow seemed to have disappeared. Not just a bit of it. Not just an arm or a leg of it. The whole thing, which meant that the hose he was holding now appeared to be holding itself upright, much like a snake, hence the confusion. Needless to say, whatever relief he felt about the snake situation was quickly overshadowed by the concern he now felt about the shadow situation.

He wiggled the hose and watched its shadow wiggle in return. He walked up and down the yard, raising and dipping his arm so the hose looked like it was slithering up and down the side of the bus. He did all of this with an expression not unlike the expression of somebody over forty watching a TikTok video for the first time.

'Oi, Ronnie!'

Ronnie flinched as Carl's voice snapped him back to reality.

'You all right, mate?' he shouted from the doorway of the bus. 'You're acting weirder than usual.'

'My shadow,' muttered Ronnie, pointing to the side of the bus.

'You what?'

As much as he would have liked a second opinion on the matter, Ronnie knew that Carl would never let him hear the end of it should it turn out to be nothing more than a bizarre figment of his imagination.

'Nothing,' said Ronnie.

Carl shrugged. 'Whatever,' he said and went back to work.

Ronnie frowned and looked around like the unsuspecting victim of a practical joke. But how could a practical joke make his shadow disappear? How could *anything* make his shadow disappear? Not only was he shocked to learn that his shadow had vanished, he was shocked to learn that his shadow *could* vanish. He'd never read about such a phenomenon, he'd never been warned about it and he'd never been informed by internet ad banners about how to remedy it with one simple life hack involving an unexpected household ingredient. It was quite possibly the only problem in the world for which no YouTube tutorial existed explaining how to fix it. The only person who might have even the slightest inkling about what was going on was his GP, Dr Sterling, with whom he already had an appointment booked after work for an unrelated matter. He decided to bring it up then.

Chapter Two

First-time visitors to Bingham would no doubt question why such a little town required such a large bus station. They would also probably wonder why a place that even Google had a hard time locating was once a popular target for German bombing practice, and why rebuilding efforts had yet to begin almost eighty years after the war had ended. Anybody who paid a visit to the Bingham Heritage Museum (open 2 p.m. – 3 p.m. every other Tuesday) would therefore be surprised to learn that the town's aesthetics could not be blamed on foreign artillery but were in fact a product of good old British industrial collapse.

It hadn't always been that way. Back when people could still suggest a holiday in a northern seaside resort and not have their spouses wait nervously for the punch-line, when the idea of rummaging around for chips in a soggy bundle of newspaper while standing on a drizzly beach still sounded quaint and not like the catalyst for a midlife crisis, before low-cost airlines decimated home-grown tourism by giving people the chance to have crap holidays in other countries instead of crap holidays in the UK, Bingham was quite the draw. People came from far and wide to ride the Bingham Eye (once the tallest Ferris wheel in the northeast, now the rustiest in England), stroll along the pier (now reduced to blackened posts that jutted from the sea like Twiglets after the Great Bingham Fire of 1987) and eat deep-fried bacon sandwiches (AKA the Bingham Butty) in a time when calories were measured on a value-for-money basis and not by their impact on your arteries.

But those days were long gone and so too were the people, not just the tourists who used to pass through the bus station in their thousands every week but also the people whose livelihoods depended on them. The hoteliers, fairground workers, street performers and restaurateurs now did different jobs in different towns, many of them working in the car insurance call centre to the north or manning the production line at the silicone factory to the south. The only people to pass through the bus station these days were locals going to and from work, and the only people to visit were the ones who did so ironically, posing for selfies beside boarded-up windows or in front of the derelict Ferris wheel and posting them on Instagram with hashtags such as #urbandecay, #welcometohell and #ghosttown. Whereas people once dreamed of visiting Bingham, now people had nightmares about never being able to escape.

Doctors were also in short supply. Because of this, anybody with a medical complaint could either take it to a neighbouring town where the facilities were slightly better, ask the local priest to say a prayer for them, ignore the problem in the hope that it magically went away or, as a very last resort, visit Dr Sterling, Bingham's only qualified medical professional, although 'qualified' was a word that people used loosely when referring to the doctor, as too were the words 'medical professional'.

The doctor had wispy white hair and a thick white moustache that covered his lips and jiggled whenever he talked. He also had the most immaculate fingernails, which Ronnie had found reassuring on his first visit ('I'd no sooner trust a doctor with dirty fingernails than I would a mechanic with clean overalls,' his dad used to say, even though he didn't trust doctors *or* mechanics, regardless of their approach to hygiene). He'd since come to learn that Dr Sterling's nail care regime was the only reassuring thing about him.

'Do you feel it?' said Ronnie. 'The round thing?'

He was stretched out on the oddly narrow bed that lurks in the corner of all doctor's offices, lying on his front with his head resting on his folded arms and his trousers around his ankles. It was not a comfortable position, made all the more uncomfortable by the fact that Dr Sterling was roughly kneading his buttocks.

'Yes,' said Dr Sterling. 'I can feel it.'

Ronnie swallowed and braced himself for the news. 'What . . . what do you think it is?'

'I think it's your bum cheek.'

Ronnie sighed. 'Not *that* round thing, the other round thing. What's the other round thing?'

'That's your other bum cheek.'

'I don't think you're taking this very seriously.'

'You're right,' said Dr Sterling as he peeled off his rubber gloves and threw them at the bin in the corner. 'I'm not.'

'Well, that's comforting,' said Ronnie, pulling up his trousers and sitting on the edge of the bed.

'I'm not here to comfort you. Watch *The Golden Girls* if you want comforting. I'm here to tell you whether or not you have a legitimate medical complaint, and as per usual, you do not.'

Ronnie had first met the doctor six months ago when he'd come to his surgery complaining of a lump in his armpit. The doctor had taken one look at the lump before asking Ronnie to stand on one leg. When Ronnie complied, Dr Sterling asked him to flap his arms like a chicken. Only when the doctor convinced him to start yodelling did Ronnie finally ask what any of this had to do with his armpit.

'Nothing at all,' replied Dr Sterling. 'I just fancied a laugh. The lump's a pimple, nothing to worry about.'

Failing to see the funny side, Ronnie had left vowing never to return, but two weeks later he was back, this time with a series of random chest pains that, according to Google, could only be stage four lung cancer, but was, according to Dr Sterling, nothing more than a mild chest infection.

Ronnie had seen the doctor several times since then. In fact, he'd visited Bingham Medical Centre more times in the last six months than in the previous forty-two years combined, but Dr Sterling had given him the all-clear every time. Ronnie never felt all clear though. Something always felt off, like the feeling you get in the hours and minutes leading up to the dreadful realisation that you've forgotten to lock your front door or turn off the oven or collect your grandmother from the supermarket.

Whereas he'd once spent his free time watching television or mooching about online, now Ronnie spent his Friday nights trawling WebMD and the NHS website for proof that he was dying. One time, he was convinced he had Crimean-Congo haemorrhagic fever, despite having never been to either Crimea or the Congo, and despite not having a fever. Another time, he feared he had a fatal case of leptospirosis after drinking a can of Fanta that he believed may have been peed on by a rat. And once he'd visited Dr Sterling complaining of various symptoms of botulism after eating a can of beans with a dent in it. According to Dr Sterling, however, the only thing that Ronnie was suffering from was an overactive imagination.

'How do you know it's not cancer?' asked Ronnie. 'Men get bum cancer all the time.'

'No, they get colon cancer, or prostate cancer, or cancer of the anus. I've never heard of anybody getting cancer of the bum cheek before.'

'I'm sure I felt something.'

'Yes, you did. You felt me squeezing your bum. Still, you're more than welcome to get a second opinion on the matter.'

'From who? You're the only doctor in town.'

'From Doctor Socktor.'

'Doctor Socktor?'

Dr Sterling opened a drawer behind his desk. His hand emerged inside a sock puppet with googly eyes and a miniature stethoscope around its neck. Ronnie had never seen the puppet in person before, but he recognised it from the various posters in the surgery waiting room. They were aimed at children and carried slogans such as 'Doctor Socktor says eat your greens,' 'Doctor Socktor says get off your iPhone,' and 'Doctor Socktor says don't stick things up your nose.'

'I'm Doctor Socktor, and you must be Onnie,' said Dr Sterling. He spoke in a high-pitched voice from the corner of his moustache, with his teeth clamped together like a ventriloquist. 'Onnie. *Onnie. Honnie.*' He sighed. 'Sorry,' he said in his own voice. 'I always struggle with the Rs. Can I call you something else? Ian? Ian is an easy one.'

'I'd rather you didn't.'

'OK, I'll do my best. Hello, Onnie—'

'No, I mean I'd rather you took that thing off your hand.'

'He's called Doctor Socktor.'

'Whatever.'

'Suit yourself,' said Dr Sterling, removing Doctor Socktor and returning him to the drawer. 'It was going to be the same opinion as mine anyway. Doctor Socktor and I don't like to undermine each other's professional integrity.' He opened a jar of lollipops and offered it to Ronnie.

'Do you treat all of your patients like this?' said Ronnie, ignoring the jar.

'Like what?' said Dr Sterling. He popped a lollipop into his mouth and screwed the lid back on.

'Like, I don't know, a burden?'

'I'm sorry you feel that way. Please don't think of yourself like that. I never feel like my patients are a burden. I prefer to think of them as . . .' Dr Sterling searched for the right words, but found the wrong ones instead. 'A necessary evil.'

'Is that what it says in the Hippocratic oath? Patients are a necessary evil?'

'No, it says do not convert your neighbour's wife.'

'I think you mean "covet".'

'Yeah, that one.'

'That's the Ten Commandments.'

Dr Sterling drummed his fingers on the desk. 'Oh, you mean *that* Hippocratic oath. Do no harm, blah blah blah? No, it doesn't say that. I don't think.'

'Well then.'

The doctor plucked the lollipop from the corner of his mouth and pointed it at Ronnie.

'You want to know what your problem is?'

'Well, I'm not here for the conversation,' said Ronnie.

'I think you're lonely.'

Ronnie laughed. 'That's your diagnosis? I come in here with a lump on my arse and you tell me that I'm lonely?'

'You don't have a lump on your arse, Ronnie. I think you have a lump on your *brain*.'

'Wait, what?' said Ronnie, suddenly panicked.

Dr Sterling chuckled. 'Not a *physical* lump. Well, you might do. I have no idea without a CT scan. I mean a *psychological* lump. Your problem is in here' – he tapped his temple with the sticky end of his lollipop – 'not in here,' he said, vaguely gesturing to Ronnie's midriff.

'Great, so you're saying I'm mad. Is that it?'

'I'm not saying you're mad. I'm saying you're a hypochondriac.'

'Oh, well, that makes me feel a lot better,' said Ronnie sarcastically.

'Ronnie, you're one of the healthiest patients I have. You must have been here at least a dozen times in the last six months, and I've never found anything wrong with you. What do you think that means?'

'That you're not very good at finding things?'

'It's a common trait among lonely people. I see it all the time. You substitute your lack of social engagement with an increased focus on yourself. You're not ill. You just have too much time on your hands. You don't need a doctor. You need Kindle.'

'Kindle?'

'Yeah. Get yourself on Kindle, start meeting people.'

'I have no idea what you're talking about,' said Ronnie.

'Kindle. The dating app.'

'That's Tinder.'

16

'Pretty sure it's Kindle,' said Dr Sterling.

'Kindle is for ebooks.'

'Oh. Tinder then. Why do they all sound so flammable? Tinder, Kindle, Firefox, Amazon.'

'Amazon?'

'Don't you watch the news? The Amazon's on fire again. How does that even happen? It's a rainforest. Wouldn't it be too wet to catch fire?'

'That's your idea of professional advice, is it?' said Ronnie, steering the conversation back to the topic in hand. 'Online dating? Are you going to write me a prescription for that?'

'Would you like me to?' said Dr Sterling. 'I could. Betty got the order wrong, so I have quite literally hundreds of these.' He rapped the prescription pad with his pen.

'No, I wouldn't.'

'Maybe I'll put a few on eBay,' he said, thinking aloud.

The telephone rang. Dr Sterling picked it up. He yepped and nodded and hmmed and then hung up.

'Oh dear,' he said. 'Mr Gilligan has come about his flatulence, and Betty wants him out of the waiting room asap.'

'Isn't that information private?'

'If he wanted to keep it private, then he wouldn't be farting all over the shop, would he?'

'Well, I hope you don't tell other patients about *my* confidential medical information.'

'Of course I don't. There's never anything worth telling!' Dr Sterling laughed. Ronnie didn't. Dr Sterling stopped laughing. 'Anyway,' he said, adjusting his tie, 'is there anything else I can help you with today?'

Ronnie stared at the floor where his shadow should have been but wasn't. He shook his head. 'No,' he said. 'Nothing else.'

'See you in two weeks then?'

'What's happening in two weeks?'

Dr Sterling shrugged. 'I'm sure you'll think of something,' he said.

Chapter Three

Ronnie was soaked by the time he got home, the heavens having opened up the minute he'd left the doctor's surgery. That was the thing about the rain in Bingham. It wasn't just ill-timed – it was often downright spiteful.

Standing in the hallway, he listened to the drip-drip-drip of his clothes on the mat and thought how loud it sounded. Even after a year, he still hadn't got used to the silence of living alone. It wasn't the sort of peaceful silence that came with sitting in the park or the library. It was the awkward sort of silence that made him feel like the house had been talking about him right before he'd walked through the door. Today was worse than usual. Coming home to a quiet house was bad enough, but coming home without your shadow made the silence even worse somehow.

'Hello?' he shouted, half expecting his shadow to come galloping round the corner like an energetic puppy, but his greeting went unanswered, which was probably a good thing. If being reunited with his shadow came at the expense of having his shadow talking to him, then he wasn't sure that was necessarily a decent trade-off.

He hung his wet clothes on the side of the bath and threw on some dry ones. Then, going from room to room, he went in search of his shadow. The search didn't take very long because the house was small: a simple two-up two-down terrace like the vast majority of houses in Bingham.

Ronnie looked in all of the usual places that seemed to attract missing things – between the couch cushions, at the bottom of the laundry basket, behind all the doors, underneath his bed – but all he found was dust, fluff and a few dead flies. He also found a sock behind the washing machine that he didn't remember losing. Only when he saw the words 'World's Best Dad' stitched into it did he realise who it belonged to. He stared at the sock, wondering what to do with it. There were so many reasons why he should throw it away and only one reason to keep it, and it wasn't even a good reason, not really. It was just a sock, and a tatty one at that, with a hole in the heel and another at the toe and a loose thread dangling from the cuff. But even though it belonged in the bin – what use was a single sock to anybody? – Ronnie couldn't bring himself to get rid of it. At least not yet.

Best to put it to one side and deal with it later, he thought, ignoring the fact that he'd spent the last twelve months doing precisely the same thing with everything else that belonged to his dad, including his ashes. He'd vowed to scatter them the day after the funeral, but the urn still sat upstairs on the windowsill of his dad's bedroom. Despite never having anything to do on the weekends, Ronnie somehow always managed to keep himself just busy enough to ensure that he didn't have the time to give his dad his final send-off.

Returning to the living room, he turned off the lamp and stood very still in the hope that his shadow could be lured out of hiding when the lights were out, much like the common cockroach, but when he flicked the lamp back on a few seconds later, he was disappointed to find that everything still had a shadow but him, including the cockroach he'd accidentally coaxed out of the skirting board. Realising he'd been tricked, the insect scurried beneath the bookcase, while Ronnie flopped onto the couch and tried to make sense of his increasingly disconcerting situation.

He started with the most rational explanations. Then, concluding that there *were* no rational explanations, he quickly moved on to the irrational explanations.

His first thought was that he was having some kind of delusional episode. After all, if people could see and hear things that weren't actually there, surely it was possible to *not* see things that *were* there? He grabbed his laptop and googled several variations of 'shadow has disappeared/I have no shadow/why does my shadow hate me?' but all he could find were some lyrics for a song called 'I Didn't Ask to be Born' by a teenage metal band called You're Not My Real Dad.

Google suggested he read up on Carl Jung, who claimed that the shadow was the animal side of oneself, like Freud's id. Ronnie didn't know what an id was. Nor did he feel like he'd ever had, or recently lost, anything resembling an animal side. Also, it turned out that Jung wasn't even talking about actual shadows, but rather a subconscious element of the personality that he referred to as the shadow, which gave Ronnie no greater understanding of his condition but did at least succeed in giving him a greater understanding as to why he never read much psychology.

He closed his laptop with a sigh and stared into the void, or what would have been the void had his television not been in the way. The screen was blank, though, so it looked a bit like a void. His reflection stared back at him.

'At least you're still here,' he said. That was something. Losing his shadow was bad enough, but losing his reflection would be infinitely worse, mainly because it would mean that he was a vampire. Ronnie really didn't want to be a vampire, partly because he wasn't charming enough, but mainly because he couldn't stand the sight of blood. Even a rare steak was enough to make him woozy. He also didn't want to live forever. Sometimes even *this* life felt like an eternity.

He wiggled around on the sofa and tried to locate the lump that was, until a few hours ago, very much present and very much terminal cancer, but it was clearly that super rare strain of terminal cancer that terminated itself instead of the host because all he could feel now were the bony bumps of his ischium. It had definitely been there, though. He even had a photograph to prove it, although the picture was far from flattering. The only mirror in his house was situated above the sink in the bathroom, which meant that he'd had to perch awkwardly on the edge of the basin in order to take the photograph, and such a pose was not becoming for a slightly out of shape forty-two-year-old man, especially one with his pants around his ankles.

Ronnie took out his phone and looked at the image while trying to ignore the oddly coquettish pose he was striking. He frowned and then zoomed in a bit. Then he frowned a bit more and zoomed in a bit more until his screen was nothing but buttock, but he could no longer see whatever he'd thought he could see and feel when he had taken the picture. Still, thought Ronnie, it must have been the lighting or the angle. He wasn't a hypochondriac. Dr Sterling was wrong about that.

The doctor was right about something else he'd said though. Even though he didn't like to admit it, Ronnie *was* lonely. It wasn't an active sort of loneliness. He didn't go through life mourning his solitude in the same way that others went through life mourning their hard luck, or their misshapen ears, or their hideously hairy backs. The sight of a happy couple did not evoke a dewy-eyed desire to have somebody to hold hands with and wake up to and share spaghetti with like the dogs from *Lady and the Tramp*. Nor did the sight of a group of friends in a pub make him want to buy them a round of drinks in the hope that the gesture would compel them, no matter how reluctantly, to pull up an extra chair and ask him to join them.

Loneliness for Ronnie was more of a peripheral concern. Like the thinning hair around his crown or the leftover Chinese food he'd hidden behind a wall of condiments because he was too afraid to touch it given how long it had been living at the back of his fridge, he didn't need to see it to know it was there, lurking like expired noodles at the back of his mind.

But now that his shadow had disappeared, his loneliness no longer felt peripheral. It felt very real, not to mention very personal. How could it just abandon him like that? What had he ever done to warrant such betrayal? It was hard not to feel just a little bit insulted by the whole thing.

Ronnie yawned and rubbed his eyes. Perhaps a good night's rest would do the trick. He hadn't been sleeping well recently. Maybe he was just overtired.

'That's probably it,' said Ronnie, trying to reassure himself. 'A good sleep will sort me out.'

But when he woke up the following morning, his shadow was still nowhere to be seen.

Chapter Four

Ronnie didn't take pride in much – he didn't think he had much to take pride *in* – but if he had to choose something he was good at, say for a job interview perhaps, 'taking care of things' would probably be that something (although further context would no doubt be required so that the interviewer understood that this wasn't some kind of sinister metaphor).

Whereas many people couldn't get through the day without temporarily or permanently misplacing their phone, their keys, their wallet or some combination of the three, Ronnie knew where everything was at any given time. His phone was always snugly encased in the little holster with the Velcro flap on his belt, the Velcro as stubborn as the day he'd bought it because he rarely made or received a call; his keys were always at the end of the curly plastic bungee cord that once belonged to his dad and now lived on his belt loop; and he never worried about losing his wallet for the simple fact that he didn't own one. Instead, he chose to distribute his valuables throughout his various trouser pockets, with his money going into one pocket and his cards going into another. It was, he reasoned, much harder to lose your trousers than it was to lose your wallet, a theory that Ronnie stood by despite Carl categorically disproving it during one particularly boisterous Christmas party.

Ronnie liked to think that this was the reason he'd been put in charge of the lost property office six months ago, that his higher-ups had noticed his propensity for orderliness and rewarded him with a job that best suited his skill set. It wasn't an easy illusion to maintain, however, mainly because his boss, Alan, had explicitly told him that he was being assigned the job for one reason and one reason only, and that was because the previous lost property manager, Kendrick, had died unexpectedly while fixing his television aerial.

'It's a real shame,' Alan had said while adding several sugars to his tea in the break room.

Ronnie nodded solemnly. 'It is a shame,' he agreed. 'He was a good man.'

'No, I mean it's a shame he couldn't have given me any warning. He's really buggered up the roster this week.'

'He fell off the roof. I'm not sure how much warning he could have given you.'

Alan took a sip of his tea. He winced and added another spoonful of sugar. 'Do you think it was . . .' he trailed off, hoping that Ronnie would fill in the blanks, but filling in blanks was not Ronnie's forte.

'Do I think it was what?' he said.

'You know,' said Alan. 'Do you think he did it on purpose?'

'What? Like . . . jumped?' said Ronnie. Alan nodded almost enthusiastically. 'No. No way. He wasn't that sort of bloke.'

Alan shrugged. 'Never know what's going on inside people's heads though, do you?'

'Well, no, I suppose not.'

'Anyway, here.' Alan handed Ronnie the key to the lost property office. 'Don't lose it, it's the only one we've got. And let me know if you're planning on falling off any roofs.'

Ronnie didn't get paid any extra for looking after the lost property office. He didn't particularly mind though. It wasn't exactly a difficult or time-consuming addition to his regular workload, after all. In fact, it didn't necessitate any work whatsoever. All he had to do was guard the key to the office and return anything to anybody who came to collect whatever they'd misplaced.

The room was filled with the humdrum things you'd expect to find in a lost property office. There was a whole shelf dedicated to umbrellas of all shapes and sizes and another to gloves, which Ronnie had sorted into left and right piles in the hope that at least one pair would match (they didn't). There were enough hats and scarves to keep an army of snowmen warm, and there were so many pairs of glasses that you could melt them all down and make a giant monocle for the Bingham Eye. There were various earrings, bracelets, necklaces and rings, some of which looked like they might be worth something, until the station had them

27

valued by a local jeweller ('mostly shite' was the verdict). One shelf held a box containing several pairs of tangled headphones, and another shelf housed a collection of books – romance and thrillers mostly, no doubt because life in Bingham was about as romantic and thrilling as a colonoscopy.

The only other person besides Ronnie who had any interest whatsoever in the lost property office was Pearl, sixty years old and of no fixed abode. Pearl had been banned from the premises for repeatedly attempting to claim things that didn't belong to her. The staff were under strict instructions to escort her off the property if she ever stepped foot inside the bus station, but Pearl always managed to evade detection. It wasn't because she was a master of disguise – with her bright pink fake fur coat, her chequered black-and-white skirt and her shock of multicoloured hair that reminded Ronnie of the multiple layers of wallpaper he'd discovered while decorating the bathroom with his dad one time, she was, if anything, a master of making herself stand out like a mangled thumb. Nobody wanted to kick her out for the simple reason that kicking her out meant approaching her, and nobody wanted to approach her because nobody wanted to get bitten. Not by Pearl, who didn't have enough teeth to pose a threat to anything other than a piece of paper in need of a hole punch, but by the various ferrets that lived inside her coat.

Nobody was quite sure how many there were exactly. Some said two, others said three, and when a rookie

police officer had made the mistake of trying to appre-
hend her after she'd kicked his vehicle and told him to
drive more carefully (he'd been sitting in his parked car
eating his lunch at the time), Zelda the cleaner, who
happened to be passing by at that very moment, swore
blind that she'd seen at least five of the critters drop
from Pearl's coat and scurry up the officer's trouser leg
while he hopped around and screamed into his radio
for backup. Bicycle clips had become standard issue for
the Bingham police force since then.

Sometimes Pearl would turn up on one of Ronnie's
days off. Sadly for Ronnie, today wasn't one of those days.

'I've come to collect my umbrella,' she said with a
straight face. She always opted for the straight face, as
if the business of claiming other people's belongings
was a highly serious matter.

'OK,' said Ronnie, knowing where this was going
but obliged to go through the motions anyway. 'Do
you have a picture of the item?'

'Yes.'

Ronnie waited. Pearl waited. Ronnie stopped waiting.

'Can I see it?' he said.

Pearl tapped her temple with her gnarled finger. 'It's
in my mind.'

'Right. Well, could you describe the item for me
then?'

'Yes.'

More waiting. More nothing.

Ronnie sighed. '*Will* you describe the item for me?'

'It's got a handle and you press a button and these metal things pop out and it keeps you from getting wet when it rains.'

Ronnie pinched the bridge of his nose and tried to count to ten. He got to three. 'You've just described an umbrella.'

'You asked me to.'

'I asked you to describe *your* umbrella.'

'I just did.'

Ronnie looked at his watch. It suddenly felt like it must be home time. It wasn't.

'What colour is it?' he asked.

'It doesn't matter,' said Pearl with a shrug. 'I'm not fussy.'

'That's not how this process works, Pearl. You can only claim something that actually belongs to you.'

'Fine,' she said. 'I'll buy one then.' She rummaged around in her pocket and slapped her hand on the desk. Ronnie stared at the items that Pearl was attempting to pass off as currency, namely a dried kidney bean, a large button, an even larger button and a Uruguayan peso.

'That's also not how this process works, Pearl. This isn't a shop. These things belong to other people.'

'But nobody's using them,' said Pearl. 'And it's raining.'

The office didn't have a window, but Ronnie could see from Pearl's sodden coat and the way her hair was plastered to her forehead that it really was raining quite heavily outside. Either that or she'd just been for a swim in the local duck pond. It wouldn't have been the first time. He wondered how long a coat like that would take to dry out. Even somebody who had the luxury of a radiator to drape it over could not expect it to take any less than a couple of days, and Pearl didn't have a couple of days because it was, as far as he knew, the only coat she owned. Nor did she have the luxury of a radiator because Pearl didn't have the luxury of a home.

Ronnie looked down at the random items she'd dumped onto his desk. He was pretty sure there'd been a kidney bean there a minute ago, but now there were just the buttons and the peso. Suddenly, a ferret popped out of her pocket and snatched one of the buttons before disappearing into the coat. A second later, it re-emerged and spat the button back out. It was hungry but clearly not that hungry, unlike Pearl, who looked like she hadn't had a decent bite to eat since ASDA had stopped giving free samples at the deli counter (due to Pearl eating them all).

He was just about to ask how many more ferrets she was harbouring so he could put that argument to bed once and for all when he heard Alan yelling from the other end of the corridor.

'Is that Pearl? Don't tell me that's Pearl!' he shouted, as if it might not actually be Pearl, as if Pearl were just one of countless women who roamed around Bingham in pink fur coats and hair the colour of Michelangelo's overalls.

'Uh-oh,' said Ronnie. 'You better get out of here.'

Pearl turned to leave, but Alan appeared in the doorway before she could make her escape.

'How many times do I need to tell you?' he said, careful to keep a safe distance from Pearl for fear of entering The Bite Zone. 'You're banned!'

'I'm taking a bus!' said Pearl defiantly. 'You can't stop me from taking a bus. It's a basic human right, like the right to a fair trial and the right to party.'

'Oh yeah?' said Alan doubtfully. 'Which bus are you taking?'

Pearl scanned the forecourt. 'That one,' she said, pointing to a bus that was idling nearby.

'Better hurry up then,' said Alan. 'It leaves in a minute.'

'Right,' said Pearl. She lingered for a moment. 'Where's it going?'

'Fingle Bridge,' said Ronnie. Pearl frowned. 'It's miles away,' he added.

'Right,' said Pearl. 'Yes. Of course.' She cleared her throat. 'Actually, I just remembered that I left my purse at home.'

'Not a problem,' said Alan, digging into his pocket. 'I'll get you a ticket. Come on.' He gestured for Pearl to follow him.

'Wait,' said Ronnie. Pearl paused. 'What did you say your umbrella looked like again?'

'It . . . well, it had a handle and . . . this thing you pushed up and then . . . then these metal things popped out and . . .'

Ronnie leaned down and grabbed something from behind his desk. 'Did it look like this one?' he said, holding up a black compact umbrella. Pearl looked at the umbrella and then back at Ronnie. He smiled and nodded almost imperceptibly.

'Yes,' she said, reaching out and taking it. 'That's the one. Thank you.'

Ronnie watched Pearl board the empty bus while Alan had a quick word with the driver. The bus departed a minute later and Alan waved as it left the forecourt.

'That should get rid of the mad old bag for a while,' said Alan with a grin.

Alan was thirty-six, but he was one of those thirty-six-year-olds who looked old enough to have thirty-six-year-old children. His face was worn and devoid of features, like the ground-floor button in a high-rise lift, and he swaggered about with a bravado that was more transparent than the armpits of his shirt after even the mildest of exertion. Also, if the rumours were true (and they probably weren't because the rumours generally came from Carl, who was well known for making stuff up), Alan wore a toupee. When Ronnie had pointed out that Alan clearly wasn't wearing a toupee because he was clearly half bald, Carl had told him that the toupee was designed to look like that so nobody would suspect that it was in fact a toupee. Sometimes there was no winning with Carl.

Alan had taken over as the station manager ten months ago. It was shortly after Ronnie's dad had died and so

Ronnie was willing to concede that his first and lasting impressions of his boss had been somewhat clouded by this fact. Still, Alan hadn't exactly done much to endear himself to Ronnie or the rest of the team. He had started by laying off several members of staff, some of whom had been there for years. Then he got rid of the vending machine in the lunch room because it kept breaking down and he said it cost too much to fix. He also started turning off all the lights that weren't being used, or that he thought weren't being used, even though they often *were* being used, like the lights in the bathroom, for example. Ronnie had lost count of the number of times he'd been plunged into darkness while sitting on the toilet. Knowing the financial difficulties that the bus station (and Bingham in general) was facing, however, he grudgingly accepted the cost-cutting measures as the inevitable consequence of living in a part of the country that the government refused to fund because the Prime Minister didn't know where it was and was therefore unconvinced of its existence.

The thing he had a harder time accepting was why Alan had recently instructed him and Carl to swap jobs. Ronnie had always cleaned the insides of the buses, Carl the outsides. Ronnie's job was undoubtedly easier – especially during winter when the freezing sea wind howled through the bus station and chased the hunched and red-faced townsfolk through the snickets and ginnels of Bingham; or when it rained, which it did approximately four hundred and twelve days per year, according to the town's Wikipedia page – but he felt like he'd earned it after so many years of service. Alan had a different opinion though, and their relationship had been strained ever since. The fact that he was mean to Pearl only made Ronnie dislike him more.

'You shouldn't call her that,' said Ronnie.

'Call her what?'

'Mad,' said Ronnie. 'Or old. Or bag.'

'But she *is* old.'

'Fine. The "mad bag" part then.'

'Why?'

'Because,' said Ronnie, 'she's a human being.'

'Good one,' said Alan, as if the idea of Pearl being human was about as believable as the idea of Pearl being a fridge-freezer.

'She lost her umbrella. That's why she was here. That's what people do when they lose things. They come to the lost property office.'

'They don't though, do they?' said Alan. 'I mean, look at all this crap.' He gestured to the shelves. 'When was the last time anybody claimed any of it?'

'Pearl,' said Ronnie. 'Just now.'

'Aside from Pearl.'

Ronnie drummed his fingers on the desk. 'Somebody called up about a missing teddy bear a couple of months ago.'

'And did we have it?'

'No,' said Ronnie. Then, as if it were some sort of consolation, he added, 'We have other bears though.'

He pointed at the shelf of forgotten stuffed toys that were clustered together as if for safety.

'I know. That's the problem. We're trying to get rid of them, not collect them!'

'Actually, somebody came looking for something just the other day,' said Ronnie.

'What were they looking for?'

'The mop.'

'Which mop?'

'Zelda's mop.'

'Zelda the cleaning lady?' said Alan. Ronnie nodded. 'Why would somebody be looking for Zelda's mop?' Alan asked. Ronnie shrugged. Alan sighed. 'It was Zelda, wasn't it? Zelda was looking for her mop.'

'Yeah.'

'See, this is what I'm talking about. Nobody gives a shit about any of this stuff. Some of it's older than you are, for Christ's sake.'

'I'm not *that* old,' said Ronnie.

'You're not *that* young, either,' said Alan. 'What are you, fifty?'

'I'm forty-two!' said Ronnie, more than a little defensively.

'That's like the average life expectancy in Zambezi. Probably higher. You'd probably be dead by now if you lived in Zambezi.'

'Everybody would be dead if they lived in the Zambezi because the Zambezi is a river,' said Ronnie.

'You're missing the point.'

'What *is* the point?'

'My point is that this isn't a lost property office anymore. It's a landfill. It's like Bingham pond, but without the shopping trollies and syringes. Just look at it. It's all rubbish.' He grabbed something from Ronnie's desk. 'I mean, who's going to come looking for this piece of shit?'

'That's my phone,' said Ronnie.

'Really?' said Alan, inspecting the phone like an amateur geologist trying to decide if he'd just unearthed a rare mineral or a mummified dog turd. 'Wow. I haven't seen one of these since . . . Actually, I don't think I've *ever* seen one of these.'

'It has excellent battery life,' said Ronnie, which was true, but only because he never used it.

'So does a vibrator, but I still don't want one,' said Alan.

'I think we have one of those in here somewhere, actually,' said Ronnie, looking around.

Alan looked perplexed. 'Why would you keep something like that?' he said.

'Because it's lost property?'

'And you think somebody's going to come and collect that, do you? You think they're just going to waltz in here and politely enquire about the vibrator they left on a bus several years ago?'

Ronnie shrugged. 'You never know.'

'See, this is what I'm talking about,' said Alan. He shook his head as he scanned the shelves like a plumber inspecting a previous plumber's handiwork. 'You know what? Get rid of it.'

'Get rid of what?'

'All of it,' he said, sweeping his arm around the room. 'Keep anything recent, but get rid of everything else.'

'What do you want me to do with it?' asked Ronnie.

'Whatever you want. Sell it. Bin it. Bury it. Dump it on the side of the A1. I really don't care. Just get rid of it.'

Orders dispensed, Alan marched out of the room with the air of somebody who had just given a directive of much greater importance than the emptying of Bingham bus station's lost property office.

Ronnie sighed. 'I wish you'd told me that *before* I gave Pearl my umbrella,' he said to himself.

Chapter Five

Not wanting to throw away a perfectly decent collection of junk, Ronnie sorted the contents of the lost property office into various cardboard boxes and set about trying to rehome it all.

It was a bittersweet process. Being the lost property manager gave him something to do when he wasn't cleaning buses, and he wasn't cleaning buses very much these days for the simple fact that there weren't many buses to clean anymore. Downtime was something he could only dream about when he first started working at the bus station twenty-five years ago. There used to be a whole team of cleaners back then – they called themselves The Clean Machine – and even though there were five of them, they still sometimes struggled to keep up with the workload.

Now, he and Carl comprised the entirety of the cleaning department, and sometimes it still felt as if they were overstaffed. They often had to pretend to be busy, and if there's one thing more exhausting than working, it's pretending to be working. The lost property office allowed him to feel slightly less redundant, and slightly less like he was going to be made redundant like the countless other employees who had come and gone over the years.

Still, despite all of the above, it pained Ronnie to admit that Alan had a point. Nobody was coming back for this stuff. They were unloved relics of a time gone by, much like the bus station, and much like the town itself. And when the station was finally bulldozed (and it was only a matter of time, if the rumours about a new shopping centre were true), then the lost property office and everything inside would be flattened right along with it, unless Ronnie found a new home for everything.

Alan had suggested hiring a skip and dumping everything into that. Actually, he hadn't suggested hiring a skip because they didn't have the budget for that sort of thing. Instead, he'd instructed Ronnie to dump everything into somebody else's skip, namely the one belonging to the builders who were busy reducing a nearby factory to rubble. But Ronnie didn't want to do that, so he made a list of all the charity shops in town and divided the items accordingly. Bingham lacked many things – law enforcement, basic services, hope – but there were more charity shops per square mile than there were bus stops. They'd started to appear about a decade ago, shortly after the mayor of Bingham – Mayor Roberts – wrote his now-famous opinion piece in the *Bingham Bugle*. In it, he had not-so-subtly implied that the town was basically bankrupt, before even less subtly instructing everybody to go and work at the silicone factory which had just opened a few towns over. When asked if he'd been paid to promote the factory, Mayor Roberts indignantly replied that he would never dream of taking a backhander and that he simply had a soft spot for silicone (and having seen his wife, three-time winner of the Miss Bingham Beauty Pageant, it was hard to dispute this statement).

As people sold up and moved away and others had their houses repossessed, more and more charity shops had popped up to deal with the influx of belongings that were left behind during The Great Exodus. Now they made up roughly twenty per cent of the Bingham shopping experience, the other eighty per cent being split fairly evenly among the nail salons, betting shops, pawn shops and takeaways that lined the town's main thoroughfare.

Every evening on his way home from work, Ronnie took a different box to a different charity shop. The books went to the Oxfam bookshop next to the Betfred and the clothes went to the British Heart Foundation that was situated opposite Chips in the Night, the chip shop on Brewer Street. The jewellery went to the RSPB, for no particular reason other than the fact that they seemed to do a lucrative trade in shiny things (Ronnie wondered if crows were their main suppliers). Anything random went to Help the Elderly because the shop would literally take anything (their window display included a traffic cone, a single wellington boot and half a box of After Eights) and anything *really* random went into the bin.

Slowly but surely the office was emptied, until only a box of dog toys remained. Either many dogs had lost many toys between them, or one particularly scatterbrained dog had, over time, lost its entire cache of punctured tennis balls, squeaky bones and ratty pieces of rope. Whatever the truth of the matter, nobody had come to claim any of it since Ronnie had taken over lost property duties, which made a lot of sense when he thought about it. After all, a dog couldn't exactly explain to its owner that it had, in a moment of absentmindedness, forgotten to grab its malformed Frisbee before alighting the 32b to Radlington. Nor was the animal likely to turn up at the lost property office to claim whatever slobbery piece of gnarled rubber it originally thought it had buried but had since come to realise, having dug up all the flowerbeds, that it may in fact have left on the bus.

Ronnie offered the toys to several charity shops, but nobody wanted them. Even Help the Elderly said no when he tried to donate them one Saturday morning.

'They're used,' said the man behind the counter with the untamed sideburns as he peered at the contents of the cardboard box.

'Yep,' said Ronnie, thinking the statement was a question. Then, realising that the statement was in fact a statement, and a closing statement at that, he said, 'Is that a problem?'

'We can't accept them.'

'But isn't everything in here used?' asked Ronnie, looking around the shop.

'Yeah, but these are *used* used,' said the man.

'*Used* used?' said Ronnie. 'What do you mean, *used* used?'

'I mean that they've been chewed. We don't accept things that have been chewed.'

'You think those haven't been chewed?' said Ronnie, pointing to a pile of children's books.

'Chewed by an animal, I mean.'

'Why not?'

'Because it's unhygienic.'

'I don't think dogs are that particular,' said Ronnie. He didn't know much about dogs, but he'd always been under the impression that any animal that licked its own arse wasn't that fastidious when it came to oral hygiene.

'You've obviously never met my sister's dog,' said the man.

'You are correct. I have never met your sister's dog.' Ronnie waited for the man to elaborate. He didn't. 'I disinfected them all, so they're very clean, I promise,' he said.

'You could disinfect a severed finger, but I'm still not going to chew on it,' said the man.

'I'm . . . not asking you to.'

'I mean, would you?'

'Chew on a severed finger?' said Ronnie, concerned at the direction the conversation was taking.

'Chew on one of those,' said the man, pointing to the box.

'Obviously not.'

43

'But you said they were clean.'

'They *are* clean.'

'So, prove it,' he said, fishing out a rubber bone and waggling it at Ronnie.

'No.'

'Why not?'

'For the same reason I don't pee on lamp posts or hump people's legs,' said Ronnie, which wasn't strictly true because he had once peed on a lamp post, a long time ago. He'd never humped anybody's leg, though.

The man thought about this. 'And what reason would that be?'

'Because I'm not a dog!'

'If you were though.'

'Would I chew on that if I was a dog?' said Ronnie, pointing at the rubber bone. 'That's what you're asking me?' The man nodded. 'Yeah, why not?' said Ronnie.

The man pulled a face not unlike the face of somebody who'd just accidentally taken a mouthful of cold tea.

'Only if I was a dog, though,' said Ronnie, keen to clarify his statement.

'I'm glad you're not my dog,' said the man.

'*I'm* glad I'm not your dog,' said Ronnie, unsure how exactly the conversation had arrived at this point.

'Good,' said the man.

'Good,' said Ronnie.

They stood in silence for several awkward seconds. Then, picking up his box of toys, Ronnie pretended to peruse the shelves while edging his way towards the door.

It was raining by the time Ronnie left the shop, the fine sort of rain that you barely noticed until your feet started squelching in your shoes.

Reaching for his umbrella but finding nothing but pocket, Ronnie frowned before remembering that he'd given it to Pearl.

He sighed and took a seat on the bench beneath the awning while he waited for a lull in the rain. After a few minutes, he sensed that he was being watched. Wondering if the man from the charity shop was silently judging him through the window, Ronnie turned to find him posing in front of the mirror while trying on a cowboy hat that somebody had donated (a cowboy, perhaps). It was only when he turned back round that he noticed the large plastic bear a few feet away on the pavement. It looked just how he imagined Paddington Bear's uncle might look, if Paddington Bear's uncle had sustained major head injuries after falling down the stairs while drunk. On top of his hat was a slot for donations, and written across the briefcase that he clutched to his chest in the same way that old ladies hold their handbags on the bus was the name of a local charity for deaf children.

Standing to attention beside Paddington's alcoholic uncle was a large yellow plastic dog, also with a hole in its head. It had the mournful expression of a real dog that was still waiting to be collected from the lamp post it had been tied to three days ago. A plastic sign hung around the animal's neck with the words 'Help us or we'll die!' written on it in bold urgent lettering. 'Have a great day! Bingham Dog Shelter' was written beneath it in jarringly perky cursive.

Ronnie pulled his hood up and grabbed the box of toys.

Chapter Six

Ronnie looked at the funeral parlour and then back down at his phone.

'You have arrived at your destination,' insisted Google Maps.

Either the map was wrong, the dog shelter no longer existed or his phone was trying to tell him something. He'd recently overheard a couple of the bus drivers talking about how 'Big Tech' was gathering so much information about you these days through your telephone calls and your photographs and your internet search history and whatnot that they basically knew you better than you knew yourself. And come to think of it, he *was* feeling a little bit under the weather (although he was, to some degree, always feeling a little bit under the weather).

He was halfway through checking his pulse when he noticed a small hand-painted sign at the mouth of a muddy lane that ran alongside the funeral parlour. 'Bingham Dog Shelter, 100 metres,' it read.

Ronnie heard the place long before he saw it. It wasn't the sound of barking dogs but the sound of Kate Bush singing 'Hounds of Love' at the top of her lungs that tipped him off, although some would argue that the two sounds weren't entirely dissimilar.

'Hello?' he shouted over the gate, more out of habit than a genuine belief that his voice could ever compete with Kate Bush on full blast, or even Kate Bush on half blast.

Letting himself into the courtyard, he made his way towards a large outbuilding where the music seemed to be coming from. Before he reached the door, a woman in her early twenties walked out with a bucket in one hand and a shovel in the other. She wore a sleeveless puffer jacket with a jumper underneath and wellington boots with her trousers tucked into the rims. She looked familiar in that way that everybody in Bingham looked slightly familiar, even if you'd never seen them before, which Ronnie was pretty sure he hadn't.

'Hi!' he yelled, trying to be heard over the music. That was his intention, anyway, but as soon as he opened his mouth, the music cut out and he ended up yelling at the woman through almost perfect silence, making for a somewhat terrifying greeting, not to mention an equally terrifying first impression.

The woman, who hadn't yet noticed Ronnie, did what most people would do in a situation where they think they're alone and then somebody yells at them. She screamed, which caused Ronnie to scream, and then she screamed again, perhaps in response to Ronnie's scream or perhaps because she hadn't yet got all of the screaming out of her system.

'Christ!' she said, rubbing her heart through her puffer jacket. 'Are you trying to give me a flippin' myocardial infarction or something?'

'My cardigan what?' said Ronnie.

'A heart attack!'

'Oh!' said Ronnie, wondering why she couldn't have just said that in the first place. 'No. I'm sorry. I didn't mean to scare you.'

'Yeah, well, Leopold Lojka didn't *mean* to get Archduke Franz Ferdinand Carl Ludwig Joseph Maria of Austria and his wife shot when he took a wrong turn in Sarajevo on 28 June 1914, but we all know how *that* turned out, don't we?' said the woman in one long breath.

'Yeah,' said Ronnie, despite having absolutely no idea how *that* turned out. 'Absolutely.'

'What are you doing sneaking about like that anyway?' said the woman. 'Don't you know it's dangerous to creep up on a girl when she's carrying a bucket full of dog turds?' She jiggled the bucket for emphasis.

'I wasn't sneaking. Or creeping. I was actually doing the opposite of sneaking and creeping,' said Ronnie, although he wasn't entirely sure what the opposite of sneaking and creeping was exactly. 'You might have heard me if your music wasn't so loud,' he added with a nervous laugh.

'Don't hate on Kate,' she said. 'This right here is a Kate-hate-free zone.' She vaguely gestured to their surroundings to indicate the invisible perimeter of the Kate-hate-free zone. It seemed to go far beyond the confines of the shelter.

'I'm not!' said Ronnie. 'I like Kate Bush.' This wasn't entirely true. Ronnie had inherited an aversion to Kate Bush from his dad, who had banned her from the house on account of the fact that Ronnie's mum loved her and her songs always reminded him that she no longer loved *him*, or at least not enough to stop her from running off with Mr Higgins, a seemingly happily married man who lived across the road. 'That woman is not welcome in this house!' he'd bark while changing radio stations, as if it wasn't just her music, but Kate Bush herself that was banned, leading eight-year-old Ronnie to wonder if the singer lived in the neighbourhood and, if so, what he was supposed to say to her if she ever turned up on the doorstep and asked to use the telephone or borrow a cup of sugar.

'Good,' said the woman, 'because she's basically my identical twin. I mean, she's obviously a better singer than I am, and she's also a lot richer, and more famous. And a *lot* older. And I'm not a vegetarian like she is. And I've never done a duet with Elton John. Not yet anyway. And her birthday is in July, whereas mine is in September. But otherwise we're pretty much the same person. We even have the same name! Well, first name at least. And I'm a Cate with a "C", not a "K". But still, it's got to mean something, hasn't it?'

'Yeah,' said Ronnie, even though he had no idea what this could possibly mean exactly.

'The dogs love her music as well,' she added, nodding towards the building she'd just walked out of. 'It calms them down. Sometimes they have these mad barking sessions, kind of like a Mexican wave, but with barks. A Mexican bark, where one barks, and then another, and then another, until they're all barking like crazy. I don't know who starts it, but we do have a chihuahua, so I'm guessing it might be him. You know, because he's Mexican. Hey, did you know that the longest Mexican wave according to the *Guinness Book of Records* went on for seventeen minutes and fourteen seconds?'

Ronnie shook his head. 'I did not know that,' he said.

'It happened at a concert for a Japanese band called Tube.'

'Really?' said Ronnie, trying to sound like this was something he'd always wanted to know.

'Yep. On 23 September 2015 if I remember correctly.'

'Right.'

'At Hanshin Koshien Stadium in Nishinomiya.'

Ronnie nodded. 'Got it.'

'That's in Japan.'

'I thought it might be,' said Ronnie, still trying to feign interest but fearing his feigning might have reached its limits.

'It's quite funny if you think about it,' said Cate.

Ronnie thought about it. 'Is it?' he said.

'Yeah. Because it happened in Japan. Not Mexico. Even though it's a Mexican wave!'

'Oh. Yeah. Ha!' Ronnie laughed, despite not finding it half as funny as Cate clearly did.

'I can't really blame them,' she said.

'Well, no, I mean, if the Mexicans aren't going to make the effort, then—'

'No, the dogs, I mean. I can't blame them for barking. They get quite bored, being locked up all day.'

'Well then, maybe these will help,' said Ronnie, shaking the box.

Cate came over to have a look. She left the bucket where it was, much to Ronnie's relief.

'Wow!' she said, picking up a rubber bone. 'This is great, thank you so much.'

'No problem. I'm not sure they're going to save any lives, but still.'

'How do you mean?'

'"Help us or we'll die",' said Ronnie, reciting the words from the plastic collection box he'd seen outside the charity shop.

'Oh! Ha, yeah, that was me. I thought it might catch people's attention.'

'It worked,' said Ronnie. 'So, do you actually . . . you know . . .' He made a gun with his fingers and pressed the makeshift barrel to his head.

'What? Kill them? God, no. I just want people to think that we do so they'll come and rescue the poor little buggers.' She rummaged through the box. 'Where did you get these?' she said. 'They aren't . . . I mean . . . Oh dear. Did these belong to *your* dog?'

'What?' said Ronnie, momentarily confused. 'Oh! No, no, I work at the bus station. This is just some old lost property that nobody came to claim.'

Cate frowned. 'So . . . your dog didn't die?'

'No,' said Ronnie. 'I don't have a dog.'

'Are you allergic?'

'I'm sorry?'

'To dogs. Are you allergic?'

'Not that I'm aware of.'

'Are you scared of dogs?'

Ronnie shook his head. 'No. Well, maybe that one from that Stephen King book.'

'Does your tenancy agreement prohibit you from keeping pets?'

'I don't have a tenancy agreement,' said Ronnie. He wondered where all of this was going.

'Do you share your home with any territorially aggressive animals, such as geese or otters?' continued Cate.

'Does anybody?'

'You'd be surprised,' said Cate. 'Do you have a controlling partner who determines what you can and cannot do with your life?'

'No.'

'Do you have a controlling cat that determines what you can and cannot do with your life?'

'No,' said Ronnie, who was starting to feel like he was on the wrong end of the Spanish Inquisition.

'So,' said Cate, smiling now, 'just to recap, you don't have a cat or a partner, you're not scared of or allergic to dogs, and you're not barred from keeping pets by a landlord who stupidly believes that animals are somehow noisier or dirtier than the average human being after a couple of drinks on a Friday night?' She counted each point off on her fingers.

'That's correct.'

'Then why don't you have a dog?'

Ronnie opened his mouth to speak, but he suddenly found himself lost for words. He'd never had to explain why he didn't have a dog because it was one of those things he never thought he'd *need* to explain. It was like somebody asking him why his feet were so big, or why he had a mole on his ear, or why he couldn't grow a proper beard. There *was* no reason.

'I . . . don't know,' he said.

Cate grinned. 'Then follow me,' she said, making her way back towards the outbuilding.

Chapter Seven

Ronnie had been a little suspicious when Cate had told him that the music had a calming effect on the animals. He didn't doubt that certain music had soothing properties. Enya had built an entire career out of it. He'd just never thought of Kate Bush as a calming influence, for humans or for animals, and perhaps she wasn't. Perhaps she hadn't calmed the dogs but terrified them into silence, but whatever the truth of the matter, there was no denying that the room had the aura of a canine monastery when Cate walked into it. Only when Ronnie walked in behind her was the spell abruptly broken.

'Oh,' said Cate as the dogs collectively threw themselves at their cage doors while they barked and snarled at Ronnie. 'Sorry, they're not usually like this. Are you wearing Lynx Africa? They hate Lynx Africa.'

'I'm not wearing Lynx Africa,' said Ronnie, who was wearing a home-brand deodorant from ASDA. There was every possibility that the dogs did not like this scent either, but Ronnie had another theory, namely that the dogs could sense that his shadow was missing and wanted him to know just how much they were not OK with this.

'Well, let's see which one might be a good fit for you, shall we?' said Cate, leading him towards the mass of gnashing teeth and saliva at the other end of the room.

Ronnie reluctantly followed her over to the large cages that ran the length of the back wall.

'How big is your house?' asked Cate.

'Not very big,' said Ronnie. 'Tiny really,' he added, hoping that Cate would get the hint.

'Then you'll want something small,' she said, scanning the cages.

'I mean, I'm not sure I actually *want*—'

'How about Oggie?' she said, pointing to a black cairn terrier. 'He's quite the bundle of joy.'

'I can see,' said Ronnie, watching as the bundle of joy in question attempted to chew its way through its wire enclosure so it could chew its way through Ronnie.

'Toto from *The Wizard of Oz* was also a cairn terrier, but you want to know what's funny? Toto was actually a girl!' Ronnie smiled, more amused by Cate's amusement than by the anecdote itself. 'She also did her own stunts, *and* she got paid more than a lot of the human actors in the film. Imagine how annoyed you'd be if you found out you were getting paid less than a dog!'

Ronnie thought about several of his colleagues and felt he could relate to some degree.

'Why do you know so much about, well, everything?' he said.

Cate shrugged. 'I read a lot.' Then, frowning as if she'd just had déjà vu, she said, 'Why – is it annoying?

Tell me if it's annoying and I'll shut up. Sometimes I
don't know when to shut up.'

'Not at all. It's impressive.'

Cate smiled, clearly not used to being impressive.
'How do you feel about chihuahuas?' she said, pointing
to a bug-eyed creature that was yapping away near
Ronnie's leg.

'I think the real question is how do chihuahuas feel
about *me*?' said Ronnie, backing off in case the animal
somehow broke free from its cage and clamped its jaws
around his leg, or as much of his leg as it could fit
between its mini Mexican mandibles.

'Hmmm,' said Cate as she scanned the cages in search
of a good fit for Ronnie.

Ronnie also scanned the cages, not because he was
looking for a good fit but because he was rapidly trying
to think of excuses as to why none of them were suitable,
he had nothing against dogs, even if these particular dogs
had something against him, he just wasn't sure he was
ready to let one into his life just yet, if ever. Owning
a pet was a really big deal. You didn't just pick up a
dog on your way home from work in the same way
you'd pick up a carton of milk or a four-pack of toilet
rolls. It was something that required a lot of time and
thought. It was in many ways like entering into a new
relationship, but one where the other person did none
of the chores and contributed nothing to the rent yet
still expected you to pick up their poop. Ronnie didn't
know if he was ready for that kind of commitment.

His eyes were drawn to a little black dog in a cage at the far end. The animal caught his attention for two reasons. The first was that the dog was the only one that wasn't barking at him. Instead, it quietly observed Ronnie in the same way that a shopkeeper might quietly observe a group of teenagers with oversized jackets. Well, one of its eyes seemed to be observing him at least. The other one appeared to be following a fly around the room.

The second reason was that the animal was by far the ugliest thing that Ronnie had ever seen. It had the kind of face that not even a mother could love, Mother Teresa included. It'd be easier to pretend you hadn't shat your pants during a game of musical chairs than it would be to love a face like that. It looked, at best, like the sort of dog that a toddler who had never seen a dog and who had absolutely no artistic merits whatsoever would draw. At worst, it looked like something the plumber might extract from the clogged drain of the only shower in a crowded student dormitory. It wasn't ugly in that 'so ugly it's sort of cute' kind of way. It was ugly in that way that made people question whether God existed, and if so, why he had such a mean sense of humour.

'That's Hamlet,' said Cate, following his gaze.

'That makes sense,' said Ronnie.

'What makes sense?'

'Naming him after a tragedy,' replied Ronnie. 'I mean, look at the poor bugger. It's like a Brillo pad had a one-night stand with a tumbleweed.'

'He wasn't named after the play,' said Cate a little irritably. 'He was named because he was found in Hamlet.' Hamlet was the next town over.

'Oh,' said Ronnie. 'Right. Sorry.'

'It's not me you should be apologising to.'

Ronnie smiled. Cate didn't. Ronnie stopped smiling.

'No, of course.' He turned to Hamlet. 'Sorry,' he said. Hamlet looked at Ronnie and then at his own leg, as if he were trying to decide which one had just spoken to him. He bit the leg, just to be on the safe side.

'He's what we call a lifer,' said Cate, as if Hamlet were a hardened criminal banged up without parole. If being ugly were a crime, then Ronnie had no doubt that this dog was guilty as charged. 'Other dogs come and go, but Hamlet's been here forever, haven't you, mate?'

'That's a shame,' said Ronnie, and he meant it. It *was* a shame. But even though he could see how unfair it was that this poor animal was destined to spend the rest of its days alone in a cage in a breezy outbuilding with terrible acoustics and very little in the way of entertainment except for a walk or two every day and a second-hand rubber toy to chew on, and all because he wasn't cute enough, or Instagrammable enough, or sane enough to realise that his own leg couldn't talk, Ronnie also couldn't bring himself to do the right thing, which was to offer this otherwise hopeless creature a home, which made him feel awful, it really did, but despite how awful it made him feel right now in this moment, he knew it wasn't half as awful as he'd feel if he had to look at that dog every day from now until the day that one of them met their maker, and when poor Hamlet finally *did* meet his maker, Ronnie sincerely hoped that he asked the silly bugger responsible just what the heck they were playing at.

'It is,' said Cate. 'It is a shame.' She looked at him eagerly, as if the two of them were on stage and it was Ronnie's turn to speak, preferably the words 'OK, fine, I'll take him.'

'Still,' said Ronnie, gazing at the ceiling, if only to avoid making eye contact with Cate. 'At least he's got a roof over his head.'

'Not quite the same as a loving home though, is it?'

'No, I suppose not,' said Ronnie, eyeballing the exit. 'Anyway, I really better—'

'He likes you,' said Cate. 'I can see it in his eyes.'

Ronnie looked at Hamlet. Hamlet's dodgy eye also looked at Hamlet. 'Really?' said Ronnie. 'And which eye would that be exactly?'

'The gammy one. It only rolls around like that when he likes somebody.'

'Well, that's very flattering, really, but I just don't feel like we're compatible. I don't get that . . .' he groped around for the right word, '. . . spark, you know?'

'Spark?' said Cate. 'I thought you were looking for a dog, not a date.'

'Well, I'm not really looking for either, to be honest. I just . . . I don't think I'm ready for a dog right now. I need time to think about it.'

'It's because you think he's u-g-l-y,' she said, spelling out the word in a whisper. 'Isn't it?'

'I never said he was ugly—'

'Don't say it in front of him!' said Cate. 'You'll hurt his feelings.'

'Sorry. Look—'

'Here,' said Cate, opening the cage. Ronnie winced as she picked up Hamlet with her bare hands and put him on the floor. 'He's a lot friendlier when he's out and about, aren't you, mate?'

Hamlet looked at Ronnie, not at his face, but at the floor around his feet where his shadow should have been. Ronnie fidgeted nervously, wondering if Cate would notice what Hamlet was staring at, or not staring at in this case, but if she did, then she didn't say anything, which meant that she probably hadn't noticed, because if there was ever a time when the rules regarding wilful ignorance for the sake of politeness could be circumvented, asking where the bloody hell somebody's shadow had gone was most certainly one of those times.

'You were saying?' said Ronnie as Hamlet started to back up towards Cate until he bumped into her leg. Even then he didn't stop, his little legs still attempting to propel him backwards as if the only thing needed to overcome physics was good old-fashioned perseverance.

'Don't take it personally,' said Cate. 'He just needs a bit of time to get used to you. Go on, Hamlet. Go and say hello to the man.' She spun him around and they both watched as a clearly disoriented Hamlet began

61

to moonwalk towards Ronnie. 'He doesn't have much faith in humans, I'm afraid. I think his previous owners were what we in the dog-rescuing profession commonly refer to as disgusting pieces of human garbage that deserve to be burnt at the stake.'

Noticing Hamlet's arse edging dangerously close to his trouser leg, Ronnie sidestepped out of the way and Hamlet continued his moonwalk across the room towards the exit.

'I'll tell you what,' said Cate. 'Just take him out for a walk. The beach is just down the hill, he likes it there. See if the two of you bond. If not, then you can always bring him back. How does that sound?'

'I'd love to, honestly, but I really need to get going,' said Ronnie, throwing his thumb over his shoulder. 'I have a thing I need to do.'

'It's a Saturday morning in Bingham. What could you possibly have to do so urgently on a Saturday morning in Bingham?'

Ronnie opened his mouth to speak and hoped a decent lie would fall out. It didn't, so he closed it again.

'Look, I'll give you a tenner,' she said, fishing around in her pocket. She plucked out a fiver. 'Oh. I've only got a fiver. Will you take a fiver? I can owe you the rest.'

'You don't need to *pay* me . . .'

'Then please, just take him for a walk. One quick walk on the beach. An hour, tops. Let him feel the sand beneath his paws. Let him feel the wind in his hair. Let him chew on random sea junk. He loves chewing on random sea junk. Please. You'll make his day.'

Ronnie sighed. He hadn't expected to be rewarded for bringing the box of toys to the shelter, but he certainly hadn't expected to be punished for it either. He felt like the victim of something, even if he couldn't quite figure out what. Life maybe? He turned round and looked at Hamlet, who was almost out of the door.

'Is he going to walk backwards all the way to the beach?' he said.

Chapter Eight

There were two beaches in Bingham, North Beach and East Beach. The fact that these names were chosen from hundreds of suggestions during a community 'Rename the Beaches' campaign several years ago told you everything you needed to know about the people of Bingham.

They weren't the sorts of beaches you sunbathed on, largely because there was never really much sun to bathe *in*. Nor were they the sorts of beaches you would walk barefoot across, not unless the soles of your feet were thick and leathery enough to withstand the minefield of broken bottles and other jagged bits of detritus that poked out from beneath the sand and in between the rocks. Given that East Beach was full of quicksand and North Beach had currents that were strong enough to drag a cargo ship off course (at least according to local legend), swimming at either location was also not advised. Because you couldn't actually do any of the things that most people would expect to be able to do at a beach, Ronnie always thought that calling them beaches at all felt a little bit like false advertising. It was like calling the top floor of the council flats on Warren

Hill a viewing point, for example, or calling Bingham a UNESCO World Heritage Site just because somebody had jokingly spray-painted 'Bingham: Eighth Wonder of the World' on the crooked welcome sign that could be found on the main road into town.

North Beach was about a ten-minute walk down the hill from the dog shelter. Ronnie hadn't been there for years, not since he was a child, and even then, he never actually went onto the beach. Instead, he'd sit in the back of his dad's Ford Escort, while his parents sat up front, the windows closed and the heating on and the air warm and tangy with the smell of salt and vinegar from the chips in the bundles of newspaper on their laps. They'd stare ahead through the rain-speckled windscreen and watch the waves crashing onto the shore, nobody speaking and no music playing because his dad couldn't afford to replace the stereo that somebody had nicked one night. Occasionally, his dad would break the silence by pointing to the shore and saying, 'Look at that one!' as if they were all on safari and he'd just spotted a leopard or a rhino or something else thrilling or majestic and not just another of an infinite number of waves.

Ronnie always thought of those memories fondly, but as he grew older he came to realise that they weren't fond memories at all. They were memories of a marriage that was falling apart, even if he didn't know it then. Thinking of his mum staring out to sea, he couldn't help but wonder what was going through her mind, whether she really was just watching the waves like the two of them or whether she was watching the horizon and wondering what lay beyond it. And while the thought of his dad pointing at waves and exclaiming how big they were or how loud they were or how wet they were once made Ronnie smile, he understood now that his dad wasn't doing it because the sight of the sea doing what the sea did best filled him with an inexplicable sense of excitement. He did it because he didn't know what else to do to fill the awful silence.

Aside from the fact that the chip shop was now boarded up, the beach was pretty much exactly the same as it was when Ronnie last visited. It was still drizzling, it was still windy and the waves still crashed into the shore with such ferocity that it seemed as if Bingham had once offended the sea and the sea had never forgotten it.

Ronnie walked along the beach with his shoulders hunched against the cold and his hands stuffed deep into his pockets. Junker's Rock loomed in the distance, its peak partly hidden by the gloom. The landmark was named after all the boats that the sea had wrecked against its cliffs. Nobody called it Junker's Rock anymore though. These days, the locals called it Jumper's Rock. It was Bingham's own version of Beachy Head, just not as high, or picturesque, or full of tourists taking selfies or influencers striking tasteless diving poses. Instead of trying to deal with the problem through community outreach programmes and mental health awareness initiatives, the council had attempted to combat the issue by putting a fence around the edge of the cliff. This fence had also ended up in the sea, the strong winds that battered the peak having ripped it from its roots and flung it into the waves, although the locals preferred to say that even inanimate objects were prone to want to kill themselves after spending more than a few weeks in Bingham.

Hamlet scoured the beach as if searching for his car keys. He looked behind him at regular intervals, perhaps because he kept forgetting what the chain around his neck was attached to, or perhaps, as Ronnie suspected, because he wanted to make sure that the weird shadowless man he'd been lumbered with wasn't creeping up behind him to infect him with whatever shadow-sucking virus he was currently playing host to.

'Don't worry,' said Ronnie when Hamlet turned round and eyeballed him for the umpteenth time. 'I don't want to come near you either.'

Ronnie checked the time. Cate had said an hour, but following some aggressive haggling on her part and some defensive haggling on his, they'd eventually settled on fifty-five minutes. Relieved to see that almost half of that time had already elapsed, he was just about to turn round and start heading back to the dog shelter when he noticed some sort of structure a little further along the coast. Ronnie squinted down the beach, hoping he could identify whatever it was without actually having to walk any further, but his eyesight, while not particularly bad, was also no match for the fine misty drizzle that made everything around him look as formless and indiscernible as Hamlet. Reminding himself that he didn't actually have anywhere else to be that morning, and reasoning that he was already so sodden that he couldn't possibly get any wetter, he allowed Hamlet to lead him down the beach until he was close enough to satisfy his curiosity.

In front of him stood a lookout tower, the sort of thing that lifeguards used. It looked like a baby's high chair, but for adults, with almost vertical stairs leading up to an elevated seat where somebody would sit and watch the sea for people in need of assistance. That in itself was strange enough. Nobody swam at North Beach, or East Beach, or any other beach within a twenty-mile radius of Bingham. Nobody in their right mind, anyway. And even if some daft bugger did decide to take a dip, there weren't enough daft buggers in the region to justify the presence of a lifeguard. It was because of this that Ronnie, try as he might, could not figure out why there appeared to be a lifeguard sitting in the lookout tower. More confusing still was the fact that the woman sitting in the chair seemed to be in her mid-to-late sixties. Even though age often brought with it both wisdom and knowledge, Ronnie couldn't immediately see how said wisdom and knowledge was going to help this woman drag a drowning person from the sea, or even see or hear a drowning person to begin with. He might have been inclined to think that she was just somebody who'd been out for a stroll and, spying a seat, decided to rest her legs for a bit (although the fact that she had to climb up there in the first place sort of defeated the point), but the bright red one-piece bathing suit she was wearing made it startlingly clear that she was not there to simply recharge her batteries.

'Morning,' said the woman cheerily. Ronnie shivered just looking at her.

'Are you not cold?' he asked.

'The fat keeps me warm,' she said with a chuckle.

'You're not *that* fat,' said Ronnie, even if she was a little on the round side.

The woman stopped chuckling. 'Goose fat,' she said. 'I'm covered in goose fat.'

Ronnie was suddenly thankful that the biting wind had turned his cheeks as red as they could possibly go. Still, he wished they were on East Beach instead of North Beach so the quicksand could swallow him up.

'Swimmers use it when they cross the Channel,' said the woman after a few awkward seconds of silence.

'Why?'

'Have you ever seen a cold-looking goose?'

Ronnie tried to picture what a cold goose might look like, but all he could see was the freezer section in the supermarket. 'No,' he said after some deliberation. 'I suppose I haven't.'

'Exactly.'

'I haven't seen a cold-looking duck either, though.'

'Duck fat also works. And porpoise fat. The first person who swam the Channel used porpoise fat. That

69

was back in the 1800s though; it isn't so easy to get your hands on these days. Also, I quite like porpoises. And ducks. Ducks are nice and friendly and peaceful. Not like geese. Geese are just mean. They hiss at you and attack you for no reason whatsoever. They're like the bullies of the bird world.' She stared at the horizon and shook her head, momentarily reliving whatever traumatic encounter she'd once had with a goose. 'No, sir, I don't have any problem using goose fat.'

'I don't think this one has a problem with it either,' said Ronnie, nodding at Hamlet, whose claws were clacking against the bottom step of the ladder as he tried to scramble his way up. 'You're lucky you're out of reach.'

'What a little cutie he is. Aren't you a little cutie?' she said, adopting that voice that everybody seems to adopt when talking to animals. 'What's his name?'

'Hamlet.'

'Who's there?'

'I'm sorry?'

'Who's there?' she repeated, this time more theatrically.

'Who's where?' said Ronnie, looking around.

The woman sighed. 'You're supposed to say, "Nay, answer me, stand and unfold yourself."'

'Oh. Yes. Sorry,' said Ronnie, realising that she was quoting the opening lines from *Hamlet*. 'He's not actually named after the play though. He just comes from Hamlet.'

'My husband was born in Hamlet.'

'When did he leave?' asked Ronnie. It was a regional

joke that nobody who was born in Hamlet stayed in Hamlet.

'He didn't,' she said. 'He's buried there.'

Ronnie stopped smiling. 'I'm sorry,' he said.

The woman shrugged. 'It is what it is.'

Ronnie nodded. He'd used the very same words on several occasions after his dad had died. It is what it is. What else could you say when somebody said they were sorry for your loss? That life was unfair? That the world was shit? That existence was meaningless and we're all going to die at some point anyway? All of that might very well be true, but it didn't mean the postman wanted to hear it. Not at 7 a.m. Not when he still had the whole day in front of him.

'He died right here, actually,' said the woman, gesturing to the beach and the sea beyond. 'Two years ago last month.'

'He must have been a brave man. I heard those currents are strong enough that—'

'They can drag a cargo ship off course. That's what they say,' replied the woman. 'He didn't drown though. He choked on a sherbet lemon, silly sod. A dog walker found him just over there,' she said, pointing down the beach.

'My grandad once choked on one of those,' said Ronnie, which wasn't totally true, because while his grandad really did once get a sweet stuck in his throat, it only got stuck there for a second or two before a robust cough dislodged it onto the carpet. Also, he couldn't remember if it was a sherbet lemon or a mint

71

humbug, but still, he thought a little solidarity might bring the woman some comfort, even if the particulars weren't entirely the same.

The woman shook her head. 'If only I'd been there,' she said, as if to herself. 'I used to work in a care home, for goodness' sake. I stopped so many people from choking that they used to call me Heimlich Harriet. But when he asked if I wanted to go for a walk, I said I was too busy. I wasn't busy though, not really. I was just sitting on the couch and doing a bit of cross-stitch, nothing that couldn't wait until later, but I was so close to the end, and you know what it's like when you've spent ages on a pattern and you can't wait to finish it.'

Ronnie wasn't sure if this was a rhetorical question or not, but he nodded like a cross-stitch enthusiast anyway.

'He said he'd be back in a couple of hours, and, well, that was the last time I ever saw him,' she said. 'Well, alive, anyway.'

Ronnie said nothing, knowing full well that even the most heartfelt words of consolation generally sounded empty to whoever was on the receiving end of them, especially if they were coming from a stranger with a weird-looking dog that was trying to nibble her toes.

'It's strange,' she continued. 'When you're standing at the altar and you're reading your vows, you're both making this pact with one another. You're saying, "I'm going to be there no matter what life throws at us. For better or worse, I'll be there. For richer or poorer, I'll be there. In sickness and in health, I'll bloody well be there too. And when death do us part, I'm going to be there as well," because that's what love is, isn't it? It's *being there*. So when Peter died, alone in the cold and without a scarf because I'd forgotten to remind him to take one, it felt like I'd broken that vow somehow. I'd been there through everything else, and, believe me, we'd been through a lot, but I wasn't there when he needed me the most, and I'll never be able to change that.'

'I'm sure he wouldn't see it that way,' said Ronnie.

'No,' said Harriet with a sad smile. 'I'm sure he wouldn't either.'

'Is that why you started coming down here?'

'No, I'm just working on my tan,' said Harriet, holding out her arms while she pretended to catch the non-existent sun. Ronnie smiled. 'But if somebody did happen to get into trouble, then, well, I'd like them to know that they're not alone.' Harriet forced a laugh. 'Blimey, listen to me! A right morbid Mary I am! Sorry to blather on, I didn't mean to keep you from your walk.'

'It's fine, really,' said Ronnie. He got the impression that Harriet didn't have many people to talk to. 'This is as far as we're going anyway. I need to get this one back to the shelter.'

'Shelter?'

'He's not mine,' said Ronnie. 'I just agreed to take him for a walk.'

'Well, I hope to see you again,' she said. 'Both of you,' she added with a wink.

Chapter Nine

Cate looked up from the floor she was sweeping and glanced at her watch.

'You two obviously got along well,' she said, referring to the fact that Ronnie and Hamlet had been gone for closer to ninety minutes than the fifty-five minutes they'd agreed on.

'I didn't intend to be so long, but I met a woman down there,' said Ronnie.

Cate frowned. 'Were you dogging?' she said, her eyes narrowing. 'Is that why you wanted to take Hamlet for a walk? So you could go dogging?'

'First of all, I didn't want to take Hamlet for a walk, you asked me! And second of all, no, I wasn't dogging!' said Ronnie, suddenly realising that he probably should have addressed the dogging allegation first. 'I didn't "meet" a woman,' he clarified, making inverted commas. 'I bumped into somebody and we got chatting. That's all.'

'That's all?'

'That's all!'

'Good, because Hamlet is messed up enough already without having to bear witness to that sort of thing,'

Cate said. She leaned her broom against the wall. 'How was he anyway?'

'He was fine, actually. He tried to eat a pebble, and then he tried to eat some driftwood, and then he peed on some seaweed and tried to eat *that*, and then we came home.'

'Yeah,' said Cate. She cleared her throat. 'About that.'

'About what?'

'The whole "home" thing.'

'What about the whole "home" thing?'

'Well, how can I put this,' she said. 'Basically, Hamlet doesn't have a home anymore.'

'I know,' said Ronnie. 'That's why he lives at a dog shelter.'

'No, I mean he doesn't have a home at the shelter anymore. There's no room.'

Ronnie laughed. 'No room?' he said. 'What do you mean, no room? He's got a cage, about this big.' He made the shape of a box with his hands. 'I saw it, less than two hours ago.'

'It's not his cage anymore. It belongs to another dog now.'

'What other dog?'

'That one,' she said, pointing to Hamlet's cage. 'Somebody brought him in after you left.'

Ronnie walked over and looked inside to find a chihuahua chewing on one of the rubber toys he'd donated. Ronnie frowned. 'That dog was here before,' he said.

'No it wasn't.'

75

'Yes it was. There was one chihuahua when I first arrived, and there's one chihuahua now. If somebody just brought another chihuahua, then there should be two chihuahuas.'

Cate thought about this. 'The man took it.'

'What man?'

'The man who brought the dog.'

'Hold on,' said Ronnie. 'Let me get this straight. You're telling me that the man who brought a chihuahua to the dog shelter then decided to adopt the *other* chihuahua?'

'Yes,' said Cate, a little unsurely.

'Then why didn't he just keep his original chihuahua?'

Cate shrugged. 'Creative differences,' she said.

Ronnie wasn't one to call somebody a liar, especially to their face, which was why he didn't call Cate a liar, even though he thought she was one. He scanned the cages while he counted them in his head. 'Then there should still be a cage free,' he said. 'Because you basically just swapped one chihuahua for another. So where's the extra cage?'

Cate scratched her head. She did this for some time. Ronnie wondered if she had fleas. 'It broke,' she said finally. 'The door fell off. It's the sea air, the salt damages the hinges and . . . yeah. That's what happened.'

When it became clear that Cate wasn't going to change her rather elaborate story, Ronnie looked at Hamlet and shrugged.

'Looks like you've got yourself a cellmate,' he said.

76

'It doesn't work like that,' said Cate.

'What doesn't work like what?'

'You can't put two of them in the same cage together.'

'Why not? They do it in prison.'

'Yeah, and bad things happen in prison. Haven't you seen *Midnight Express*?'

Ronnie had seen *Midnight Express*. His dad had made him watch it when he was a teenager to dissuade him from trying to smuggle hashish out of Turkey. So far, it had worked.

'What are you going to do then?' said Ronnie.

'Well,' said Cate, drawing the word out and hanging on the 'L' for several seconds longer than necessary. 'I know this isn't ideal, but I was wondering if you could maybe keep hold of him for a little while, just until we get the whole cage situation sorted out.'

'I can't. I'm sorry.'

'It'd only be temporary.'

'I work all week. He'd be home alone a lot of the time.'

'He's very independent.'

'I'd love to, really, but it's just not possible because . . . because . . .' Ronnie frantically flicked through his mental Rolodex of excuses before remembering that he'd stupidly left himself out of excuses by answering 'no' to all of Cate's previous questions. He wasn't allergic to dogs. Nor was he frightened of them. His landlord had no problem with pets because he didn't have a landlord and he didn't have a cat or a girlfriend who would object to the presence of a dog, even one that looked like Hamlet. There was quite literally nothing stopping him from saying yes except for the fact that he didn't want to, but something about saying those words aloud made him feel uncomfortable, like he was saying he didn't want to help an old lady across the street, or he didn't want to lend somebody his ladders so they could rescue a kitten from a tree, or he didn't want to give up his seat on the bus for a pregnant woman.

'What's the worst that can happen?' said Cate.

Ronnie thought about all of the potentially catastrophic things that might happen as a direct result of him becoming Hamlet's temporary custodian. After eliminating all of the technically possible but highly unlikely scenarios – getting killed while trying to rescue Hamlet from a dog-napper with horrendous taste in dogs; drowning while trying to rescue Hamlet after a freak wave dragged him out to sea; getting run over by a bus while trying to rescue Hamlet after he forgot that he was a dog and not a speed bump; ending up with seven years of bad luck after Hamlet knocked over a mirror; ending up with seven years of bad luck after Hamlet *looked* at a mirror – Ronnie was forced to conclude that the very worst thing that could realistically happen was that Hamlet might crap on the carpet.

'That's it?' said Cate when he told her. 'That's the very worst thing that could happen?'

Ronnie shrugged. He thought that having dog poop on the carpet was one of those things that was universally accepted as being bad, like stubbing your toe or dropping your phone into a pub toilet, but Cate made it sound so trivial that he wondered if he should mention one of the technically possible but highly unlikely scenarios instead.

'He might think he's a speed bump . . .' he said before trailing off when he realised how ridiculous it sounded out loud.

'He's not going to crap on your carpet,' said Cate. 'And if he does, I'll clean it myself. How about that?'

'I don't know,' said Ronnie, squirming like a kid being forced to wear the itchy jumper his gran had knitted him for Christmas.

'Please. Just a couple of days. I'd really appreciate it. And so would Hamlet. Wouldn't you, mate?'

They both looked at Hamlet. Hamlet looked at Ronnie. The look was not the look of appreciation. The look was a look that said, 'You're a weirdo with no shadow and I don't want to be anywhere near you, but if coming with you means getting out of this place for a couple of days, then screw it, let's do this.' That's how Ronnie interpreted the look anyway.

'Just a couple of days?' he said.

'Just a couple of days.'

Ronnie sighed. A couple of days was a couple of days longer than he'd like, but still, as Cate had said, what was the worst that could happen?

Chapter Ten

It didn't occur to Ronnie until he arrived home that removing Hamlet's lead would not be a straightforward process. Only when he tried to breach the one-metre perimeter that Hamlet had strictly enforced ever since Ronnie had taken him for a walk along the beach did Ronnie realise that waking up or coming home to find dog poop on the carpet was perhaps not the worst-case scenario after all.

'Come on, mate,' he said in his best 'you can trust me because I'm speaking several octaves higher than usual' voice, but for every step he took towards Hamlet, Hamlet took a step back, and when he'd taken so many steps back that he found himself backed up against the garden wall of Ronnie's house, Hamlet started stepping sideways instead, like a hairy crab, but one you'd throw back if you found it stuck in your fishing net.

Deciding that the only way he was going to get close enough to Hamlet to remove his lead was to use said lead to drag Hamlet towards him, Ronnie tentatively reeled him in, slowly pulling inch by inch while Hamlet did his best to resist. When his collar was within arm's reach, Ronnie cautiously extended his hand in a bid to unclip the lead. The closer his hand came to Hamlet, the louder Hamlet growled until, deciding that the whole growling thing clearly wasn't having the desired effect, he lunged forward and snapped at Ronnie's fingertips. It seemed more like a warning shot than an actual attempt to sever his digits, but Ronnie yanked his hand away anyway, not wanting to take any chances.

'Well, this is just brilliant,' he muttered. Hamlet scowled at him as if he too thought that this was just brilliant. 'Could this day get any worse?' he said, half to himself and half to Hamlet.

'Hi, Ronnie,' came a voice from behind him. Ronnie closed his eyes, realising that this day actually *could* and just *did* get worse.

He turned around and saw Janet Higgins, the woman from across the street whose husband had run off with Ronnie's mum all those years ago. Ronnie tried to avoid her whenever possible, partly because he felt a strange sense of guilt for his mother's role in destroying this woman's marriage, and partly because she had a habit of cornering him whenever she saw him and asking, despite nearly thirty-five years having passed since she'd woken up to an empty house, whether his mother had been in touch with him lately, presumably in the hope that she might discover the whereabouts of her husband.

'Hi, Mrs Higgins,' he said, forcing a smile.

'I just thought I'd say hello,' she said. 'I was doing a bit of dusting in the living room and I saw you through the window.' Ronnie assumed she was telling him this so he wouldn't think she was spying on him, but she needn't have bothered because he already knew that she was spying on him. He often saw her twitching behind her curtains or pretending to water the plants while staring across the street at his house. Sometimes he waved at her, just to let her know that her cover had been blown.

'How are you?' asked Ronnie.

'Oh, you know. Battling on,' she said with the weariness of somebody who really had just stepped off the battlefield for a quick breather and some half-time refreshments. 'And how about you?'

'Fine, fine,' he said, even though he wasn't fine, fine at all. He was crap, crap – how had he managed to come home with a dog?! – but he hoped that a positive response might elicit fewer questions than a negative one.

Ronnie waited as Mrs Higgins tried to steer the conversation around to the topic she'd come over to talk about. She finally found her cue in the flowerbed.

'Those geraniums have come up nicely this year,' she said, nodding at the pink flowers near the gate. 'I remember when your mum first planted that flowerbed. Blimey, how long ago would that have been now?'

'A long time,' said Ronnie.

Mrs Higgins nodded. 'Yes,' she said. 'I suppose it would have been.' She plucked an imaginary piece of fluff from her cardigan. 'Have you heard from her at all? Your mum?' she asked, her face momentarily lighting up with the dying embers of hope that she'd been stoking for over three decades.

'I'm afraid not, Mrs Higgins,' said Ronnie. 'I'll be sure to let you know if I do.'

Mrs Higgins nodded, her smile fading with every bob of her head.

It used to annoy Ronnie whenever Mrs Higgins would ask about his mum. Her question always sounded like a thinly veiled accusation, as if she somehow considered him guilty by association of robbing her of her husband and wanted him to know it. Over time, the question started to feel more like an insult, as if she were deliberately trying to upset him with her constant reminders that his mother had abandoned him. But as he got older he came to realise that neither of these things were true. She wasn't looking to stir up trouble. She was simply looking for closure.

'Who's this then?' she asked, pointing at Hamlet as if she'd only just noticed him.

'Hamlet,' said Ronnie. 'He's not mine,' he added, keen to emphasise this point. 'He lives up at the shelter. I'm just looking after him for a couple of days.'

'To be or not to be?' she said. 'That's *Hamlet*, isn't it?'

'I think so,' said Ronnie, 'although "To be on a lead or not to be on a lead" is probably more appropriate for this one.' Mrs Higgins frowned. Ronnie explained. 'He won't let me get close enough to take this thing off,' he said, shaking the lead in his hand.

'Is that true, Hamlet?' she said. 'Are you making trouble for poor Ronnie here?' She crouched down and put her hand out. Hamlet moved backwards and forwards, unsure what to do.

'Careful,' said Ronnie. 'He's got a mean streak.'

'He doesn't look like a meanie, do you, Hamlet? No, you don't,' said Mrs Higgins as her hand edged ever closer to Hamlet until her fingertips finally made contact. 'There you go,' she said, gently scratching him behind the ear. 'You're not a meanie weenie, you're a good boy, aren't you?'

Hamlet looked perturbed for a moment, as if he were trying to figure out whether Mrs Higgins's question was rhetorical or whether she actually expected an answer, and if she did expect an answer, then what answer would that be? *Was* he a meanie weenie? He didn't know, but the question seemed to have opened up an emotional can of worms that he looked like he was struggling to close. Still, the more Mrs Higgins scratched his ear, the less he seemed to care about those worms until his eyes began to close and his body began to sway before he keeled over on his side and lay there without moving.

'I don't suppose you're looking for a dog by any chance?' said Ronnie. 'He clearly likes you.'

'I'd love to, but I don't think my cat would be too happy about it.' She unclipped his collar with one hand while continuing to scratch him with the other. 'Voilà,' she said, holding up the end of the lead.

'Well, let me know if you change your mind,' said Ronnie, opening his front door. 'And thanks for your help, I really appreciate it.' He looked at Hamlet. 'Come on, you,' he said.

Hamlet remained lifeless for a moment, temporarily unreachable on whatever far-off galaxy that Mrs Higgins's ear tickles had transported him to. Then, realising he was no longer being petted, he lifted his head and looked around groggily, as if the jet lag from the return journey was already kicking in.

'Go on,' said Ronnie, nodding at the open door. Hamlet stood up and galloped inside.

'My pleasure,' said Mrs Higgins. 'It's nice to be needed sometimes.' Then, as if not wanting to sound self-pitying, she added, 'Speaking of which, I better get home and feed Winston before he tears the house apart.'

As Ronnie watched her cross the road and disappear into her house, it occurred to him that the conversation they'd just had was the longest exchange they'd ever had together. It made him wonder about the last time she'd had such a long conversation with anybody.

Chapter Eleven

Ronnie didn't know a great deal about dogs, but he'd always been under the impression that A) they liked to play poker and B) they liked to lie in front of fires. The only fireplace in the house was in the living room, and even though the fire wasn't on, he wagered that Hamlet was not the sort of dog who would notice such a detail. But Hamlet wasn't there. Nor was he in the kitchen, the pantry, the closet in the hallway, the cupboard beneath the stairs or the bin beside the back door.

'They should have called you Houdini, not Hamlet,' muttered Ronnie as he traipsed upstairs to continue the search in his bedroom, and then the bathroom, and then the bedroom again, all to no avail.

The only room he didn't check was his dad's old bedroom. The latch was loose and needed replacing, causing the door to swing open at seemingly random intervals. It hadn't started doing this until his dad had passed away, and Ronnie had almost shat himself the very first time it had happened. Today, however, the door was firmly closed, which Ronnie was rather relieved about. The last thing he wanted was a dog like Hamlet sniffing about in his father's room, or any animal for that matter. Even he didn't like to go in there unless he had to. Ronnie wasn't scared or anything like that. He'd never been scared of his dad in life and he certainly wasn't in death. Nor was the room a shrine, at least not intentionally. He just preferred to leave things as they were, much in the same way that his dad's favourite armchair still inhabited the living room and his favourite mug still lived in the cupboard. It wasn't like he needed the extra space for anything – he had no intention of converting the room into a home gym or a man cave or a meth lab or whatever else people usually did with their spare bedrooms these days.

Also, keeping his dad's things in there made it easier for Ronnie to imagine that his dad was still in there, doing a crossword in the chair in the corner or standing at the window and watching the birds in the garden with his binoculars. He'd once heard a poem by Henry Scott Holland read at his grandmother's funeral. The poem was called 'Death Is Nothing At All', and Ronnie always remembered the line 'I have only slipped away into the next room'. That's how he liked to think of his dad, and most of the time he succeeded. It was only when the door creaked open that this illusion was shattered. He made a mental note to get it fixed.

Thinking he could lure Hamlet out with food, Ronnie opened one of the tins of dog slop that Cate had given him and dumped it into a bowl that he put on the kitchen floor with some newspaper underneath it. And then he waited. And waited. And waited some more. Then, realising he'd be waiting all night if he continued to rely on this particular strategy, he picked up the bowl and carried it from room to room, hoping to entice Hamlet out from whatever obscure hiding place he'd wedged himself into with the meaty odours that Ronnie was grudgingly spreading all over his house.

When that didn't work either, he returned the bowl to the kitchen floor, sat down in the living room and pretended to watch TV for a while in the hope that Hamlet would come looking for him, much like a child playing hide-and-seek comes looking for his mates when it's clear they've given up trying to find him and gone to play football instead. The plan was to trick Hamlet out of hiding with a bit of good old-fashioned reverse psychology, but when Hamlet still didn't appear, Ronnie wondered if reverse psychology even worked on an animal whose psychology already seemed somewhat reversed. Maybe Ronnie needed to use the opposite of reverse psychology, otherwise known as psychology, but then he remembered that stuff he'd read by Carl Jung and decided to pass on the whole psychology thing altogether.

Ronnie eventually found Hamlet when he went to do his laundry. Throwing his clothes into the washing machine, he became aware of a presence that he imagined people feel right before they decide to put their house on the market. He peered into the drum and saw what he thought was a grotesque ball of lint staring back at them. Then, remembering that lint didn't have eyes, he realised that it was in fact Hamlet.

'What are you doing in there you daft bugger?' he said. 'It's a good job I found you before I put the washer on. You would have ruined my whites.'

Hamlet growled and continued to growl until Ronnie had shuffled back to the regulation distance. He sat on the floor with his back against the wall and sighed.

'OK, look. I know what you're thinking. Actually, I don't know what you're thinking because I'm not entirely sure that *you* know what you're thinking. But I know that you know that I don't have a shadow, and I also know that it's a pretty weird thing to happen to a person, so I don't blame you for being a bit freaked out, because honestly, I'm a bit freaked out myself. But still, we need to learn to live together, if only for a couple of days, so we should probably try to make an effort to get along as best we can until I take you back to the shelter on Monday. Agreed?'

Hamlet's expression was unreadable, not in the way that a book written in Greek is unreadable to somebody who doesn't understand Greek, but in the way that a computer program is unreadable because it's riddled with malware.

'Agreed,' said Ronnie. 'Now, first things first, a few house rules. Rule number one: no crapping on the carpet. If you need to, you know, do your business, then, I don't know, bark or stand by the front door, or do whatever dogs normally do when they need to go to the loo. Understand?'

Hamlet looked at him like he was trying to calculate how many hamsters could fit into the glovebox of a Ford Fiesta.

'I'll take that as a yes. Rule number two: no chewing on things that shouldn't be chewed on. That includes anything and everything that doesn't look like this.' He rummaged around in his pocket and pulled out one of the rubber bones that he'd rescued from the box before leaving it with Cate. 'This belongs to you. Other things you are permitted to chew on include food, but only your food, and legs, but only your legs. Got it? Good. Rule number three: no biting. Biting will not be tolerated in this household, or out of this household either for that matter. Violence doesn't solve anything, Hamlet. Not unless some maniac breaks into the house and tries to kill me in my sleep or something. If that happens, then you have my permission to disregard the no biting rule, provided that you bite them and not me. Otherwise, no biting. If you bite me, then I'll bite you back. Don't think I won't.' Ronnie would sooner sink his teeth into a used urinal cake, but he hoped that his bluff wouldn't need to be called.

'Rule number four: no barking between the hours of . . . Actually, just no barking. At all. Not unless you have a really good reason, and by "really good reason", I mean the same reason that it's OK to bite somebody, namely if an intruder breaks into the house. The sound of the postman delivering the mail is not a good reason to bark. Neither is the sound of the paperboy delivering the paper. Neither is the sight of a squirrel. Not unless the squirrel is somehow in the house. Then you can bark. Otherwise, no barking. OK?'

Hamlet barked. Ronnie frowned.

'Was that a bark of agreement or a bark of defiance?'

Hamlet barked again.

'Was *that* a bark of agreement or a bark of defiance?'

Hamlet barked a third time.

'OK, we could do this all night. I'm going to assume that you're agreeing with me here,' said Ronnie, even though he secretly thought that Hamlet was barking out of insubordination. 'In return, I promise not to come near you unless absolutely necessary. For example, if we have to get into a lift together, or if we need to share an air-raid shelter due to some sort of nuclear fallout. Otherwise, I promise to respect your boundaries to the best of my abilities. Do we have a deal? Don't bark if we have a deal.'

Hamlet didn't bark, although whether that was because he now had one of Ronnie's socks in his mouth or whether he was following Ronnie's instructions was anybody's guess.

'You're breaking rule number two, Hamlet,' said Ronnie, adopting the stern voice of a dog owner trying to assert authority. 'Hamlet! Hamlet? You're breaking . . . Hamlet! Listen . . . Oh, forget it.'

Leaving Hamlet in the washing machine, Ronnie went upstairs, where he filled a bowl from the kitchen tap and placed it on the sheet of newspaper he'd put down earlier. Then, dragging a couple of blankets from the cupboard, he made a bed for Hamlet in front of the hallway radiator before fixing himself some tea.

It took Ronnie a long time to fall asleep that night. His eyes were tired, as was his mind, but his ears were wide awake, tuned in to the sounds of the house and picking up on every creak or crack to determine whether they were normal creaks or cracks or whether they were the creaks and cracks of a dog in search of something to chew or somewhere to poop.

It only occurred to him as he lay there in the darkness that this was the first night he hadn't had the house to himself since his dad had died.

He'd never planned on being one of those people who lived at home forever. Nobody planned on being one of those people, not unless you were from a culture where such a thing was considered the norm. In Bingham, living at home after thirty said nothing about what a great relationship you might have with your parents and everything about what a terrible relationship you clearly had with anybody else, because nobody with friends or a family of their own would ever dream of living at home if they didn't have to.

But even though the folks at work sometimes took the piss out of him because of it, especially Alan, who seemed to take great pride in the fact that he'd lived alone since he was eighteen (although Ronnie wondered if he took as much pride in the fact that he hadn't moved out by choice but because his dad wanted to turn his bedroom into a home cinema), Ronnie never saw much practical sense in moving out. He liked living with his dad, and his dad liked living with him. They didn't bother each other in the usual ways that parents, bothered their children and children bothered their parents. His dad never burst into his room without warning. Nor did he hammer on the bathroom door and demand to know what Ronnie was doing in there, perhaps because it was obvious what people did in the bathroom, or perhaps because he simply didn't want to know. For his part, Ronnie never played techno music at ungodly hours (he didn't play techno music at godly hours either, whatever those were). Nor did he steal money from his dad's wallet to buy cigarettes, or sell his valuables in exchange for smack, or whatever else the news and the TV led people to believe that kids habitually did these days.

He also didn't sneak women into his room after his dad had gone to bed, for the simple reason that he didn't really know any. Most people met people through work, or through friends, or through friends of friends, but there were only two women who worked at the bus station: Zelda the cleaning lady, who was old enough to be his mum, and Alice the bus driver, who was happily married with three kids. As for friends of friends, Ronnie didn't have any friends who had friends because he didn't have any friends, which only really left Tinder (or Kindle, according to Dr Sterling) and online dating as an option, but Ronnie had heard that the people who used it rarely looked like their pictures, and some of them weren't even the same gender as they said they were, and some of them lied in their profiles, like saying they liked cricket when they didn't, or saying they weren't intending to drug and rob you when they bloody well were, at least according to Phil the bus driver (although he was keen to stress that this hadn't happened to him but to somebody he knew).

Alan had once asked Ronnie in front of everybody how he ever intended to meet a woman as long as he was still living at home.

'What are you going to do, take her back to your place?' he'd said. 'Give your dad some headphones and pop the *Antiques Roadshow* on for him? That's why you're still single, Ronnie. You'll never find a missus as long as you're living with your old man.'

'So what's your excuse then?' said one of the drivers, referring to the fact that Alan lived alone and was also perpetually single. Everybody got a good laugh out of that one. Well, everybody but Alan.

What nobody seemed to understand was that Ronnie didn't care about how he was going to explain his living arrangements to a prospective partner, for the simple fact that he wasn't looking for one. This often received as many, if not more, strange looks as when he told people he still lived with his dad. It was like telling somebody that you had no desire to sleep, or to eat, or to squirt whipped cream into your mouth if you found a can of it in the fridge and there was nobody around to witness it. Some people thought he was lying by implying he was single by choice and not because nobody wanted to go out with him. Others asked with a chuckle and a sneer if he was 'batting for the other team'. But Ronnie wasn't gay. He just wasn't interested.

Did he often wish he had somebody in his life who he could share things with? Somebody who he could nudge and say, 'Hey, wow, look at that!' when he saw something of interest (provided that that something wasn't a wave), or somebody he could have a drink with or go for a walk with or talk to about things that you just couldn't talk about in the lunch room at work? Yes, he did. But you didn't need a relationship for that. You just needed a friend. He wasn't unhappy being single. He was simply fed up being alone. Because of this, he found it oddly comforting to know that there was another living, breathing presence in the house that night, even if it was the sort of presence that most people would call an exorcist about.

Chapter Twelve

Up until the age of eight, Ronnie, like most children, collected friends like rich people collected expensive works of art. Unlike rich people, however, Ronnie, like most children, did not lock his friends in vaults, mainly because vaults weren't an option. Sheds and closets and toilet cubicles were, though, so they locked each other in those instead. They called the game 'The Prisoner' because they weren't very imaginative, and it was generally quite fun, just as long as you weren't the one being incarcerated.

One day he thought it would be fun to play the game with his mum, although it only occurred to him afterwards that he probably should have asked her if she wanted to participate first. He hid beneath the basement stairs and waited for the washing machine to stop spinning. The moment it did, his mum appeared like clockwork with the empty laundry basket. He watched as she descended the stairs and started to unload the washing machine. Then, creeping out of the basement, he quietly locked the door behind him and waited for the door handle to start jiggling. Two minutes later and nothing had happened, and because two minutes was the rough equivalent of a bajillion minutes to an eight-year-old, Ronnie got bored and went to watch cartoons instead. He wasn't gone for *that* long, but as anybody who's ever been locked in a basement will know, it doesn't take *that* long to start freaking out when you realise the door won't open. Needless to say, his mum did not see the funny side, and by the time she'd finished yelling at him before sending him to bed without any tea, neither did Ronnie.

He woke the next day to find his dad at the kitchen table with a letter in his hands. He looked like he'd been crying, but Ronnie couldn't be sure because he'd never seen him cry before and therefore didn't know what the crying version of his dad was supposed to look like. His dad wouldn't read him the letter, but he gave him the gist, and the gist was that his mother had gone and wasn't coming back. It was a pretty rough gist.

His dad never explained the reason behind his mum's disappearance, so Ronnie did what any kid would do in such a situation – he blamed himself. It took him a long time before he could bring himself to lock another door without worrying that somebody might be trapped on the other side of it. It took him even longer to realise that his mum hadn't left because of him, but because she'd run off with the bloke who lived across the road.

Instead of hitting the bottle or having a meltdown or burning every last remnant of his wife on the front lawn like any normal person would do, Ronnie's dad did something much worse; he pretended like everything was fine. More than fine, in fact. He acted like things couldn't be better, as if his wife leaving him to raise their son alone while she started a new life with a man who used to frequently borrow his lawnmower was like one big picnic on a sunny day with infinite sandwiches and not a wasp in sight.

He started smiling for no apparent reason, like when he was driving or listening to the news or watching something that wasn't even remotely funny, like a hard-hitting BBC drama or anything starring Jim Davidson. Ronnie found this sudden onset of smiling unnerving, not only because his dad usually dispensed smiles with the same regularity that broken vending machines dispensed bags of Wotsits, but also because the sentiment his mouth was attempting to express was not shared by the rest of his face, and a smiling mouth minus smiling eyes equalled a smile not entirely unlike the smile of somebody who may or may not have a body in their freezer. He looked like he'd stubbed his toe in church or trodden barefoot on a piece of Lego at a children's birthday party, smiling through the pain no matter how much he wanted to curse the gods and their grandmothers. Only once he'd read Ronnie a bedtime story (something Ronnie's mum usually did, and something she was much better at because she did all the voices and pulled all the faces, but Ronnie didn't tell his dad that) and tucked him in, would he finally allow his smile to fade, and when it did, he looked exhausted, as if the smile were a parasite that lived off his energy and only dropped off when it had gorged itself on every last ounce of his strength.

Ronnie sometimes crept from his room and watched his dad when he couldn't sleep, sitting on the stairs in the dark and peering through the banisters while his dad sat in front of the television with a glass of whisky in his hand that he never seemed to drink, still on his side of the couch as if his wife had just popped out of the room and would be back to join him any minute. It made Ronnie sad to see his dad like that, sitting there alone with an expression he couldn't quite place. It looked a bit like his 'I'm not angry, I'm just disappointed' face but with way more disappointment in it than Ronnie had ever managed to induce (including the time he hid a bunch of McDonald's mayonnaise sachets beneath the living room rug like landmines and then promptly forgot about them until his mum found the ruptured condiments while searching for the source of whatever was making the house smell so funky).

The smile would always be back by morning, beaming at him across the breakfast table as if his dad had just told a joke and was waiting for Ronnie to get the punchline. But every morning it seemed to grow wearier, sagging just a little more with each passing day, like a second-hand tent bought on Facebook Marketplace, until one day Ronnie came downstairs to find his dad sitting at the breakfast table with a mug of tea in his hand and a blank look on his face. He looked like he'd gone into some sort of mental hibernation, like somebody on public transport whose phone had died when they still had multiple stops to go. His eyes reminded Ronnie of the eyes of the fish that watched him from the seafood counter at ASDA, their pupils dark and glassy and oddly mournful, despite fish not being able to form meaningful expressions even when they were alive, never mind when they were gutted and displayed on ice in a supermarket.

Ronnie had watched his dad in between mouthfuls of home-brand Coco Pops, wondering if humans could break down like cars and, if so, how you'd go about fixing one. The radio murmured away in the background, which usually irritated Ronnie because it played the kind of music that grown-ups listened to, namely the boring kind. Had anybody told eight-year-old Ronnie that forty-two-year-old Ronnie would listen to that sort of music out of choice and not because somebody was pointing a gun at his head, he probably would have drowned himself in his cereal right there and then. He was thankful for the radio that day, however. Even kids aren't immune to the awkwardness of awkward silences.

The radio was a recent addition to the household, having appeared a few weeks after Ronnie's mum had left. Since then, it had never been switched off, not even at night, when it was turned down low but never all the way. Ronnie had no idea why his dad was treating the radio like the Olympic flame. He wondered if his mum hadn't run away at all but had in fact been kidnapped and his dad was keeping the radio on in case it broadcast news of her whereabouts. It didn't occur to him that the police would probably contact them directly, instead of forcing them to listen to Bingham FM all day and night. Only when he grew up and started to live alone did he understand why his dad took comfort in the sound of the radio. Sometimes any sound was better than nothing.

Somebody had called the radio station and requested a song. Usually, people requested something perky and upbeat, a drive-time song to make their commute to work a little more enjoyable. This person asked for 'No Man Is an Island' by Joan Baez, a song that Ronnie had never heard before, or since, that morning. It would have seemed like an odd request even during the station's Odd Request Hour (2 a.m. – 3 a.m. every Sunday), but it was a particularly obscure choice given that most people asked for Duran Duran, Phil Collins or Bon Jovi at that time of the day—something to pep them up for the day ahead instead of plunging them into an existential crisis before they'd even finished their breakfast.

Ronnie's dad had given no indication that he was listening to the radio. He'd given no indication that any of his senses were functioning as they should be, so when he laughed – not a proper laugh, but one of those short, sharp nasal exhalations that people often perform when they think they have a bug up their nostril – Ronnie flinched a little.

'No man is an island,' he said. 'What do you think, Ronnie. Is no man an island?'

Ronnie shrugged. The question confused him as much as the sentence formulation. 'Yes?' he said through a mouthful of cereal.

'We're all islands, Ronnie, whatever people say. Every one of us.'

Ronnie had never heard anybody say that no man was an island. It just wasn't the sort of thing you heard in the playground. He thought that men were men and islands were islands and that was all there was to it, so to learn that men were islands and islands were men was something of a revelation. Only after Ronnie's dad had been called into school following a heated argument between his son and the geography teacher did he feel the need to clarify that men and subcontinental land masses surrounded by water were in fact different things.

'People are trouble, Ronnie. That's what I'm trying to say. Society wants us to think that we need each other, that we're somehow better off together, but it's a lie. Don't trust anybody, they'll only let you down. The only person you can trust is yourself.'

'What about you?' said Ronnie.

'OK, fine, yes, you can trust me.'

'And Spider-Man?'

'No, don't trust Spider-Man. He wears a mask. Never trust anybody who wears a mask.'

'Granny wears a mask.'

'That's not a mask. That's a ventilator. Your granny has emphysema.'

'So I can trust her?'

'Yes. Just not with a packet of cigarettes. Never trust your granny to look after your cigarettes.'

'I don't smoke.'

'Even better,' said his dad.

'Can I trust my friends? They don't wear masks.'

'No, definitely not. Never trust your friends. Your friends are your enemies.'

Ronnie frowned. 'Then what are my enemies?'

'Your enemies are also your enemies.'

'So who are my friends?'

'Nobody. That's my point.'

'Not even Gavin?' said Ronnie. Gavin was his best friend.

'Especially not Gavin.'

'Why?'

'First of all, he never blinks. It's super weird, and you can never trust a weirdo. Secondly, he's your best friend, which means he's closer to you than anybody, and let's not forget what happened to Caesar.'

'What happened to Caesar?'

'He was killed by Brutus.'

'Who's Brutus?'

'Caesar's best friend.'

'Oh,' said Ronnie. He nodded thoughtfully and then stopped. 'Who's Caesar?'

Ronnie's dad sighed. 'Look, the closer people are, the easier it is for them to betray you, get it? You expect your enemies to attack you, not your friends, which is why it's so easy for them to hurt you. They strike when your guard is down,' he said, slashing the air with his teaspoon, 'but they can't strike if they're not close, and they can't get close if they're not your friend. People can only hurt you if you let them, Ronnie, so don't let them. Be a lone wolf. Nobody can hurt a lone wolf.'

Ronnie found this wolf metaphor even more confusing than the island one.

'A lonely wolf?'

'A *lone* wolf.'

'What's the difference?'

'A lonely wolf is lonely. A lone wolf is alone.'

Ronnie frowned. This was very much potato/potahto territory, and he wasn't sure which potato was which.

'Being alone doesn't necessarily mean being lonely, Ronnie,' said his dad. 'You can be alone without being lonely.' He laughed. 'You don't feel lonely when you're on the toilet, do you?'

Ronnie nodded. 'Sometimes,' he said.

Ronnie's dad laughed before realising his son was serious. 'Really?'

Ronnie shrugged a shrug that said, 'Yes, really, but thanks for making me feel awkward about it.'

'Oh. Right. Well, I don't know what we can do about that, son.'

'Maybe we could put a picture of Mum in the bathroom.'

'We're not putting a picture of Mum in the bathroom.'

'Why?'

'Because. People don't put pictures of other people in their bathrooms. It's just not what people do. And people *definitely* don't put pictures of people in their bathrooms when those same people walked out on their families to start a new life with some arsehole from across the road.'

Ronnie stopped chewing. 'You said a bad word,' he said.

'I know, I'm sorry.'

They sat in silence for a moment.

'I miss Mum,' said Ronnie.

'Me too,' said his dad, momentarily forgetting he was supposed to be pretending that he didn't. He cleared his throat. 'That's why you can't trust anybody, Ronnie. All they do is make you sad, and it's better to be a lone wolf than a sad wolf.'

Being only eight and therefore unequipped to deal with this level of profundity, Ronnie had thanked his dad for the warning before promptly returning to being a kid. He didn't want to be a lone wolf or a sad wolf or any other kind of wolf, except for perhaps a werewolf or a Teen Wolf like Michael J. Fox. He just wanted to play with his friends, so that's what he did. The next time one of them wronged him, though (Gavin went to play at another kid's house despite he and Ronnie having already made plans to throw stones at a recently discovered wasps' nest in the local park), Ronnie, who was usually quite pragmatic about such things, remembered what his dad had told him and wondered if there was in fact a modicum of truth to his paranoid ramblings.

'That's what you get for having friends,' said his dad in a tone that sounded so much like 'I told you so' that he may as well have just come out and said 'I told you so.' 'Don't rely on other people, Ronnie, they'll only let you down. If you want to do something, then do it on your own.'

Had he known that Gavin and Ronnie were plotting to piss off a wasps' nest, he probably wouldn't have suggested doing it alone, if at all. Also, had the wasps' nest been full of angry wasps, then there was every chance that Ronnie would have roundly rejected his dad's 'lone wolf' philosophy, mainly because he could run much quicker than Gavin and would therefore have been thankful for the presence of a friend who could double as a human sacrifice should things go south. But the nest turned out to be empty. Not only that, but when he struck it with a rock, the nest fell to the ground in one piece, which meant that Ronnie got to keep the whole thing instead of having to share it with Gavin by either breaking it in half or coming up with some kind of joint custody agreement, like they'd done with the dead mouse they'd once found (they'd also discussed breaking it in half) before it started to smell and neither of them wanted it anymore.

Realising there were certain benefits to doing things alone, Ronnie began to do other things on his own. He often played football with his friends at lunchtime, scurrying around the playground and yelling 'offside!' and 'goal hanger!' and 'man on!' but mainly he just yelled 'pass!' because nobody ever gave him the ball without explicit verbal instruction. In fact, nobody ever gave him the ball *with* explicit verbal instruction, especially his mate Stuart, who fancied himself as something of a Maradona, but without the cocaine addiction (he had one now, though, according to Stuart's brother's mate's ex-girlfriend). The reason for this was simple. Ronnie was crap at football. He didn't know it, but he was. Nobody could deny that he put a lot of effort into running around and waving his arms and generally *looking* like he knew what he was doing, but none of this ever equated to anything remotely close to talent.

When Stuart refused to pass the ball even though Ronnie was the only other member of his team who wasn't lying on the ground clutching his leg due to a flurry of violent tackles by a crazy-eyed kid called Dylan, and even though Ronnie was in the perfect position to score because the goalkeeper was momentarily preoccupied with trying to stop the wind from blowing away their piles of jumpers that comprised the makeshift goalposts, Ronnie decided enough was enough and refused to play football with his friends anymore. Instead, he started bringing his own ball to school and spent his lunch break kicking it against the wall. It was so much more fun! The wall always returned the ball without having to scream 'pass!' at it, and if it didn't, then you could simply take your ball and leave without the wall accusing you of being a bad sportsman. The wall also never kicked you in the shins, so it wasn't just win-win – it was win-win-win! Sometimes his ex-teammates would ask him if he wanted to join them, usually when another kid was sick or injured and they needed to make up the numbers, but Ronnie always declined their offers, until eventually they just stopped asking.

It was in this way that Ronnie's circle of friends slowly began to dwindle. First, the circle became a semicircle, and then a semi-semicircle, and then a semi-semi-semicircle. Eventually, he had so few friends that they couldn't form a circle even if they wanted to, so for a time he had a square of friends. Then he lost another and the square briefly became a triangle. One corner of that triangle was occupied by a kid called Martin who lived down the street. Ronnie didn't really like Martin because Martin had a tendency to grope around beneath tabletops and chew whatever gum he happened to find stuck to the underside. He was also one of those kids who, when standing at the urinal, would insist on dropping his trousers completely, baring his arse to the world. Ronnie found this habit disconcerting. Still, Martin had an impressive collection of wrestling action figures and nobody else to share them with, so Ronnie tolerated the occasional mooning in exchange for unbridled access to Jake the Snake, Hulk Hogan and Macho Man Randy Savage.

Gavin made up the other corner of the triangle, or he did until he came over to Ronnie's house one day and saw the wasps' nest proudly displayed in Ronnie's bedroom, on the trophy shelf that his dad had put up in the days before his son's lack of sporting prowess became apparent.

'You stole it!' said Gavin, pointing at the nest.

'You can't steal from wasps!' said Ronnie.

'You stole it from *me!*' said Gavin, prodding himself in his little bony chest. 'I found it first!'

'Yeah? Well, I don't see your name on it!' said Ronnie.

'I don't see *your* name on it!'

'That's because it's written in really small letters!' lied Ronnie, unsure how else to get out of the corner he'd just argued himself into.

'Show me then!' said Gavin, reaching for the nest.

Nothing settles an ownership dispute among children quite like seeing your name on something. You could literally write your name on somebody's cat and it would rightfully belong to you before the ink had even dried.

'Get off!' said Ronnie, trying to prise Gavin's fingers off.

A scuffle ensued, and as anybody who's ever scuffled over a delicate ball of wood pulp and wasp saliva will no doubt be aware, such scuffles never end well.

'You broke it!' said Ronnie, staring at the papery residue as it fell through his fingers.

JAMES GOULD-BOURN

'Serves you right for stealing it!' said Gavin.

Those were the last words the two friends ever exchanged with each other, although somebody with handwriting very similar to Gavin's wrote 'Rony luvz girls' on the toilet wall at school shortly after their fallout, which was pretty much the most inflammatory thing you could say about an eight-year-old boy.

Gavin wasted no time in telling everybody that Ronnie was a thief and not to be trusted. It was a pointless rumour to spread because Ronnie only had one friend left by then and so it wasn't like he had much to lose from the negative publicity. Also, despite the best efforts of his ex-best friend's smear campaign, Martin still wanted to be friends, no doubt because nobody else would hang out with him. But Ronnie, preferring to have no friends than a friend who chewed the pre-chewed gum of strangers, decided to cut his losses and navigate the treacherous terrain of adolescence alone. His dad was right. Friends were trouble. They let you down, they never passed the ball, they called you names and they ruined your things. Lone wolves didn't have these sorts of problems. They didn't care if anybody passed the ball or not. Wolves didn't even play football!

'Good for you,' said his dad when Ronnie announced over tea that night that his solitudinarian metamorphosis was complete (he didn't use those exact words). He seemed as proud of his son's lack of friends as most dads would be of their sons' abundance of them. 'Forget about them lot. Who needs friends when we've got each other?'

'Can we still be lonely wolves if there's two of us?'

Ronnie's dad shrugged. 'I won't tell anybody if you won't.'

Encouraging your children to jettison their friends by projecting your own insecurities onto them probably isn't the sort of suggestion you'd come across in any decent book about parenting, and many people could end up resenting their dad for doing such a thing. When Ronnie once mentioned to Carl how he didn't have any friends growing up, Carl had looked at him like he'd just revealed that his parents used to keep him in a cage in the basement.

'Wow,' he'd said. 'That must have been pretty shit.'

Ronnie could understand how a friendless childhood might sound pretty terrible to somebody like Carl, whose own father was, in the words of Carl himself, as emotionally present as a fire hydrant, and one that Carl wouldn't even let his dog piss on if it was on fire (Ronnie got the impression that Carl didn't quite understand how fire hydrants worked), but whenever Ronnie thought about his childhood, all of his happiest memories came from the age of eight onwards. His dad filled the shoes of his friends so snugly that he soon forgot he'd ever had friends to begin with. The two of them did everything together, even things that men approaching middle age probably shouldn't be doing. They climbed trees, they melted Lego men with magnifying glasses, they rang their neighbours' doorbells and ran away (never Mrs Higgins's doorbell though – she'd been through enough) and one time, when Ronnie's dad found him digging a hole in the garden for no other reason than to see how deep he could dig it, instead of being angry that his lawn now resembled a sinkhole, his dad grabbed a shovel from the shed and started digging with him. They made it several metres down before they had to stop when their shovels collided with the neighbourhood water pipe.

The only time that Ronnie became aware of the downside of having your dad as your only friend was when a kid in the year above him at school decided that Ronnie was the perfect pebble on which to sharpen his bullying skills. With nobody to watch his back for him, Ronnie found himself on the wrong end of mean words and pudgy fists on an ever-increasing basis. Only when the kid made fun of him for not having a mum ('Did she run away because you're so ugly?') did Ronnie finally tell his dad, mainly because he wanted to know if his mum had in fact run away because he was so ugly. Ronnie wasn't sure what his dad would do about the situation, but he imagined that he'd maybe have a talk with the school's head teacher or perhaps the kid's parents. He didn't expect him to confront the kid directly, and the kid probably didn't expect it either, which was why he looked so surprised when Ronnie's dad told him the following day while picking up Ronnie from school that if he didn't leave his son alone then he could very well expect a kick up the arse in the very near future. The kid threatened to have his dad beat him up, which Ronnie's dad dismissed as the sort of empty threat that all kids throw about when all other options have been exhausted.

When he dropped Ronnie off at school the next day, however, he learned that the kid, while clearly a little shit, was also, somewhat annoyingly, a man of his word. He also learned that the kid's dad, who was right there beside his son with a look on his face that suggested his lower lip was attempting to consume his upper lip and everything above it, took the whole 'my dad could beat up your dad' thing really quite seriously, which he promptly demonstrated by beating him up in front of the other parents.

'I think I hurt him,' said Ronnie's dad once the scuffle was over.

'You didn't hit him,' said Ronnie.

'No, but he hit me and I think I hurt his fist.'

Ronnie couldn't argue with this logic.

'That showed him, huh?' said Ronnie's dad.

'*What* did it show him?' asked Ronnie, not quite following.

'That we're a team,' said his dad, touching his lip and flinching from the pain. 'We might not be the *winning* team, but we're still a team.'

It was only when his dad died of a sudden heart attack many years later, sitting in his favourite chair in front of the television after Ronnie had gone to bed, that Ronnie belatedly realised that putting all of your friends into one basket would one day result in putting all of your friends into one casket. It hadn't occurred to him until that moment that the one person who had always been there for him would not be able to comfort him during the darkest moment of his life. He looked around for somebody to share his grief with, but the only other person present was the vicar, who also kept looking around, not because he needed a hug but because he seemed reluctant to commence his sermon.

'Do you know how long the others will be?' he whispered to Ronnie. 'I have another funeral at three.'

'The others?'

'The other attendees.'

'There is nobody else,' said Ronnie. 'It's just me.'

'Oh,' said the vicar. He nervously cleared his throat. 'Right. I'll get started then.'

As the vicar half-heartedly read his sermon like a warm-up band without an audience, Ronnie tried to imagine what his own funeral would look like now that his dad was gone. He wondered who would turn up if he suddenly dropped dead, or failed to wake up, or fell off a bridge, or choked on a fish bone alone in his living room, but he couldn't think of a single person who would come, at least not for the right reasons. Some of his colleagues might attend, but only because it would give them a chance to skive off work for a few hours. Gary from the corner shop might stop by, although probably not. Their conversations never went any deeper than lamenting the state of the weather (it didn't matter what the weather was doing, there was always something to complain about) and discussing Bingham FC's never-ending free fall through the ranks of non-league football (Ronnie knew nothing what-soever about football, but he'd become quite adept at nodding and frowning during Gary's impassioned monologues). Also, Ronnie didn't even know Gary's last name, and Gary didn't even know Ronnie's first name (he always called him Ramón for some reason), which meant that Gary wouldn't even know if Ronnie had died because he'd be looking for the wrong name in the *Bingham Bugle* obituaries.

The only person he could bank on to be there at his graveside was the person whose graveside he was currently standing beside. He didn't have any other friends. Not real friends. Not the sort of friends who would back you up in a pub fight, even if you were the one at fault. Not the sort of friends you'd turn to if you desperately needed to hide a body. Not the sort of friends who would turn to you if *they* needed help with hiding a body. And not the sort of friends who you could talk to if your dad had just died and you didn't know where else to turn.

Ronnie had never felt more alone than he did that day. But then his shadow disappeared, and Ronnie found himself feeling more alone than ever.

Chapter Thirteen

When Ronnie woke up the following morning, fully rested from a night of unbroken sleep, his first thought – how fully rested I feel from a night of unbroken sleep! – was quickly elbowed out of the way by his second thought – *why* did I have a night of unbroken sleep? He'd expected to be woken in the night by a bark or a growl or the sound of water pouring from somewhere other than the tap onto something other than porcelain, and the fact that he hadn't meant that Hamlet had either A) crumbled a sleeping pill into his food, or B) hadn't caused the mischief that Ronnie had fully expected him to cause. He was willing to entertain either possibility.

Sliding his feet into his slippers, cautiously, in case there were any unpleasant surprises lurking inside, Ronnie shuffled out of his room to find his dad's door had swung ajar at some point during the night. He pulled it to and went downstairs to find Hamlet's makeshift bed empty.

'What are you up to?' he muttered as he stared at the faint indentation of Hamlet's little body in the blankets.

A sense of déjà vu followed him around as he made his way from room to room in search of his furry housemate. This time, however, instead of starting with the most logical places, Ronnie went straight for the washing machine, convinced he could shave off valuable time from his search and rescue mission by thinking like Hamlet instead of like a normal person. But Hamlet wasn't in the washing machine. Nor was he anywhere else in the house, not unless he'd managed to wedge himself into the teapot or the biscuit jar.

Ronnie was just about to check inside the oven when he remembered how his dad's door had been slightly open that morning.

'Hamlet!' he yelled, stomping up the stairs and coming to a halt outside his dad's bedroom. 'Are you in there?' he said before realising how pointless this question was.

He put his ear against the door and listened for any sign of life. Hearing nothing, he placed his fingers on the handle, took a deep breath and counted to three before slowly exhaling and opening the door.

The faint odours of Old Spice, even older books and Fox's Glacier Mints greeted him as he walked into the room. Even individually, these smells never failed to evoke memories of his dad, but together the effect was cruelly illusionary, so much so that Ronnie had to take a moment to pull himself together and remind himself that his dad was gone and had been for quite some time.

The second thing to greet him was the sight of Hamlet curled up on the bed. He was dead to the world in a way that made Ronnie wonder if he might actually be, well, dead to the world, until his back leg twitched ever so slightly.

Ronnie felt a rare sort of anger well up inside of him, the sort he hadn't felt since he'd seen the paperboy taking a shortcut across his dad's flowerbed shortly after the funeral. He'd yelled at the paperboy in a way that had startled himself almost as much as it had startled the kid (who was that surprised by Ronnie's outburst that he ran off before he'd even delivered the morning paper). He felt the same urge rising up in him now, and if he wasn't gripping the door handle so tightly, then he might have yanked the duvet out from under Hamlet like a magician performing the tablecloth trick. But as he stood there and watched the rise and fall of Hamlet's scratty little ribcage, he felt his anger slowly subsiding. It was no secret that Hamlet was not the most pleasant creature to behold when awake, but when he was asleep, he looked oddly sweet, or sweetly odd perhaps. He was bathed in an almost celestial glow from the morning sun that beamed through the window. Ronnie had forgotten how bright this room could be, and as he turned round and followed the light that streamed past him and into the hallway, which was often gloomy at all times of the day because there were no windows in the stairwell, he was surprised to see how warm it now seemed.

'Would you look at that,' said Ronnie quietly. He shook his head and smiled, as if he'd just spent the morning searching for his glasses only to find them on his head all along. The house had often felt like a very dark place in the months since his dad had passed away, and all he had to do to bring a little light back into it was to open the door.

Leaving Hamlet gently snoring on the bed, Ronnie crept out of the room, propping the door wide open behind him. Then, creeping back in a minute later, this time with the lead in his hand, he tiptoed across the carpet and carefully attached it to Hamlet's collar before quietly backing out of the room.

Ronnie flicked the kettle on and made himself a cup of tea. Returning the milk to the fridge, he looked at the fridge light before tentatively putting his hand beneath it and moving it back and forth. Still no shadow. Ronnie sighed and closed the door.

Had it run away? he wondered as he sat down at the kitchen table and took a sip of tea. Was being his shadow really so bad that it would rather cut itself adrift and float through the world untethered than spend another second attached to him?

He tried to imagine what sort of hardships he'd unknowingly subjected his shady sidekick to over the years, and the more he thought about it, the more he realised that shadows had a pretty bum deal in life, regardless of who they were paired with. Even the shadows of movie stars and fashion models and members of K-pop bands didn't exactly have it easy. After all, for all of the glitz and the glamour, for all of the fancy awards ceremonies and lavish rooftop parties in Malibu or St. Moritz, or wherever famous people had lavish rooftop parties, there came a point, as there came a point with every person on the planet with a functioning digestive system, where those movie stars and fashion models and K-pop band members needed to go to the bathroom, and every time they did, their shadows would be forced to go with them. Ronnie was no exception. He went to the bathroom like everybody else, and sometimes, during his weekends or his lunch breaks, he spent a lot of time in there, scrolling the internet or playing Fruit Ninja or reading the latest additions to the toilet wall that had been scrawled by nameless scrawlers since his last visit. He never once spared a thought for his shadow, who was forced to sit in there beside him, or, given the unfortunate location of most bathroom lighting, directly beneath him.

He thought about all the times his shadow had seen him naked, and shuddered, not because he felt exposed, but because he felt bad for his shadow. It probably knew every wrinkle, mole, crease and crevice that his body had to offer, whether it wanted to or not, and it most likely didn't, because even Ronnie didn't want to know about those things. Not only that, it also had to witness him doing various undignified things that people usually did alone, like singing 'Baby Shark' in the shower or stalking ex-classmates on Facebook or reading the TV & Showbiz section of the *MailOnline*, or any other section of the *MailOnline*. It had to observe him flossing, a highly undignified endeavour due to the fact that his mouth was small and his hands were big and his molars lived so far back that he couldn't get to them without repeatedly triggering his gag reflex. And it also had to watch him dance, which he sometimes did alone at home, and nobody deserved to watch him dance, which was why he did it alone at home.

Ronnie concluded that the life of a shadow was really quite miserable. Aside from dogs, who the hell wanted intimate and uncensored warts-and-all access to the private lives of their human companions? Especially when there was nothing in the form of recompense. Dogs got treats and head scratches and toys, but there were no such perks for a shadow. Nor were there any bonuses or holidays or sick days. They couldn't complain because they didn't have a voice, and they couldn't lobby for change because, well, they didn't have a voice *or* a union. It was just work, work, work, day in and day out, and even though the 'work' wasn't physically demanding, being a passive observer could feel like work if what you were passively observing made you hanker for a lifetime of hard labour. It was like being forced to watch the film adaptation of *Cats* on repeat for eternity. Nobody deserved that, not even shadows.

Ronnie understood why his shadow might want to run away. What he didn't understand was *how* it could run away. He didn't want to sound too arrogant about the whole arrangement, but he was fairly certain that his shadow was quite literally nothing without him. He didn't mean that in the way an angry mentor might mean it while yelling at the back of the protégé they'd raised like a son and was now betraying them by taking all their hard-earned knowledge to the mentor's most bitter rival. He meant it in the very literal sense of the word. His shadow only existed because he existed, which meant that it could only run away if he ran away with it, thereby defeating the entire point of running away.

So if it hadn't run away, then where was it? And how would he find it? Losing your shadow wasn't like losing your keys or your wallet or your phone. Lose any of those things and you could at least go back to the train station or the cinema or wherever else you'd last seen them and hope that some kind stranger had found whatever you'd dropped and handed it over to the lost property office. You couldn't hand a shadow over to the lost property office, not without risking some funny looks and a very awkward conversation. And even if you could, who paid enough attention to their shadow to know when and where they'd seen it last? Nobody, that's who, because you shouldn't have to keep an eye on your shadow. It was just one of those things that you should not have to keep an eye on. That was what made this whole thing so much worse.

Not only was it utterly bizarre, it was also completely unfair. Ronnie felt like the victim of some weird glitch in the system. It was like the time he received a court summons through his door for failing to pay a parking ticket, even though he'd never received the parking ticket in question, for the simple fact that he didn't own a car.

He didn't know Hamlet had entered the room until he saw something lurking in the corner of his eye. He turned to find Hamlet staring at him with the confused expression of somebody who had gone to sleep in a bed and somehow woken up in a skip.

'Morning, sleepyhead,' he said. Hamlet continued to glower at him. 'What's up?'

Hamlet looked at the lead that had mysteriously attached itself to his collar.

Ronnie shrugged. 'Don't look at me,' he said, trying to sound innocent.

Chapter Fourteen

Realising that he couldn't leave Hamlet dragging his lead around the house all day without risking an accidental strangulation, and noticing that the sky was if not blue, then certainly a lighter shade of grey than usual, Ronnie decided to take Hamlet out for what was supposed to be a short walk but ended up being much longer than intended, mainly because Hamlet insisted on stopping every few seconds in search of a decent place to go to the bathroom.

'To pee or not to pee?' said Ronnie, chuckling at his own joke. He hoped it was only a pee because he didn't have any poop bags with him. Perhaps aware of this fact, Hamlet decided after several more impromptu pitstops that it wasn't just a pee he needed.

'Not there!' said Ronnie as Hamlet proceeded to go right in the middle of the pavement.

Ronnie tugged a little on the lead, hoping that the gesture might make Hamlet suck in whatever was about to come out, but he stopped when he thought about how annoying that must be, having somebody pulling on your neck while you're trying to use the toilet. He knew that some people paid good money for that kind of thing, but he also knew that he wasn't one of them.

'Feel better now?' he said as Hamlet finished his business and casually tried to continue his journey before the length of his lead yanked him to a halt. He turned round and looked at Ronnie as if wondering why he too wasn't actively trying to flee the crime scene. 'We can't just walk away, Hamlet. We live in a civilised society! We need to clear this up!'

But as he looked around for something to clean it up *with*, it quickly became apparent that doing so would not be easy. The combination of a blasé attitude to littering and a town that seemed to attract more wind than a charity baked-bean-eating contest meant that you could walk down any street in Bingham full in the knowledge that you wouldn't get to the other end of it without a plastic bag slapping you in the face, getting stuck on your foot or dancing around you as if rehearsing for the stage adaptation of *American Beauty*. Today, however, just happened to be the only windless and therefore plastic-bagless day that Ronnie could remember. In fact, he'd never seen the streets so clean, which on a normal day would fill him with joy, but today filled him with a mild sense of despair.

Ronnie sighed. If there was one thing he hated more than anything else in this world, it was people who played their music on the bus without using headphones, but if there were *two* things he hated more than anything else in this world, that other thing would be people who didn't clean up after their dogs. The thought of joining their ranks was not something he'd ever imagined having to entertain before, yet here he was, thinking about doing the unthinkable.

'OK, look,' he said to Hamlet. 'I'll tell you what we'll do. We'll leave it here *temporarily* while we go and buy some bags, and then we'll come straight back and pick it up and hope that nobody treads in it in the meantime.'

He scanned his surroundings, keen to ensure that nobody was present to bear witness to the heinous sin he was about to commit. Then, confident that the coast was clear, he set off at such a brisk pace that Hamlet's little legs could barely keep up. Fortunately for Hamlet, yet unfortunately for Ronnie, the brisk pace lasted only a few seconds before Ronnie came to a sudden halt when somebody yelled 'Oi!' from somewhere behind them.

He turned round to find a stocky man with a red face standing a few metres away. Having checked the street just seconds earlier, Ronnie couldn't figure out where the man had come from until he realised that the car in the middle of the road with the driver's door open belonged to him. The man appeared to be in his mid-sixties, an age that wouldn't normally be considered threatening, but what the man lacked in youthful prowess, he seemed to make up for with that sort of simmering rage that many men of his age carried around with them. It was the sort of rage that came from a lifetime of being forced to do unpaid overtime by shithead bosses because they had too many responsibilities to risk putting their job on the line, but now that the mortgage had been paid off and the kids had left home and the winter fuel allowance had kicked in, the gloves were off and they were looking to unleash those years of pent-up frustration on the first poor sod who let their dog crap on the pavement without first checking that they had a roll of poop bags in their pocket.

'I hope you're going to clean that up!' he shouted, despite the fact that he was most certainly close enough to Ronnie to convey his message at a normal volume. He pointed at Hamlet's turd in the same way that angry people point at things in newspaper stories with headlines such as 'Kerb nearly killed me!' or 'Thieves stole my wheelie bin from this spot right here!'

'I am!' said Ronnie. 'I just don't have anything to pick it up *with* so—'

'So you thought you'd bugger off and leave it for somebody to step in.'

'No!' said Ronnie incredulously. 'I'd never do that.'

'You just *did* do that.'

'I wasn't *leaving* it. I was on my way to the shop down the road so I could buy some bags to clean it up with. I'll be back in a minute.'

'Yeah, right,' said the man dismissively. 'Pick it up.'

'I'm going to.'

'Now.'

'With what?' said Ronnie, holding out his arms to emphasise the distinct lack of nearby poop-scooping apparatus.

'That's not my problem. You can use your hands for all I care, just get rid of it,' said the man. 'Before I call the police.'

Ronnie sighed and looked at Hamlet. He thought about offering him up as collateral while he went to the shop, just so the man would believe he was going to return, but he didn't think that doing so would help his attempts to prove that he was in fact a responsible dog owner. Also, even *he* didn't believe he was going to return.

'Fine,' he muttered, looking around while he searched for something that could double up as a poop bag. While he did so, another car came down the road. The driver pulled up behind the man's car and waited for a few seconds. When it became clear that the man wasn't going to move his car, the driver wound her window down and stuck her head out.

'What's going on?' she said, shouting to be heard over the large German shepherd that was barking away on the back seat behind her.

'You'll never believe this,' said the man.

'Believe what?' she said.

'This bloke was trying to leave without picking up his dog shit.'

'That's not true!' said Ronnie.

'Well I never,' said the woman. She turned off the engine and got out of her car. 'You should be ashamed of yourself,' she said, standing next to the man.

'I was coming back!' insisted Ronnie, but neither of his roadside judges seemed interested in giving him a fair trial.

Noticing a crisp packet folded up and wedged into the gutter, he plucked it out, opened it up and tried to poke Hamlet's poop into it with a stick, while the man and the woman tutted and sighed in turn. Failing that, he looked around for something more suitable and, after rummaging through the litter wedged in somebody's hedge, found a polystyrene tray, which he tried to use as a makeshift poop scoop.

'You're smearing it all over the place!' complained the man while Ronnie chased the turd around the pavement.

'You're meant to be cleaning it up, not making it worse!' shouted the woman.

'There,' said Ronnie, slightly out of breath. He held up the tray while proudly displaying his quarry.

'What do you want, a medal?' said the man. 'Don't let me catch you doing it again, or else!'

'Yeah,' said the woman. 'Next time do yourself and the rest of us a favour and carry some of these with you!' She pulled out a roll of poop bags from her pocket and waggled it at Ronnie.

'You've had those in your pocket the whole time?' said Ronnie, but the man and the woman were already climbing back into their cars. He looked at Hamlet. 'She had them in her pocket the whole time!' he said.

If Hamlet shared Ronnie's outrage, then he didn't show it, being far too busy trying to eat his own ear.

'Come on,' said Ronnie, setting off down the road with Hamlet trailing from the lead in one hand and a polystyrene tray awkwardly held at arm's length in the other.

The suspiciously dry weather lasted only as long as it took them to reach the outskirts of town.

Having jettisoned their unwanted cargo, Ronnie and Hamlet ducked into the doorway of Bingham Library while they waited for the downpour to pass.

'Such a shame,' said Ronnie as he peered through the grimy window and into the wreckage of the library. It had closed for renovations about two years ago and never reopened after the council decided to reallocate the budget, but not before the contractors had torn out the interior, ripped up the floor and generally left the place in such a state of disrepair that even Bingham's homeless hadn't bothered to break in.

Ronnie remembered going there with his mum about a year before she disappeared. She'd left him in the children's section while she'd gone to look at the romance novels, or so she'd said, but when Ronnie had flicked through all of the children's books and his mum still hadn't come back for him, he went to look for her. Finding the romance section empty, he'd eventually found her in the dark and unfrequented corner of the library where the military history was kept, which he thought was strange because his mum had no interest in military history, or any sort of history as far as he was aware. But then he saw that she was chatting to Mr Higgins from across the road and realised that she'd probably seen him in the military history section and gone over to talk to him. Not thinking any more of it back then, he'd aimlessly wandered around the library until, spying a deck of cards in the play area, he'd kept himself busy by slipping them into random books like bookmarks until the entire pack was empty. It was only later, when his mum had left, that it dawned on Ronnie that Mr Higgins probably wasn't that interested in military history either.

The community centre was directly across the road from the library. It looked as derelict as the library but was, miraculously, still in use. Along with the church and a handful of other buildings, the community centre was one of the oldest buildings in Bingham that still served its original purpose. Everything else had been converted into takeaways, souvenir shops and pubs, most of which were also now closed. Every time he passed the noticeboard outside, Ronnie would stop and read about the coming week's events. They were never anything interesting – dance classes, bingo, jumble sales, cake bakes – but it was reassuring to know that *something* was still happening in Bingham, even if that something was no more exciting than a tango class for the over-sixties.

Curious as to what was on the board today, Ronnie crossed the road and swapped one doorway for another.

'Zumba?' he said to Hamlet. 'Fancy a bit of Zumba?' Hamlet did not seem to fancy a bit of Zumba. 'Suit yourself,' said Ronnie as he continued down the list of events. As he did so, a car pulled up outside and a woman got out with a small dog in her arms.

'Here for the class?' she asked on her way into the community centre.

'Class?' said Ronnie. 'What class?'

'Dog training,' she said, nodding at the board. 'I'm hoping they can give me some tips about how to stop this little menace from chewing the couch to pieces.' The little menace in question was a grumpy-looking Yorkshire terrier with a pink bow wrapped around a bunched-up sprout of hair between its ears. Ronnie wondered if the couch-chewing and the pink bow were somehow connected. The dog eyeballed Ronnie with suspicion.

'We were just sheltering from the rain, actually,' said Ronnie while he scrolled down the noticeboard until he found the class in question. Dog Training, Sunday, 1:30 p.m. – 3:30 p.m.

'Then you may as well shelter inside,' she said, heading through the door. 'It's a free class.'

Aside from the recent pooping incident, which was, in hindsight, his own fault for not being prepared, Ronnie didn't think that Hamlet needed to attend an obedience class. Despite expecting to wake up that morning to find the couch cushions shredded, the carpet sullied and the wallpaper riddled with damp spots from a night of overzealous territory marking, Ronnie had been surprised at how well behaved Hamlet had been (although he still hadn't ruled out the possibility that unwanted presents were currently festering in various corners of the house). Also, while Hamlet clearly had problems, Ronnie had a feeling that they weren't the sorts of problems that could be solved by a free obedience class in Bingham community centre. Still, given how stacked the odds were against Hamlet ever getting adopted, Ronnie thought that it was only fair to give him a fighting chance.

'What do you think, mate?' he said to Hamlet. 'Shall we give it a go?'

Hamlet turned round and tried to walk away, perhaps because he understood and objected to the proposal, or perhaps because he simply wanted to play in the rain.

'Come on,' said Ronnie, leading him inside. 'Don't think of it as obedience training. Think of it as improving your life skills. You could put this on your CV!'

The class was held in the main function room. It was the same room that people used for wedding receptions, birthdays, office parties and wakes. Ronnie would probably have booked the room for his dad's wake, if his dad had had a wake, but Ronnie had skipped the tradition on account of there being nobody to invite. If there was one thing even more depressing than a funeral, it was a wake with nobody there, and Ronnie hadn't fancied the idea of sitting in an empty room and eating his way through a platter of cold drumsticks and soggy sandwiches on his own.

It hadn't occurred to him just how well behaved Hamlet was until he saw the other attendants. Ten flustered people were struggling to restrain ten dogs that varied in shape, size and breed but were similar when it came to acrobatic displays of disobedience. Some of them were jumping up and down, others were doing actual flips, a few were barking incessantly and a couple were whimpering like they thought the training was a smokescreen for a covert veterinary check-up. All of the owners were staring at Ronnie as if he were somehow to blame. Then, remembering how the dogs at the shelter had responded to him, he realised he most likely *was* to blame for the pandemonium unfolding before him.

'Actually,' he whispered to Hamlet, 'I don't think this is such a good idea after all.'

Nor did the trainer, who sidled up to Ronnie and gently ushered him into the corner furthest from everybody else.

'I'm really sorry,' she said, 'but would it be OK if you didn't attend our session today?'

'That's fine,' said Ronnie, making a move for the door, 'we were just leaving.'

'Thanks so much for understanding,' said the woman, who looked like the sort of person who asked for the manager the moment things weren't going her way. 'It's just really difficult for the other dogs to concentrate when there's something like that in the room.' She pointed at Hamlet.

Ronnie stopped. '*That?*' he said.

'Your dog.'

'He's called Hamlet,' said Ronnie, surprised by how defensive he sounded.

'That makes sense.'

'What makes sense?'

'Naming him after a tragedy.'

'Are you saying my dog is ugly?'

'Are you saying he's not?'

Ronnie stuttered. 'Well, I mean, he might not be a looker in the conventional sense of the word, but that doesn't mean he isn't beautiful in his own way. You know, on the inside.'

'Well, could he be beautiful on the outside?' she said, pointing to the door.

'I thought you were supposed to be a professional trainer?' said Ronnie, surprised by her attitude. He thought that animal trainers were animal lovers, and that animal lovers loved animals regardless of what they looked like, but clearly that wasn't the case.

'I am, but I can't teach your dog to stop being ugly, can I?'

'No, but maybe *he* can teach *you* some manners!' said Ronnie. They both looked down to find Hamlet's nose embedded so far up his own arse that he'd need a headlamp if he went any further. Ronnie cleared his throat. 'Come on, Hamlet,' he said, heading for the door.

A man with a black-and-white cat on a lead was on his way into the community centre as they were on their way out. He was young, early twenties at most, with large eyes set into a skinny face. He looked slightly haunted, in that way people do when they've narrowly avoided getting hit by a car.

'After you,' said Ronnie, stepping aside as he held the door open for them.

'Thanks,' said the man. 'Is this the place for the training?'

'Yeah,' said Ronnie, a little confused. 'The *dog* training.'

'Great,' said the man, seemingly oblivious to Ronnie's attempts to emphasise the canine angle. His cat, however, seemed perfectly aware of the situation. Either that or it just had an inherent dislike of community centres. Whatever the reason, it wouldn't move its legs when the man tugged the lead, and when he tugged it a little bit harder, the cat fell over and refused to get up. 'Come on, you,' said the man, scooping up the limp animal and carrying it inside as if this wasn't the first time he'd had to deal with such protests.

Ronnie watched the door close behind them and then looked at Hamlet.

'Did any of that make sense to you?' he said. Then remembering who he was talking to, he quickly added, 'Actually, don't answer that.'

Chapter Fifteen

On the way home, they took a detour through Bingham Park.

The council had run out of funding for the park years ago, but a team of local volunteers did what they could to keep the hedges in line and the undergrowth at bay.

Ronnie wished he could let Hamlet off his lead so he could dash around the open space like a normal dog. It looked like they had the park to themselves, and it seemed like such a shame to let the wide-open space go to waste. It was only when Ronnie saw the massive Rhodesian ridgeback galloping towards them at full speed that he realised they weren't as alone as he thought.

Ronnie panicked and went to grab Hamlet, afraid that the bigger dog was about to tear him to pieces, but Hamlet refused to comply, preferring to take his chances with the ridgeback than allow himself to be manhandled by Ronnie.

'Fine,' said Ronnie, 'but don't blame me if you get eaten!'

The ridgeback lurched to a halt a few feet away and started to bark at Ronnie. Ronnie slowly backed off, keen to show his aggressor that he had no interest in a turf war and was more than happy to relinquish his claim to this random square metre of park if it meant escaping with his jugular intact.

'Easy now, easy,' said Ronnie in a tone he hoped would not betray how close he was to needing to buy new underpants.

The ridgeback stepped forward and closed the gap between them, clearly growing in confidence. It was close enough to lunge at Ronnie and it looked like it was about to do just that until Hamlet suddenly planted himself between the two of them and proceeded to chew his own leg.

'What are you doing!' hissed Ronnie, afraid that Hamlet, as usual, had not adequately assessed the situation. But Hamlet stood his ground, staring down the ridgeback while casually gnawing his scrawny shank. Was he trying to assert dominance? Was he communicating with the bigger dog in some ancient canine code? Or was he simply doing what he did best, which was to inject his own particular brand of confusion into the situation? Whatever it was, it seemed to be working, as the big dog wavered, unsure what to do. It was still trying to make sense of Hamlet when a man came bounding over the hill with a face as red as the lead that was flailing about in his hand.

'Don't worry!' he shouted. 'He won't bite unless you upset him!'

'How do I know if I'm upsetting him?!' yelled Ronnie.

'He'll bite you!'

'Well, that's helpful,' muttered Ronnie.

The two men didn't recognise each other until Alan lumbered onto the path and grabbed the dog by the collar. Ronnie had never seen his boss outside work before, and it took him a second to reconcile Boss Alan with Citizen Alan.

'Oh, hi, Ronnie,' said Alan, a little disappointedly. 'I didn't realise it was you.'

'Nice to see you too,' said Ronnie.

'Sorry, I just wouldn't have bothered running if I'd known.'

'Thanks for your concern.'

'Ah, you would have been OK. He's a teddy bear at heart. Aren't you, Henry?' said Alan as he patted Henry's head.

'I didn't know you had a dog,' said Ronnie.

'I didn't know *you* had a . . . dog?' said Alan, tilting his head as if a different angle might help to clarify what exactly he was looking at.

'I'm just looking after him for a little while. He belongs to the shelter; he's not actually mine.'

'Neither's this one,' said Alan, nodding at Henry, who had taken to cautiously sniffing Hamlet, not in the way that dogs usually sniff one another but in the way a person sniffs milk to check whether it's expired. 'He's my dad's dog.'

'It's good of you to walk him,' said Ronnie.

'I don't do it for my dad,' said Alan. 'I just like his company.'

'I'm not sure he feels the same.'

'What do you mean?' said Alan, smiling nervously.

'Well, he *was* trying to run away from you . . .'

'Oh! Yeah. Good point. So much for man's best friend!'

'I never thought I'd hear myself say it, but, well, this one's also starting to grow on me.'

'He's quite the character, isn't he?' said Alan.

'That's one way of putting it.'

Knowing that Alan wouldn't be able to help himself, Ronnie waited for the inevitable comments about Hamlet's less-than-conventional appearance. To Ronnie's surprise, however, his boss simply crouched down and tickled Hamlet behind the ear. Hamlet looked at Ronnie as if to say 'See? This could be us if you weren't such a weirdo.'

'What's he called?' asked Alan.

'Hamlet.'

'Hello, Hamlet,' said Alan, stroking Hamlet's back. He looked up at Ronnie. 'Are you going to adopt him?'

'I don't know yet. I don't think he likes me very much.'

'Well, I can't blame him,' said Alan.

Ronnie smiled. In the ten months they'd been working together, he couldn't ever remember having a laugh with his boss, yet here they were, standing in the park and bantering like old friends. It was a strange and not entirely unwelcome experience.

'Hey, know what we should do?' said Alan enthusiastically. 'We should start a dog-walking club.'

Ronnie frowned. 'What, like . . . you and me?'

'Yeah, and anybody else who wants to join.'

'I don't know anybody else with a dog,' said Ronnie.

'Neither do I, but, I don't know, we could put an advert in the *Bugle* or something. You never know, it could be fun.'

'Yeah, maybe,' said Ronnie, trying to sound both polite and noncommittal. As much as he preferred this version of Alan to the Alan he knew from work, he didn't like him enough to spend any more time with him than was absolutely necessary.

Perhaps sensing Ronnie's reluctance, Alan's smile faltered. 'For the dogs, I mean,' he said. 'It could be fun for them. I read somewhere that it's good for dogs to socialise with other dogs. You know, for their mental health and stuff.'

'That makes sense, yeah . . . it's just . . . like I said, I'm not sure if I'm going to have Hamlet much longer, so, you know, I can't really commit to anything when—'

'That's OK, it was just a thought—'

'It's a good idea though—'

'Sure, no problem—'

'You should definitely—'

'Yeah,' said Alan, clearing his throat and checking his watch. 'Anyway, I better be getting this one back before my dad sends out the search party.'

'We should probably be heading back as well.'

'See you tomorrow.'

'Yep, see you at work.'

Ronnie watched Alan trudge back up the hill, this time with Henry in tow.

'Well, that was strange,' he said to himself before looking down at Hamlet. 'Don't you think that was strange?'

Hamlet was too busy eating a leaf to weigh in on the conversation at hand.

'Hey, thanks for trying to protect me by the way,' said Ronnie. 'If that was in fact what you were trying to do. Which I'm not sure it was. But still, if you were trying to do what I think you were trying to do, then, you know, thanks. That was very brave.'

Ronnie held his hand out and wiggled his fingers in the air above Hamlet. He looked like he was trying to cast a spell on him.

'This is me giving you a head scratch. It's like an air-five but, well, an air-scratch.'

Hamlet continued to chew his leaf while trying to pretend as if he didn't know Ronnie.

Given how unexpectedly eventful his Sunday had so far been, not to mention stressful, Ronnie decided to stop into his local for a quick pint on the way home.

When most people referred to their local, they generally meant the pub where they went to meet their mates, or at the very least where they were guaranteed to find somebody they knew or somebody who knew them. If nothing else, they usually knew the name of the land-lord. Their local didn't even need to be geographically convenient to be considered their local. It was just the pub they frequented the most.

For Ronnie, however, his local was his local because it was local and no other reason than that. It was two minutes down the road from his house, which was a convenient staggering distance following any heavy drinking sessions, although such convenience was wasted on Ronnie because he didn't really have heavy drinking sessions, primarily because there was something inherently sad about drinking heavily on your own. He didn't go there often, once per month at most, and when he did, the landlord didn't greet him by name because the landlord didn't know his name, and Ronnie didn't greet him by his name because Ronnie didn't know his name either. Nor did he know the names of the other patrons, and although he recognised a few of them, a wordless nod and a mumble of salutation was pretty much the extent of their communication.

Ronnie ordered a pint of bitter and carried it to the empty table in the corner. Hamlet lay by the open fire, his fur steaming while he dried himself. His dodgy eye was closed, while his slightly less dodgy eye followed Ronnie across the pub.

'Don't get too close to that fire,' said Ronnie, concerned that Hamlet was not the sort of dog that would necessarily take measures to extinguish himself should he happen to catch fire. Hamlet rolled his eye, perhaps in response to Ronnie's fussing or perhaps because he had no control over the eye in question.

The rusty cowbells above the door jangled and Ronnie looked up to see a black-and-white cat on a lead saunter in with the man from the community centre in tow. The man ordered a drink at the bar and then, noticing Ronnie in the corner, paid for his pint and made his way over.

'Mind if I join you?' he said, unclipping the lead from his cat's collar.

'Not at all,' said Ronnie, which wasn't strictly true, but the man had already taken a seat, so he couldn't exactly say no. The cat immediately made a beeline for the fire, seemingly unperturbed by the presence of Hamlet, who was distinctly less unperturbed by the presence of a cat.

'I'm Brian,' he said, extending his hand.

'Ronnie.' The two men shook hands. 'How was the training?' he asked, although given that he'd last seen the man only thirty minutes ago, and given that the training was still very much in progress, he was fairly confident that he already knew the answer to this question.

Brian shrugged. 'Dunno,' he said. 'They kicked me out. They said cats weren't allowed to attend. Which is ridiculous if you think about it.'

'Is it?' said Ronnie, struggling to find the ridiculous angle.

'Yeah. I mean, why does a dog need dog training? It's a dog, it knows how to be a dog. Maybe it's just me, but I'm pretty sure that if there's one animal in this world that doesn't need to be taught how to be a dog, it's a dog, am I right?' Ronnie said nothing, hoping the question was rhetorical. 'But a cat, well, that's a different story, isn't it? A cat has absolutely no idea how to be a dog. It needs all the help it can get, but the woman at the training didn't seem to understand that, which makes me wonder if she's even qualified to be running these sorts of courses.'

'I don't think the training was designed to teach animals how to be dogs,' said Ronnie once it was clear that Brian was being serious.

'Then why was it called dog training?'

'Because it was training dogs how to be more obedient. You know, how to stop them eating the furniture or barking all night or whatever. It wasn't training them how to actually be dogs.'

'Are you sure?'

'Pretty sure, yeah.'

'Oh,' said Brian. He let this sink in. 'Right,' he said. He didn't seem totally convinced.

'Why are you trying to train your cat to be a dog anyway?' asked Ronnie.

'Because he doesn't do any of the stuff that a dog does.'

'Because he's a cat.'

'Yeah.'

'Not a dog.'

'Right.'

'If you don't mind me asking,' said Ronnie, still massively confused, 'wouldn't it be easier to just get a dog? There's plenty up at Bingham dog shelter. That's where I got him.' He pointed to Hamlet.

'Yeah, it would, but I live with my mum and she's super allergic to dogs,' said Brian. 'She knew I really wanted one though, so, I dunno, I guess she thought cats were the next best thing or something because she got me him for my birthday.' He nodded towards the fireplace, where his cat was asleep in front of the fire while Hamlet lingered in the shadows looking cold and miserable. 'It's not like I hate cats or anything. I don't. I quite like them actually, but, well, I just prefer dogs, so I thought that maybe I could train him up. I even gave him a typical dog's name so that it might help him to, you know, get into the zone.'

'What's he called?' asked Ronnie, expecting to hear 'Max' or 'Rex' or 'Rover' or 'Fido'.

The man took a sip of his pint. 'Beethoven,' he said.

'Beethoven?'

'Yeah. You know. Like the Saint Bernard from the *Beethoven* films?'

'It's not exactly a typical dog's name though, is it? I mean, most people wouldn't think of a Saint Bernard when they hear the name Beethoven, would they?'

Brian frowned. 'What else would they think of?'

'The composer maybe?'

'Oh. Yeah. That's more your generation though.'

'My generation?' said Ronnie. 'Beethoven was born in the seventeen hundreds!'

Brian looked over at Beethoven, who was splayed very catlike across the carpet in front of the fireplace.

'Do you think your dog might be able to teach him a thing or two? You know, just some of the basics?'

'Hamlet?' said Ronnie. He laughed. 'I think somebody needs to teach *him* some of the basics. In fact, I'm not sure he even knows that he *is* a dog.'

'You fellas up for the pub quiz on Friday?' said a woman who was busy collecting glasses from a table nearby.

'Yeah!' said Brian. 'Definitely!' He looked at Ronnie. 'Want to join my pub quiz team?'

'I'm not really very good when it comes to general knowledge,' said Ronnie.

'That's part of the fun!' said Brian.

Ronnie could understand this philosophy when doing, say, karaoke, for example. Nobody was expected to be able to sing karaoke very well. In fact, it was kind of boring when somebody *could* sing karaoke well. The fun came from the amateurishness. But Ronnie couldn't see much fun in not being able to answer a bunch of questions. That just sounded a little disheartening. In fact, it sounded a lot like school. But then he thought about all of the times he'd sat there in that pub alone, surrounded by other customers who were busy laughing and joking and drinking with their friends or their family or their partners or their colleagues while he stared into his pint or pretended to be texting his non-existent friends. Compared to that, doing badly in a pub quiz actually *did* sound like fun.

'OK,' he said. 'Yeah, why not?'

'Great!' said Brian. He finished his pint and stood up. 'See you here on Friday,' he said, clipping Beethoven onto his lead.

'See you then,' said Ronnie, suddenly feeling quite excited about the prospect of being part of something for once, even something spearheaded by a man who thought that dog training was designed to teach other animals to be dogs.

'Don't forget to bring your friends,' said Brian, dragging Beethoven away from the fire and heading towards the door.

'My friends?' said Ronnie, his pint halfway to his lips.

'Yeah,' said Brian. 'For the quiz. We can't have a team with only two people, can we!' The cowbells jangled as he pushed the door open.

'Wait!' said Ronnie. He half stood, ready to run after him, but then he sat back down. After all, what was he going to say? I can't bring my friends because I don't have any? He knew that he technically *could* say that – it was the truth after all – but he couldn't bring himself to admit it out loud. He could, however, simply tell Brian that he'd suddenly remembered a prior engagement on that particular day and at that particular time which would therefore, regrettably, mean that he couldn't attend the quiz after all, but by the time this thought had crossed his mind, Brian and Beethoven were long gone.

Chapter Sixteen

Mrs Higgins was in her front garden when Ronnie and Hamlet arrived home. She waved at him and he waved back, keen to keep their communication non-verbal in case she asked him about his mum again.

Closing the gate behind him, Ronnie noticed a man with a bushy beard and thinning hair standing on his doorstep. He wore a bow tie and a button-down shirt that was tucked so tightly into his trousers that he looked like he'd been vacuum-packed.

'Hi there,' said the man with a jarring cheeriness. 'Do you live here?'

'It depends on what you're selling,' replied Ronnie in a tone that simultaneously implied that he was joking but also not.

The man laughed. 'Don't worry, I'm not one of those annoying door-to-door salesmen,' he said, but before Ronnie could take any relief from this, the man continued. 'I just wondered if you had five minutes to talk about our Lord and Saviour Jesus Christ?'

'No, I'm sorry,' said Ronnie, suddenly wishing that the man was in fact one of those annoying door-to-door salesmen.

'Four minutes?'

'I'd love to, really, but I'm running late for something,' said Ronnie.

'Three minutes then?'

'Maybe another time,' said Ronnie.

'Please,' said the man, his confidence slipping. 'I must have been to fifty houses today and not a single person wants to talk about Jesus.'

'Have you thought about maybe talking to them about something else instead?'

'Like what?'

Ronnie shrugged. 'Football?' he suggested.

'Bit weird though, isn't it? Knocking on people's doors and asking if they want to talk about football.'

'Is it any weirder than knocking on people's doors and asking if they want to talk about Jesus?' said Ronnie.

The man nodded. 'Good point,' he said.

'Actually, while you're here, can you do me a favour and unhook my dog?' said Ronnie. Then, realising how strange his request sounded without some sort of context, he pointed to his lower lumbar and said, 'Bad back, you see.'

'Right,' said the man. He looked at Hamlet, clearly uncomfortable. 'I don't know.'

'What's wrong?'

'Nothing. Just . . . do you have a glove or something?'

'Why?' said Ronnie. 'Are you allergic?'

'No. Maybe. I don't know.'

'You don't know if you're allergic to dogs?'

'I don't know if I'm allergic to *that* dog,' said the man, pointing at Hamlet.

'Look,' said Ronnie, 'I'll make you a deal. Help me unclip him and I'll talk to you about Jesus for two minutes. How does that sound?'

'It's fine,' said the man, slowly backing away.

'Three minutes then.'

'Is that the time?' said the man, consulting his non-existent watch. 'I really need to be off.'

'Wait!' called Ronnie as the man fumbled with the latch on the gate as if the devil himself were hot on his heels. 'Let's talk about Jesus!'

'Don't worry about it!' shouted the man as the gate clattered shut behind him. 'It's a boring topic anyway!'

'It's OK, Hamlet,' said Ronnie while he watched the man scurry off down the road. 'I'm sure God loves you.'

If Hamlet cared about the Almighty's affection, then it wasn't immediately apparent.

Ronnie looked across the street and sighed.

'Come on,' he said. 'Let's go and say hello to Mrs Higgins.'

'Did he manage to convert you then?' Mrs Higgins asked when she saw Ronnie and Hamlet approaching.

'He didn't have the chance. Hamlet scared him away.'

'Good boy, Hamlet! I'd say that makes him a keeper,' she said, crouching down and tickling Hamlet behind the ear. 'Are you a keeper, Hamlet? Are you?' She looked up at Ronnie. 'Have you thought about it?'

'Thought about what?'

'Keeping him.'

'I don't think he wants to keep *me*,' said Ronnie, deflecting the question. 'He still won't come anywhere near me.'

'I think he just needs a little bit of time to get used to you.'

'Maybe,' said Ronnie, even though he was pretty sure that he knew what the issue was. 'He doesn't seem to have a problem with anybody else though, just me.'

'Who knows what's going on in that little head of his. Hmm? What's going on inside that little head of yours?' she said. 'Let's have a look, shall we?' She lifted one of his ears and peered inside.

Ronnie smiled, wishing he had the same easy rapport with Hamlet as Mrs Higgins did.

'Maybe he can sense what you're feeling,' she said, ruffling Hamlet's fur. 'Animals are very tuned into that sort of thing. My cat always knows when *I'm* sad.'

Ronnie frowned. 'I'm not sad, though,' he said, wondering why she chose to emphasise this particular point.

Mrs Higgins stood and looked at him for a moment. Then, smiling warmly, she said, 'No, of course not. I just meant that animals can often see things that us lowly humans can't. That's all.'

'Oh,' said Ronnie, not fully convinced that's what she actually meant but keen to move the conversation along. 'Yeah.' He nodded at Hamlet. 'I think this one can even see things that other animals can't see.'

'That's what makes him so special, isn't it, Hamlet!'

'That's certainly one word for it,' said Ronnie. 'Sorry to ask, but would you mind helping me with his lead again? I managed to clip it on this morning while he was asleep, but I don't think he's going to fall for that trick again.'

Lying in bed that night, Ronnie thought about his conversation with Mrs Higgins, specifically the part about him being sad.

Was he? Sad? Mrs Higgins certainly seemed to think so, although given that Mrs Higgins was hardly a ray of sunshine, he wondered if she wasn't perhaps projecting slightly. Or was *he* the one projecting?

He wasn't *happy*, he knew that much, but that didn't necessarily mean that he was unhappy either. It just meant that he was normal, at least according to Bingham's abnormal standards of normal. If somebody with a clipboard stood on the high street and asked random passers-by about their emotional state, 'happy' would not be a common response. If 'shrug' was an option, then they'd probably go for that. Either that or 'don't know'. Those were the two most common answers in Bingham, regardless of the nature of the question.

He used to think that the weather was to blame for the general lassitude of the townsfolk, and perhaps it was, to some degree. It was hard to feel bright and breezy when the weather was always so dull and squally. But Norway, which was only a relative stone's throw away across the North Sea, had weather that made Bingham seem positively tropical, yet the country was often ranked as one of the happiest in the world. Then again, they also had the added benefits of the aurora borealis and wild reindeer and breathtaking fjords, all of which made it slightly easier to cope with the miserable weather, whereas Bingham had light pollution and foxes that tore your bin bags open and occasional sinkholes that appeared without warning to swallow people's garden sheds and sometimes the garden as well.

No, it wasn't the weather. It was the simple fact that Bingham had been abandoned and forgotten and left to rot, just like countless other coastal towns up and down the country, and now the sea was slowly claiming them piece by piece, turning once-thriving seaside resorts into driftwood and sea junk that would one day wash up on other, perhaps more prosperous shores. It was little wonder that the people of Bingham never seemed particularly happy. After all, it wasn't easy to feel cheerful when everything around you looked so sad.

But not Ronnie. Ronnie wasn't sad. At least he didn't think he was, although now that he thought about it, now that he was actively attempting to tune into his emotional frequencies, he realised that he *did* feel something. He felt anxious.

Of all the people in Bingham, people with mates and families and social circles and Facebook friends who were actually friends and not just a bunch of largely random people, how was it that the one person in town with none of those things had found themselves being tasked with assembling a pub quiz team?

If he hadn't managed to make a single friend in the thirty-five years since he'd wilfully traded his mates for a lifetime of lone wolfery, then he certainly wasn't going to make any by Friday. There was a small chance that some of his colleagues might come if he asked them, but there was a much bigger chance that they wouldn't. Also, he wasn't sure he'd want them to. Although he didn't know Brian very well, or at all, come to think of it, he felt he knew him well enough to know that he didn't deserve to have the likes of his co-workers foisted upon him. Ronnie had been to enough Christmas parties to know what they got like after a few drinks, and even if Carl was able to keep his trousers on, and Phil the bus driver didn't try to punch somebody after one too many sambucas, and Alan was rendered mute with a freak bout of laryngitis, Ronnie knew from first-hand experience that Brian, who lived with his mum and had no friends and thought taking a cat to a dog-training class was a perfectly reasonable thing to do, would be seen by his colleagues as an easy target for ridicule, which he was, there were no two ways about it, but Ronnie wanted to spare him from having to learn this the hard way.

That only left one course of action, and that course of action was inaction. He simply wouldn't show up. He didn't like the idea of leaving Brian in the lurch, but there really wasn't any viable alternative. Not unless he wanted to turn up on his own and explain to him why he didn't bring anybody with him, which he didn't. He'd probably have to avoid the pub for a while, just to be on the safe side. He'd also have to be careful that he didn't bump into him around town, which was easier said than done in a place as small as Bingham, but at least he had some experience in that department, having largely avoided somebody who lived just across the street for the vast majority of his adult life.

That's probably it, Ronnie thought, nodding to himself in the darkness. He probably just looked a little anxious about the whole pub quiz thing, not sad like Mrs Higgins thought.

But, then again, perhaps he didn't. Perhaps he looked perfectly fine. Perhaps he just looked sad to Mrs Higgins because everything probably looked a little sad to Mrs Higgins. While he couldn't remember with any real clarity what she was like before his mum and her husband ran away together, the vague recollections he *did* have of her — waving to him from her front garden while sipping gin and tonic and listening to the radio, kicking his football back to him when it bounced across the road, chatting with his mum in the supermarket, utterly oblivious to what was going to happen and what might already be happening – were a far cry from the Mrs Higgins who now spent her days shuffling around town like a ghost that had forgotten which house it was supposed to be haunting and watching him through her living-room window, holding on to the edges of her curtains in the same way that she still held on to some kind of hope that perhaps her husband might one day return. Thirty-five years without closure was bound to affect the way you looked at the world. It was like going through life wearing glasses with a crack in one of the lenses. No matter how blue the sky or how beautiful the view, everything was always going to look just a little bit broken.

Whenever she asked him whether he'd heard from his mum, Ronnie was tempted to lie, partly to put a stop to all the questions, but also because it might just be what she needed in order to finally move on with her life. The next time she asked, instead of saying no, he could say that, yes, actually, he *had* recently heard from his mum as a matter of fact. She'd called him up, out of the blue, ringing the landline, fully expecting to hear a different voice on the other end of it but hoping that whoever picked up might be able to give her the contact details of some previous occupants, namely her family, or her ex-family, or however she thought of them these days, if she thought of them at all. He'd tell Mrs Higgins that they chatted for a while, avoiding the specifics of their fictional conversation so that he didn't have to lie any more than necessary, and then he'd gently break the news to her. He'd tell Mrs Higgins that his mum hadn't seen Mr Higgins for years, that things had never worked out between them and she had absolutely no idea where he was or how to contact him anymore.

It wouldn't bring her complete closure, he understood that, but it might just be enough to set her free. She clearly considered Ronnie to be her last remaining link to her husband's possible whereabouts, even though his connection with her husband was about as tenuous as Hamlet's connection with reality. Breaking that link might also break the chain that had shackled her to the lead weight of hope that she'd been dragging around for all these years. But, then again, maybe that hope was the only thing that kept her going. Instead of setting her free, maybe it would take away the only reason she had left for getting out of bed every day. As much as Ronnie wanted to help, he wasn't sure it was worth the risk. She'd probably see right through him anyway. He was, after all, a terrible liar. He couldn't even lie to himself.

'I'm fine,' he muttered, his mind returning to the question that had kept him awake until now. A little anxious, he thought, but otherwise fine. Ask anybody. Ask the postman. Ask the people at work. Ask Gary at the corner shop. Everybody knew it. 'I'm fine,' he'd say whenever they asked, and they'd say the very same thing in return because they were fine and he was fine and everybody was fine. That was the thing about Bingham. No matter how bad the weather, no matter how bleak the town, no matter how much pain and suffering you might be carrying around inside you, everybody was fine.

Chapter Seventeen

Given how Hamlet had spent the last two days treating Ronnie with all the warmth and affection that one would treat a radioactive isotope, Ronnie assumed that his reluctant sidekick would be dying to get back to the shelter, and the way he marched along the pavement on the day of his return only seemed to confirm this suspicion.

'Anybody would think you wanted to get away from me,' said Ronnie sarcastically as Hamlet dragged him down the road like a child dragging their dad to the ice-cream van. It was hard not to feel a little insulted by Hamlet's eagerness to get rid of him. For all of Ronnie's flaws, of which there were many, he nevertheless found it hard to believe that a cage in a room full of barking dogs could ever be considered preferable to a life with him at home. Still, he tried not to take it personally. After all, if *he* had the option of living in a room full of barking dogs or in a house with a person who didn't have a shadow, he couldn't say with any certainty that he'd choose to live with himself either.

It was only when they were nearing the dog shelter that Hamlet's lead began to go slack.

'What's up, mate?' asked Ronnie as Hamlet came to a halt a few metres from the gate. 'Not a fan of "Babooshka"?' he said, referring to the music that was emanating from the shelter so loudly that it could very well wake the dead at the funeral parlour down the road.

'What have I told you about slagging off Kate?' said Cate as she suddenly popped up from behind the gate.

'Christ,' said Ronnie, flinching. 'You scared me.'

'Yeah, well, now we're even.'

'How long have you been hiding there?'

'Believe it or not, I have better things to do with my time than hiding behind gates waiting to jump out on you all day,' she said. 'With that in mind, I did see you coming down the path just now and decided to hide behind the gate so I could jump out on you.'

'Well, I hope you know first aid because you almost gave me a myocardial infarction,' he said.

Cate looked impressed. 'Well remembered.'

'I'm trying to brush up on my general knowledge.'

'What for? You look a little old for *University Challenge*,' she said. 'No offence.'

'None taken,' said Ronnie. 'I didn't even go to university, so, you know, the joke's on you.'

'Actually, the oldest person on *University Challenge* was seventy-three years old, so a little bit older than you. She was called Ida Staples and she was on the 1997 Open University team.'

'A little bit older than me?' said Ronnie, trying to hide his exasperation. 'How old do you think I am?'

Cate thought about this for a moment. 'Younger than seventy-three?'

'A lot younger, thank you very much,' said Ronnie. 'I'm forty-two.'

'That's how old my dad is.'

'Right,' said Ronnie, suddenly feeling very old.

'He always said that I should have gone on *University Challenge* because I'm such a bloody smart-arse,' she said. She smiled, but it wasn't a happy one.

'You should have, you would have been great.'

'Thanks,' she said, and she seemed like she meant it. 'I thought about it, just to spite him, but then I dropped out of uni and, well, being at uni is sort of a prerequisite for being on *University Challenge*.'

'I was a rubbish student as well,' said Ronnie, trying to show some solidarity.

'I wasn't a rubbish student. That was the problem. I was a good student. I was just rubbish when it came to that whole "playing drinking games and getting shit-faced and waking up in the beds of strangers who think that traffic cones and road signs are perfectly acceptable forms of bedroom décor" thing, otherwise known as The Uni Life. It's quite funny, if you think about it. Most people drop out because they can't cope with the studying. I dropped out because I couldn't cope with the people.' Cate shrugged. 'C'est la vie,' she said. 'What's with the sudden need to know stuff anyway?'

'I just joined a pub quiz team, but I'm useless at

general knowledge. Correction, I was recently *tricked* into joining a pub quiz team.'

'How exactly do you get tricked into joining a pub quiz team?'

'It's a long story, but basically it's all his fault.' Ronnie looked down at Hamlet, who made no attempt to dispute the allegation.

'I bet they're fun,' she said.

'You bet what are fun?'

'Pub quizzes.'

'You've never done a pub quiz?'

Cate shook her head. 'I've done quizzes though. Obviously. And I've been to pubs. Also obviously. I've just never, you know, combined the two. Actually, that's a lie. I once did a maths quiz on my phone while waiting in a pub for a friend. Well, a date. A friend-date. They didn't show up though, but I got one hundred per cent on the quiz, so, you know, it wasn't a complete waste of time.'

'You should join our team!' said Ronnie, unable to hide his excitement, not just at the prospect of having somebody with such an impressive grasp of general knowledge on his team but also at the prospect of having *anybody* on his team. Then, suddenly feeling conscious that his eagerness might be misconstrued as creepy – he was, after all, a man in his forties asking a woman who had just confessed to being young enough to be his daughter to the pub – he cleared his throat and continued in a tone that he hoped sounded more casual and less intense. 'If you want to, I mean. You don't have to. And, you know, I'd have to run it past Brian. But I'm sure he'd be OK with it. Only if you are though. No pressure or anything.'

'Who's Brian?'

'He's the team captain. He's probably about your age, come to think of it. Just in case you were worried about getting stuck with a team of crusty old people like me.'

'And you wouldn't mind me joining? Because if you're inviting me just to be polite, then, really, you don't need to, I totally understand.'

'I'm not asking you out of politeness. I'm asking you because who else would know that the oldest contestant on *University Challenge* was a seventy-three-year-old woman called Ira Staples who was on the 1997 Open University team?'

'Ida,' said Cate, smiling sheepishly. 'Ida Staples.' Being complimented on her capacity for remembering utterly random pieces of trivia was clearly something she wasn't used to. 'OK, I'd love to join, thank you.'

'Great! We still have space on the team, so feel free to bring your friends,' said Ronnie, hoping to put her further at ease with the idea of meeting up with two random men.

'They're busy,' said Cate almost immediately.

'I never told you when the quiz was.'

'When's the quiz?'

'Friday.'

'Yeah, they're busy.'

'No problem,' said Ronnie, sensing he'd stumbled into sensitive territory and eager to stumble back out of it. 'We can be the Three Amigos then.'

'Or the Three Stooges.'

'Or the Three Musketeers.'

'Or the three-headed hound of Hades.'

'Yep. Or that,' said Ronnie, trying to appear like he knew what the three-headed hound of Hades was exactly.

'You know? Cerberus? From Greek mythology?' said Cate. 'He guards the gates of the underworld to stop the dead from leaving?'

'I'll take your word for it,' said Ronnie. Then, using the topic of hounds from hell to segue into his reason for being there, he nodded at Hamlet, who was straining on his lead while his paws scrambled in the dirt in their futile attempt to carry him in the opposite direction of the shelter. 'Speaking of which, I'm here to return this little chap.'

Ronnie hadn't anticipated feeling any sort of emotional weight about the idea of parting ways with Hamlet. The two of them were hardly the most conventional duo after all. Hamlet didn't want to be near him and Ronnie didn't want to look at him, so Ronnie was surprised to feel a little lump in his throat when he handed the lead to Cate.

'We've had quite an eventful time, haven't we, Hamlet? We even got kicked out of a dog obedience class because the lady who ran it said he was u-g-l-y,' said Ronnie, spelling out the last word.

'Was it the class at the community centre?' asked Cate. Ronnie nodded. 'That's rich coming from her. She's got a face like a badger's bumhole.' She looked at the lead but didn't take hold of it. Ronnie jiggled it a little, waiting for her to grab it, but Cate simply stared at it like Ronnie was trying to hand her a gun that may or may not have just been used in a robbery.

'Here you go,' said Ronnie, pretty sure the verbal prompt was unnecessary but unsure what else to do given that Cate was making no attempt whatever to take the lead from him.

'There's a bit of a problem,' she said finally.

'Problem? With what?'

'With Hamlet.'

'You're telling me,' said Ronnie.

'No, I mean . . . we can't take him back just now.'

'What do you mean? You told me to take him for a couple of days and bring him back on Monday. I took him for a couple of days and now it's Monday, so . . .' he trailed off with a nervous laugh.

'I know, but, well, we had an unexpected visit from the animal welfare inspector yesterday and he said we weren't allowed to take any more dogs for the moment.'

'Why?' said Ronnie.

Cate cleared her throat. 'Static.'

'Static?'

'Yeah,' she said, a little unsurely. 'Static.'

'I don't understand,' said Ronnie.

'It's all the dog hair. It generates static, and the more dogs there are in one place, the more static there is, and sometimes that static can build up until there's enough electricity to start a fire. It doesn't happen often, but when it does' – she threw her arms up in the air with a dramatic flourish – 'whoosh!'

Ronnie laughed, convinced this had to be a joke. 'That's funny,' he said.

'What's funny?'

'You know. Whoosh!' he said, mimicking Cate's gesture. 'Very good.'

'There's nothing funny about a dog shelter going up in flames.'

'No, I know that, but you're obviously not being serious,' he said. Then, noticing Cate's rather serious expression, he added, 'Are you? Being serious?'

'I wouldn't joke about something like that,' said Cate with a faraway look, as if she were still haunted by the last catastrophic static dog-hair fire she'd been caught up in.

Ronnie took a second to gather his thoughts. 'So, let me get this straight. You're saying I can't bring Hamlet back today because of fears that he might . . . what? Spontaneously combust?'

He looked at Hamlet, who did not seem in any imminent danger of spontaneously combusting. He drooled too much to catch fire.

Cate sighed as if Ronnie had just asked her which of his shoes belonged to which of his feet. 'No,' she said. 'Spontaneous combustion is chemistry. I'm talking about static electricity, which is physics. Chemistry and physics are totally different.'

'Right,' said Ronnie. He knew that Cate was making this stuff up, just like she'd made up that other story about the man who had swapped one chihuahua for another. Still, even though she clearly took him for a fool, he couldn't fault her reasons for trying to fool him. She was determined to find a home for Hamlet, and she was obviously going to do whatever it took to make sure that happened. She was even more committed to getting rid of Hamlet than he was, and he couldn't help but respect her for that. 'So now what do we do?' he asked, already knowing the answer.

'Well, I know it's not exactly what we agreed on, but I was wondering if you could maybe possibly hold on to him for a few more days, just until we get the numbers down a bit.'

Ronnie sighed. 'I don't know,' he said, even though he did. He just wanted Cate to think that she couldn't exploit his good nature without a fight. Sighing and saying 'I don't know' was, however, the extent of his fight, partly because Ronnie wasn't very combative and partly because – and this thought hadn't truly occurred to him until right at that very moment – he'd actually quite enjoyed having company these last couple of days, difficult though it was to admit to himself.

Yes, Hamlet had caused him to chase poop around the pavement in front of the disapproving eyes of the general public, and yes, his refusal to allow Ronnie to breach his clearly defined perimeter had resulted in him having to interact with Mrs Higgins a great deal more than he would have liked, and yes, he was indirectly responsible for Ronnie getting himself unwittingly nominated as pub quiz team coordinator, yet despite all of this, or maybe, in a strange kind of way, *because* of all of this, Ronnie had felt something he hadn't felt in a very long time. Since his dad had died, he'd often experienced the odd sensation of being a background actor, a blurry nameless figure whose job it was to fill space and look busy and not draw attention to themselves. But over the last few days he felt like he'd gone from being a faceless extra to somebody who, while still not the protagonist, did at least now have a speaking role in the story of his life, figuratively and also quite literally. Whenever he finished work on Friday, he usually didn't have another conversation with anybody until he went back to work on Monday, where he'd chat to people about their weekends while expertly steering the conversation away from his own uneventful life. He'd chitchat with the postman on Saturday morning if the postman happened to visit (the exchange always stuck to a similar pattern – a trading of hellos, followed by a brief reference to the weather, before Ronnie said, 'Not more bills I hope?' and the postman shrugging and saying something non-committal before the two of them wished each other a good day), and he'd have another brief chat with Gary during his weekly visit to the corner shop. He'd also talk to his dad sometimes, just little comments here and there, like 'What shall we watch tonight, Dad?' or 'What shall we have for tea, Dad?' but unless somebody called him – and when they did, it was usually a wrong number or somebody trying to sell him car insurance, loft insulation or, one time, car insulation (he was pretty sure that one was a scam) – then that was generally the extent of his conversations during any given weekend.

Over the last couple of days, however, Ronnie had spoken to so many people that he had quite literally lost count, and even though not all of those interactions had been friendly – a few of them had been rather hostile and some were downright strange – he'd also had several pleasant encounters, or if not pleasant as such, then at the very least not unpleasant either. It gave him a sense of being a part of something, even if he wasn't sure what that something was or what part he played in it exactly. All he knew for certain was that his life had changed since Hamlet had arrived, and although there was every chance that such a change may not turn out to be for the better, Ronnie was willing to take that chance, at least for another few days.

'What do you reckon, mate?' he said, looking down at Hamlet. 'Think you can put up with me for a little while longer?'

Hamlet looked at Ronnie, then at the shelter and then at the rolling fields beyond the shelter. It was obvious which of the options he would have preferred, and Ronnie imagined him galloping off to fight windmills, or whatever else he thought might be lurking beyond the horizon. Still, judging by the way that Hamlet had looked at him before looking at the shelter, Ronnie liked to think that he was at least Hamlet's second-best option, even if it wasn't a particularly close second.

'Thanks,' said Cate. 'I really appreciate it. And I know that Hamlet does too. That's his appreciative face.' They both looked at Hamlet. His face often conveyed several expressions at once, many of them conflicting, and today was no exception, although 'appreciative' did not appear to be one of them.

'If you say so,' said Ronnie. 'See you at the Pig in the Pond on Friday. The quiz starts at eight.'

Chapter Eighteen

They made their way down the lane that took them back to the main road. Ronnie walked ahead, while Hamlet trudged behind him like a little black cloud on a lead. He looked like he'd been asked to choose between ringworm or tapeworm for Christmas.

Ronnie paused at the end of the lane and waited for Hamlet to catch up. In front of him were two signs: one pointing left towards town and the other pointing right to the beach. The evening was still young, even if it looked on the wrong side of middle age, and he looked at the sky as he tried to gauge the weather. It was grey but it was dry, and it was windy without being wild. That was the closest thing to a pleasant evening you could hope for in Bingham. Noticing that Hamlet seemed a little glum and remembering how much he'd enjoyed his previous trip to the beach, Ronnie turned right and headed for the coast.

Hamlet perked up the moment they arrived at the shore. He raced up and down the beach as much as his retractable lead would allow, playing chicken with the waves and chewing on things that a dog had no business chewing on while the sea breeze hit him from every direction and turned him into a galloping pom-pom. Ronnie smiled, happy to see that even an animal as complicated as Hamlet knew how to be a dog sometimes.

Spying a small piece of driftwood wedged between a couple of rocks, Ronnie decided to see if Hamlet knew anything else about being a dog, namely how to play fetch. He grabbed the stick and flinched as something jabbed his palm. Quickly pulling his hand away, he looked at the spot at the base of his thumb where a small blob of blood had formed around a tiny hole in his hand. He looked at the stick again and only then noticed the rusty nail protruding from the end of it. He washed his hand in the sea, trying and failing to time the waves so that he didn't get his shoes drenched. Then, finding another stick, he carefully checked it for nails before gently reeling Hamlet in for a bit of canine 101.

'OK,' he said. 'You are a dog. You might not agree with me on that, and many other people wouldn't either, but that's what you are. And this,' he said, holding up the piece of wood. 'This is a stick. It comes from a tree. You know, those big things that you sometimes pee on. Dogs aren't known for having any great interest in trees. They do, however, have an inexplicable fascination with sticks. Dogs and sticks go together like shepherds and pie. You can't resist them. If somebody throws one, then you have no choice but to retrieve it. This is one of the things that people love about dogs. If you can chase a stick and bring it back, then your likelihood of getting adopted increases by . . . I don't know how much, but it increases by a lot, and let's face it, Hamlet, you're not exactly rife with selling points right now, so we really need to do whatever we can to make you more attractive to the prospective adopter. Not *physically* attractive. No offence or anything, but, well, I think we can both agree that you are way beyond help in that department. But that's OK because that doesn't matter. What matters is what's on the inside, Hamlet, and you know what's on the inside of you? That's right, a dog! I know he's in there, Hamlet. He's in there and he's dying to get out, and this stick is the key to setting him free, so when I throw it, don't think, don't hesitate, don't look at the stick and wonder how many of them it would take to build a wigwam. Just listen to your inner dog and the rest will take care of itself. Got it?'

Hamlet coughed and regurgitated a wad of partly chewed seaweed.

'Great,' said Ronnie. 'Ready? Here we go. Three! Two! One! Go!' He threw the stick and they both watched it sail through the air before clattering against the rocky beach.

Ronnie stared at Hamlet and willed him to go after the stick. Hamlet stared at the stick and willed it to return to them of its own accord. The stick just sat there doing its own thing.

'Not a problem,' said Ronnie, retrieving the piece of wood and resuming his place beside Hamlet. 'You obviously weren't ready, so let's try again, shall we?

Just to recap, I throw the stick, you chase the stick, you bring the stick back. OK? OK. Operation Stick Retrieval, take two.'

Ronnie threw the stick again. Hamlet watched it land and then looked at Ronnie as if waiting for him to go and fetch it. Ronnie sighed.

'Watch,' he said, walking over to the stick and crouching down beside it. 'You're supposed to grab it, like this.' He got down on his hands and knees and pretended to grab the stick in his teeth. 'See?' he said, pointing at his mouth and then pointing at the stick. He gnashed his teeth for emphasis. Hamlet seized the rare opportunity to look at Ronnie as if he, Hamlet, was the most well-adjusted of the two of them.

'What are you doing?' said a voice from behind him. Ronnie turned round to see Harriet walking along the beach towards them. She was wearing the same red bathing suit as last time, but this time she had a blanket wrapped around her shoulders.

'Playing fetch,' said Ronnie, standing up and patting the sand from his hands and knees.

'Isn't the dog usually the one who does the fetching?'

'Usually, yeah, but nobody seems to have told Hamlet this.'

'Don't worry,' she said to Hamlet. 'You don't need to know how to chase a silly stick.'

'I thought it might improve his chances of getting adopted,' said Ronnie, a little miffed that Harriet was undermining his efforts in front of Hamlet, even though

Hamlet had no idea what Harriet was saying, or, for that matter, why Ronnie kept throwing a stick down the beach.

'Our Jenny, God rest her soul, she couldn't play fetch for all the tennis balls at Wimbledon, but that didn't make us love her any less.'

'Was she related to Hamlet by any chance?'

'No,' said Harriet. 'She was a tortoise.'

'Right,' said Ronnie. He wondered how many tennis balls it had taken for Harriet to realise that tortoises weren't into the whole fetching scene.

'Hey, I've got an idea,' she said, glancing around as if about to impart some highly confidential information. 'If you really want to make sure he gets adopted, then you know what you should do?'

'Put a paper bag over his head?'

'Adopt him!'

'Oh! Yeah. No. I'd love to, really, but, you know.' Ronnie shrugged in that way people did when they didn't know how else to end the conversation. Harriet looked at him in that way people did when they didn't understand that some people shrugged because they didn't know how else to end a conversation. Ronnie sighed. 'It's not that simple, unfortunately.'

'Why not?'

'Because, well . . .' Ronnie wracked his brains for a suitable reason as to why adopting Hamlet was objectively impossible. He couldn't exactly say that he was allergic to dogs. Nor could he say he was scared of them, even though Hamlet did sort of terrify him. Unable to think of a decent excuse, and temporarily forgetting how bad he was at lying, he decided to make something up. 'I had a dog, when I was younger. I found him in a cornfield and he followed me home. I loved him to bits, he was like my best friend. But then he got attacked by a wolf and ended up with rabies, so, well, I had to shoot him. It was so traumatic that I haven't been able to own another dog since.' It was only after Ronnie had recounted this story that he suddenly realised he hadn't made it up at all. He'd ripped off the plot from *Old Yeller*, and now it was too late to backtrack.

Harriet stared at him, her mouth slightly agape. 'You shot him?' said Harriet. 'With a gun?'

Ronnie nodded solemnly. 'Both barrels,' he said, as if doubling the barrels somehow doubled the credibility of his story.

'You couldn't have just had him put down?'

'We couldn't afford it,' said Ronnie, hoping that would be the end of it. It wasn't.

'Why did you have a gun?' asked Harriet, clearly struggling to make sense of Ronnie's story.

'My dad was a farmer.'

'Where?'

'In the . . . countryside,' he said, pointing inland towards the unspecified countryside that lay somewhere beyond the horizon.

'And you said your dog was bitten by a wolf?'

Ronnie nodded.

'How?'

'Just, you know, with its teeth.' He made a chomping motion with his fingers.

'No, I mean how did he get bitten by a wolf when there are no wolves in England?'

'Oh! Sorry. Yes. Good point. The farm wasn't in England. It was in Scotland,' he said, this time pointing north along the coast.

'There aren't any wolves in Scotland either.'

'It might not have been a wolf, I really can't remember. It might have been a rabid . . . beaver. It was so long ago.' Harriet frowned. She opened her mouth, but Ronnie cut her off before she could ask another question. 'And anyway, even if I could somehow overcome the childhood trauma of, you know, that whole thing – which I absolutely can't, I still have nightmares about it to this day – but if I could, then the fact remains that, well, Hamlet likes me about as much as slugs like salt and vinegar crisps. Isn't that right, mate?'

For the first time ever, Hamlet looked like he both understood and agreed with Ronnie.

'Don't be silly, he adores you! I can see it in the way he looks at you.'

'That's not adoration. That's suspicion. He looks at the vacuum cleaner in the same way. And traffic cones. He's very suspicious of traffic cones.'

'Nonsense. That right there is a look of love if ever I saw one. Our Jenny used to look at Sidney in exactly the same way,' said Harriet. 'Sidney is my husband.'

Ronnie tried to imagine what a loving look might look like on the face of a tortoise, but all he could picture was the one and only expression he'd ever seen on a reptile, namely that of dead-eyed indifference.

'Was,' said Harriet, pulling the blanket a little tighter around her shoulders.

'Sorry?' said Ronnie.

'Sidney *was* my husband. I said "is", but he's a "was". Even though he still feels like an "is". If that makes any sense.'

Ronnie nodded. 'My dad's been gone for a year but I still sometimes take two mugs out of the cupboard whenever I put the kettle on.'

Harriet smiled. 'I thought I was the only one who did that,' she said.

'You know, if you're looking for a bit of extra company, then I'm sure that Hamlet would be happy to oblige,' said Ronnie. 'Harriet and Hamlet. It's got a certain ring to it, don't you think?'

'I would gladly take you up on that offer if I wasn't so allergic,' said Harriet. 'Anything furrier than a kiwi fruit and I'll be sneezing for a week. That's why we got a tortoise.' She sighed and shook her head. 'Poor Sidney. He always wanted a cat, and he ended up stuck with a tortoise. He never complained though. That was the thing about Sidney. He never complained. It used to drive me a bit mad actually. Isn't that funny? Most people would love to have a husband who didn't complain, and there was me, complaining about his lack of complaining. I asked him about it once. I said, "Sidney, why don't you ever complain about anything?" and you know what he said? He just shrugged and said, "Life's too short."' Harriet shook her head. 'Life's too short,' she repeated, as if to herself.

Ronnie followed her gaze over his shoulder, but there was nothing behind him but beach.

'Anyway,' she said, flinching back to the present. 'Better get a move on. Tea won't cook itself.'

'I don't suppose you're any good at pub quizzes, are you?' said Ronnie. He hadn't been intending to ask Harriet to join the team, but he knew what it felt like to go back to a house that always seemed so full and now seemed so empty.

'Pub quizzes? I don't know, to be honest, I've never done one before,' said Harriet. 'I quite like watching quiz programmes though. I once won a quarter of a million pounds on *Who Wants to be a Millionaire?* Well, I didn't win it, obviously, but, you know, I got all the questions right. Why do you ask?'

'Me and a couple of others have formed a team, and I wondered if you'd like to join. The stakes are slightly lower than *Who Wants to be a Millionaire?* But I'm sure it'll still be good fun.'

'Oh!' said Harriet. She seemed surprised, although Ronnie couldn't figure out if her surprise came from being invited to a pub quiz by a virtual stranger or from being invited to anything by anybody. 'Well, yes, that would be lovely. I'm not sure how much good I'll be though. I only guessed the questions correctly that one time. I think it was luck more than anything. I'm usually quite useless when it comes to general knowledge.'

'It's OK,' said Ronnie. 'I'm useless as well. We can be useless together.'

Ronnie couldn't help but smile to himself as he and Hamlet made their way back to town. He didn't know how he'd done it, but he'd pulled off what had seemed impossible just a couple of days ago. He, Ronnie Porter, had singlehandedly managed to assemble a pub quiz team. For most people, such an achievement would be no more cause for celebration than the successful tying of one's shoelaces or the non-wonky application of a postage stamp to a postcard. After all, most people had enough friends to comprise a pub quiz team without having to rely upon complete and utter strangers to make up the numbers. But for Ronnie, a man whose last friendship with somebody who wasn't his dad had ended with harsh words and dramatic allegations of wasp nest thievery nearly thirty-five years ago, the magnitude of such a feat could not be understated.

'We did it, Hamlet! We did it!' he said.

Hamlet looked confused, like he was trying to recall what it was they had done exactly and whether or not he should deny all knowledge of it.

Chapter Nineteen

Ronnie wasn't sure how long he'd been staring at the teabag in his mug. It could have been a minute or it could have been ten. That was the problem with making a cup of tea you didn't really want. You didn't pay attention to what you were doing.

He'd picked up the habit from his dad, not the absentmindedness, but the instinct to make a cup of tea whenever you needed to pass some time. 'Nothing to do? Make me a brew!' he used to quip whenever Ronnie made the mistake of telling his dad he was bored. Ronnie was quite sure that his dad didn't always want a cup of tea whenever he recited this mantra. Sometimes he actually had a cup of tea in his hand when he said it. But he still made Ronnie make him one anyway. The purpose of the exercise wasn't to help Ronnie to hone his tea-making skills. The purpose of the exercise was to discourage Ronnie from ever being bored. In reality, however, all it did was encourage Ronnie to stop verbalising his boredom while still feeling just as bored as he would have been had he said it out loud. Also, instead of teaching Ronnie to do something productive with his time, the lesson that

Ronnie took away from the exercise was that you should make a cup of tea whenever you were bored, even if you didn't particularly want one, which was, Ronnie had come to accept, an equally unproductive use of one's time.

He looked at the clock on the wall of the lunch room and sighed. The next bus wasn't due to arrive for another hour, and he had absolutely nothing else to do until then. It was going to be a long afternoon.

He sipped his tea while making random words with the alphabet fridge magnets. The other magnets were mostly holiday magnets brought back from Tenerife and Benidorm by one of the bus drivers who no longer worked there. There was also one from a place called Punxsutawney in Pennsylvania, although Ronnie had no idea who'd brought that one back. The magnet had an image of a man in a top hat holding up a giant rodent which, upon closer inspection, turned out to be a groundhog.

Ronnie vaguely remembered something about groundhogs having difficulty seeing their shadows, at least according to the film *Groundhog Day*, and a quick check on his phone confirmed this suspicion. However, whereas Ronnie's shadow had quite literally disappeared, a groundhog's shadow only disappeared on cloudy days apparently, much like any sort of shadow, come to think of it. The only difference was that if a groundhog couldn't see its shadow, then it meant – according to Pennsylvania Dutch superstition – that winter would continue for another six weeks, which was a pretty ridiculous form of weather forecast, but still, at least there was some sort of meaning attached to it, which was more than Ronnie could say about his own predicament.

After researching groundhogs, he then went down a twenty-minute rabbit hole while he read about *Euprymna scolopes,* otherwise known as the Hawaiian bobtail squid. Ronnie had never felt any sort of kinship with squid before, or any other invertebrates for that matter, but he seemed to have more in common with this particular creature than he did with anybody or anything else in the world at that moment, something he found both comforting and mildly concerning. To avoid scaring off potential prey while hunting at night, the squid emitted just enough light to match the moonlight shining on it, effectively erasing its shadow from the seafloor in order to take unsuspecting shrimp by surprise. Had Ronnie's survival depended on his adeptness at hunting crustaceans, then he might have been able to better understand why such a gift had been bestowed upon him, but Ronnie didn't even like shrimp, and even if he did, he could buy them down the road at Tesco like any normal person. There was therefore no practical application to this bizarre endowment that Ronnie could see. Also, unlike the squid, Ronnie didn't have the luxury of toggling between the two options. His shadow had simply buggered off without warning, perhaps never to return.

'Hi, Ronnie.'

Ronnie flinched and turned round to find Zelda the cleaner standing behind him. He hadn't heard her come in, and as he looked around, he realised that he hadn't heard her clean the entire room either.

'How do you do that?' asked Ronnie.

'Do what?'

'Clean the whole room without making any noise. You should be a cleaner for the CIA or something. Your talents are wasted here.'

'I think being a cleaner means something else in the CIA.'

'Does it?' said Ronnie. 'Like what?'

'Assassin,' said Zelda.

'Oh! Right. Well, that's not what I meant. Although, come to think of it, you would make an excellent hitman. Woman. Hitwoman. Nobody would ever hear you coming.'

'I'll take that as a compliment,' she said. 'By the way, I see that you're, well, missing something.'

'Missing something?' said Ronnie.

'I noticed it earlier. I wanted to mention it, but you were talking to Alan and I didn't want to embarrass you.'

Ronnie frowned. 'What am I missing?'

'You know. Down there.' Zelda nodded towards Ronnie's legs.

Ronnie stared at the floor around his feet before looking at the light above his head. The room was dimly lit, but not so dim that it wouldn't cast a shadow, if only

Ronnie had a shadow to cast. Zelda had one, which Ronnie found strange, because he'd always imagined that if anybody was going to notice that his shadow was missing, then it was probably going to be somebody who had the same condition as he did. But maybe Zelda had some sort of extrasensory perception. 'Zelda' certainly seemed like a good name for somebody who had those kinds of skills.

'You mean you can *see* it?' he said.

'It depends on what you mean by *it*,' said Zelda, a little unsurely.

'No, you're right, there's nothing to actually see because it's not, well, *there*. But still, you're obviously, you know, *aware of the issue*?'

'It's quite obvious, to be honest.'

'That's great!' said Ronnie, sighing with relief. 'I'm so glad to hear that. I've been hoping that people might notice, but you're the first person to point it out. I thought I was going mad!'

'So . . . you knew about it?' said Zelda, her brow crinkling.

'Of course I knew about it!'

'And you didn't think to do anything about it?'

Ronnie laughed. 'Like what?' he said.

'Like sew it back on?'

'Very funny,' said Ronnie, rolling his eyes. 'Even if I could, I'd need to find it first.'

'It might have popped off around the station some-where,' said Zelda, slowly backing away towards the door. 'I'll check the vacuum bag, I've probably sucked it up by mistake.'

'I don't think you'll find it in there,' said Ronnie.

'You never know. It wouldn't be the first time I've found a button in the bag.'

Ronnie's eyes narrowed. 'Button?' he said.

'Yeah,' said Zelda. 'You know, for your trousers.'

Ronnie's hand instinctively moved to his fly, but all he found was a gaping hole. 'Jesus, sorry, I'm so sorry,' he said, trying to hold his trousers together in the absence of his missing button. 'I had no idea you were talking about . . . *that*.'

'What else did you think I was talking about?' said Zelda.

Ronnie knew that he couldn't tell her the truth, but nor could he think of a single substitute for the truth. It was, after all, a rather specific problem he thought he'd been discussing. He decided to compromise on *a* truth, if not *the* truth.

'There is no possible way that I can answer that question without you thinking I'm even more of a weirdo than you no doubt already think I am,' said Ronnie.

Zelda thought about this for a moment. 'We'll leave it at that then,' she said, grabbing her mop. 'I'll let you know if I find your button.' She kicked her wheelie bucket out of the room and hastily scurried after it.

'All right, mate?' said Ronnie as he closed the front door behind him and kicked off his shoes. Hamlet was standing in the middle of the hallway, eyeballing Ronnie as if he were the chimney sweep who was two hours late and he, Hamlet, were the lord of the manor, only minus the smoking jacket and, well, the peerage. 'How was your day, m'lord?'

Hamlet wasn't capable of a shrug, but if he was, then that's what he would have done.

'My day?' said Ronnie, pretending that Hamlet's body language signified an abundance of enthusiasm and not, despite all evidence to the contrary, a total lack of interest. 'It was OK. Same old stuff. Actually, I tell a lie. I made a proper fool of myself in front of Zelda the cleaning lady this afternoon. That was new.'

Hamlet looked like he could easily imagine Ronnie making a fool of himself.

'Listen to that wind!' said Ronnie as the front door shuddered in its frame behind him. 'I think we might have to skip your walk tonight, mate. You might fly away otherwise.'

Hamlet seemed to perk up at the prospect of flying.

'Anyway, let's get some food on the go, shall we?'

Ronnie was in the kitchen when he heard the thud. He thought it was the wind at first until he realised that the sound had come from upstairs.

189

'Hamlet? You OK, mate?' he called, worried that Hamlet had fallen off the bed, but Hamlet wasn't big enough to be a 'thud' kind of dog. He was, at best, a 'muffled thump' kind of dog, which led Ronnie to his next question. 'What have you done, Hamlet?' he shouted, his tone no longer concerned, but mildly accusing.

Ronnie made his way upstairs and stuck his head into his dad's bedroom. Lying on its side in the middle of the carpet was his dad's urn. The lid had rolled to the other end of the room and between them both lay a long mound of ashes. As if this sight wasn't distressing enough, Hamlet also appeared to be eating Ronnie's dad.

'Hamlet!' yelled Ronnie.

Hamlet backed away, clearly unnerved by the harsh and unfamiliar tone in Ronnie's voice.

Ronnie dropped to his knees and carefully tried to guide the ashes back into the urn. They hadn't all spilled out, but a good fifty per cent or so now lay embedded in the carpet.

'I'm sorry, Dad,' whispered Ronnie as he brushed at the ashes with his hand, but every new swipe of his palm seemed to drive the ashes further into the carpet.

Never one to read the room, at least not correctly, Hamlet crept closer to Ronnie, perhaps for moral support or perhaps out of morbid curiosity.

'Go away!' shouted Ronnie. 'You've already done enough damage!'

Hamlet lingered, unsure what to do.

'I said get out!' shouted Ronnie, angrily jabbing his finger at the door. This time, Hamlet didn't need to be told twice.

Ronnie remained on his knees, hunched over the carpet while he painstakingly tried to extract every piece of ash from it. He was so focused on what he was doing that he didn't realise the window was open until a sudden gust of wind caused it to swing on its hinges and into the bedroom.

Fearing the wind would blow away whatever ashes he'd managed to collect, he quickly closed the urn and got up to shut the window. He had no idea why it was open in the first place until he remembered that he'd ushered a fly out of it before work that morning, partly because it was annoying him, but mainly because he worried that Hamlet would eat it if the two of them were left in the house together all day.

He quietly cursed himself for leaving his house unlocked for so long (not the smartest thing to do in a town like Bingham). And then he cursed again – not so quietly this time – when it belatedly dawned on him what had just transpired. Hamlet hadn't knocked the urn off the windowsill, which made sense now that he thought about it. Hamlet could barely get onto the couch, never mind the windowsill, which was twice as high at least. The wind had blown the window, and the window had knocked it off. Hamlet was still very much guilty of eating part of his dad, but as for who caused the urn incident, Ronnie knew that the blame lay squarely at his feet.

'Well done, Ronnie,' he said to himself. 'No wonder you don't have any friends.'

He found Hamlet in his own bedroom, not on the bed, but underneath it. He was backed up so far into the corner that he was barely visible in the shadows. Ronnie was used to seeing Hamlet look scary, but this was the first time he'd seen him look scared.

'I'm sorry, Hamlet,' he said, lying on the carpet and resting his head on his arm. 'I shouldn't have shouted at you like that. And I shouldn't have blamed you either. It was my own stupid fault, and I'm sorry for thinking it was you.'

Hamlet made no attempt to extract himself from the dark corner he was huddled in.

Ronnie sighed and rolled onto his back so he was staring at the ceiling.

'None of this would have happened if I'd just scattered them when I was supposed to,' he said, half to Hamlet and half to himself. 'I kept meaning to, but, well, I was always too busy.' Ronnie laughed drily. 'Actually, that's complete nonsense. I could have done it any time I wanted to. I just, well, I guess I just never wanted to.'

Ronnie heard movement from beneath the bed, but he didn't take his eyes off the ceiling.

'Although, in my defence, Dad never actually specified where exactly he wanted his ashes to be scattered.'

Ronnie shrugged. 'I suppose he always thought he still had time for those sorts of decisions,' he said, before adding, a little sadly, 'We both did.'

He saw something move in the corner of his eye and turned his head to find Hamlet sitting on the floor nearby with his chin resting on his paws.

'You want to know a secret?' said Ronnie. Hamlet's ears pricked up, as if he did indeed want to know a secret. 'I think I'm a bit scared. You know, of saying goodbye. Which is ridiculous, if you think about it, because he's been gone for over a year. He's not here anymore. There's nobody to say goodbye *to*. That urn full of ashes – well, half full anyway – that isn't my dad, is it? It's just a pile of powder. You can't hug it. You can't go for a walk with it. You're not going to get a decent conversation out of it. And you're certainly not supposed to eat it.' He looked at Hamlet. 'I can't believe you did that by the way.'

Hamlet averted his gaze, or one of his eyes did at least.

Ronnie smiled to himself. 'This is a bit like a therapy session, isn't it?' he said. 'Me lying here talking about my feelings and you sitting there pretending to listen. Probably a lot cheaper as well. I assume you'll be charging me mates' rates?'

Hamlet gave Ronnie one of his infinite number of inscrutable expressions.

'I think he would have liked you, you know. And I think you would have liked him. He was funny and he was kind and he was a great listener. He also had a shadow, so, you know, there's another big plus.'

Ronnie's arm was going to sleep, so he pushed himself upright and leaned his back against the bed frame.

'I wonder what your dad was like,' he said to Hamlet. 'Actually, I wonder what your dad was full stop. I don't suppose you know anything about him, do you?'

Ronnie thought about how lonely it must be for Hamlet, without friends, without family and without much prospect of ever having either. It made him feel even worse about shouting at him.

'Sorry again about before,' he said. 'Think we can be friends again?'

Hamlet cocked his head as if he wasn't quite sure if he'd heard correctly.

'OK, not *friends* friends but, you know, not enemies?'

Hamlet started chewing on the black rubber door stopper screwed into the floor near the doorway.

'I'll take that as a yes,' said Ronnie, deciding not to say anything about Hamlet's flagrant disregard for rule number two. 'I really can't afford to lose any friends. Actually, speaking of losing things, I don't suppose you're any good at pub quizzes, are you?'

Chapter Twenty

'OK, Hamlet, paws on buzzers. Which UK band previously known as Skin Disease and Scab Aid had a hit single in 1997 with a song titled "Tubthumping"?'

Hamlet chewed his hind leg, perhaps for inspiration, but most likely because it still hadn't occurred to him that this particular appendage belonged to him.

'I'm sorry, Hamlet, but I'm going to have to hurry you,' said Ronnie.

Hamlet stopped chewing his leg and looked at Ronnie as if he suddenly had the answer. Then, yacking up a small clump of fur onto the carpet, he went back to gnawing his leg.

'I'm afraid that's the wrong answer,' said Ronnie. 'The correct answer is Chumbawamba. Remember that song? The one about getting knocked down and then up again and then down and then up again and then, well, down and then up again?'

Hamlet did not appear to remember any songs about getting knocked down and then getting back up again.

'Probably a bit before your time, come to think of it. I bet you're not into that sort of music anyway, are you? You're probably into, I don't know, experimental jazz or psychedelic rock or Morris dancing music or something.' Ronnie grabbed the pad he was using to keep score. 'Anyway, that's one point to me.'

He added a one beneath his name and sighed. It was one more than Hamlet's big fat zero, but it was still several points short of what he'd hoped to have accrued by this stage of the game, not least because there'd been twenty-two questions prior to the Chumbawamba one and he hadn't known the answers to any of them.

He tried to make himself feel better by reminding himself that a lot of the questions were about sport. He knew less about sport than he knew about any other topic, except for perhaps astrophysics. And all of the other sciences. And maths. And a bunch of others. What he had a harder time consoling himself about was the fact that the rest of the questions were about history, geography, film, politics, music, art, culture, architecture, literature, food and nature, yet the only one he'd managed to answer correctly was a question about Chumbawamba. He could accept not having a specialist subject. Most people didn't have a specialist subject, not unless they went to university, but everybody had some basic level of general knowledge, didn't they?

As much as he didn't know about Gary from the corner shop, he knew him well enough to know that he probably wasn't an expert in, say, marine biology, or horticultural engineering, or 1930s black-and-white Scandinavian film noir. And his postman, for all he talked about the weather, was almost certainly not a closet meteorologist, but Ronnie was pretty sure they both knew who won the Premier League in 2011 and what the real names of the Bee Gees were. They didn't know that stuff because they'd studied sport or the Bee Gees. They knew that stuff because it was general knowledge, and nobody studied general knowledge. It was just one of those things that you picked up as you went along, like scars and fleas and half-smoked cigarettes, if that was your thing. For many people, general knowledge was simply the sum total of their life experiences. They could point out places on a map because they'd actually been to those places. They knew their frittatas from their fajitas and their ragù from their ragout because they'd eaten them on holiday or cooked them at home. But not Ronnie. The sum total of his life experiences wouldn't even fill up the advert break of most people's life experiences.

The only questions he felt even slightly confident in answering were questions about serious bacterial infections – a topic he'd been extensively researching of late, not because he thought that questions about serious bacterial infections were going to pop up on the quiz, but because he was quite convinced that he had one, tetanus specifically. The cut on his hand that he'd sustained while trying to teach Hamlet how to play fetch on the beach had become progressively more painful, much more painful than it actually looked. In fact, to most people it probably looked no worse than a common graze, but Ronnie had googled the various symptoms of tetanus and he was definitely experiencing some of them, even if they were the more general and non-specific symptoms that were no more indicative of tetanus than they were of a million other benign conditions.

He looked at his hand and winced as he slowly opened and closed his fingers. He'd removed the plaster to air it a little, but the skin around the cut still looked white and wrinkly, like a sausage that had been in the bath too long. He didn't want to go to the clinic because he didn't want to further validate Dr Sterling's theory that he was a hypochondriac, but if the cut didn't start to heal in the next couple of days, then it was definitely tetanus and he was definitely going to die unless he sought proper treatment. Even Dr Sterling must know what tetanus looked like, or so Ronnie hoped.

'I think that's enough general knowledge for today,' he said, packing away the Trivial Pursuit and returning it to the shelf in the living room with the rest of the board games that hadn't been opened since he was a child. Except for Hungry Hippos. His dad always liked Hungry Hippos. The two of them had spent countless hours sitting at the living room table, bashing their respective hippopotamuses until one of them had gobbled up all the balls. It was only during their last game together, which they'd played on what Ronnie would later learn was also their last evening together, that Ronnie had finally asked his dad just what it was about Hungry Hippos that he seemed to love so much. His dad had shrugged and said that he never cared one way or another about the game and that he only suggested playing it because he thought that it was *Ronnie*'s favourite game, which it was, about thirty-five years ago. When Ronnie told him that he only ever suggested playing it because he thought it was his *dad*'s favourite game, the two of them laughed so hard that they were both in tears by the time they'd managed to calm down.

Whenever Ronnie thought of his dad now, that's the memory that often came to mind, of the two of them laughing about the years they'd spent playing Hungry Hippos together simply because they thought it would make the other person happy. And it did, looking back on it. Ronnie was happy because he thought his dad was happy, and his dad was happy because he thought that Ronnie was happy.

That was one of the things he missed the most about his father, the fact that he often did things not because they mattered to him necessarily, but because he thought they mattered to Ronnie. He once signed his son up for squash lessons after Ronnie had made a throwaway comment about wanting to learn the sport while watching a television documentary about Jahangir Khan. Concerned he'd have nobody to play against, his dad signed himself up as well, even though he suffered from tennis elbow in one arm, golfer's elbow in the other, plantar fasciitis in both feet and a chronic lack of hand-eye coordination.

Another time he'd suggested – seemingly apropos of nothing – that the two of them go fishing together. Ronnie had never been fishing before and neither had his dad. Nor had either of them ever expressed the slightest interest in learning. Still, not wanting to let his dad sit alone on the riverbank all day, Ronnie agreed to join him. After several hours hunched in the drizzle without a single fish to show for it, Ronnie's dad asked him what had suddenly inspired him to want to learn to fish. When Ronnie told him that he *didn't* want to learn to fish and that he was only there to keep his dad company, his dad frowned and asked why he was reading a book about fishing if he didn't want to learn to fish.

'What book?'

'The book on the coffee table,' said his dad. 'The one about fishing.'

It took a minute before it dawned on Ronnie just what on earth his dad was talking about.

'Dad, I wasn't reading it,' he said with a laugh when he finally remembered the book in question. It was called *So You Want to Learn How to Fish* and he'd found it on the bus on the way home. He'd left it on the coffee table to remind himself to take it to the lost property office when he went to work the following day, which he had done, but his dad had obviously noticed it and assumed that Ronnie was getting into angling. When he explained all of this to his dad, his dad looked at the rod in his hand as if it had suddenly just appeared out of nowhere.

'Then what are we doing sitting in the rain?'

'Learning to fish, I guess,' said Ronnie, laughing. 'I'll tell you what though – it's a good job the book wasn't called *So You Want to Learn How to Breakdance*!'

They laughed a lot, him and his dad, and the creak of the floorboards and the groan of the pipes and the clacking of the clock on the mantelpiece seemed so much louder now that the sound of laughter was gone from the house.

They talked a lot too, albeit not about anything too deep or meaningful. There was only really one heavy topic that either of them might be inclined to talk about, but Ronnie avoided it for the same reason he imagined his dad did, namely for fear of getting stuck in the mud of the past that his dad had tried so hard to carry them both out of. He knew he could have talked to him about the whole shadow situation though. His dad was quite possibly the only person in the world who wouldn't have judged him or ridiculed him for something like that. He'd never judged or ridiculed Ronnie even when he probably deserved a bit of judgement or ridicule, like the time he got his toe stuck in the bath tap when he was ten.

Ronnie didn't dare mention his condition to Dr Sterling because Dr Sterling didn't seem capable of treating an ingrowing toenail, never mind an outgoing shadow, and he didn't mention it to anybody else in case his shadow was actually perfectly visible to everybody but him, thereby confirming to himself and others that he'd simply lost his mind. His dad would have understood though. He probably wouldn't have understood what the bloody hell was going on – who could? – but he'd at least be able to understand Ronnie's concern and find a way to make him feel better about the whole thing.

Ronnie's fingers brushed against something on the carpet beside his chair. He picked it up and his hand emerged with a claw-shaped stick. It was the only thing his dad had caught on their ill-fated fishing trip, having become tangled up in his line and refusing to let go until his dad had reeled it in and forcibly removed it. He'd ended up taking it home with him as a funny memento of their failed fishing expedition. Only later did he realise that the gnarly piece of wood doubled as a surprisingly effective back-scratcher.

Leaning forward, Ronnie absently scratched his back while returning to his shadow conundrum.

It hadn't crossed his mind before, but he wondered if it might be hereditary. Did his mum have a shadow? She certainly had a history of running away like one. Or perhaps it came from his dad. He tried to remember if he'd ever noticed his father looking distinctly shadowless, but observing how light interacts with another human being wasn't the sort of thing a person usually paid much attention to.

He pulled out one of the photo albums from the shelf beneath the board games and flipped it open to a random page. The first picture he came across was of his dad playing snooker in his twenties. He was staring intently at the shot he was about to take, and his shadow was clearly visible on the felt as he leaned across the table.

Having eliminated his dad from his list of suspects, he flicked through the album for a picture of his mum, but the exercise proved harder than expected because his dad had removed nearly all evidence of her from the album. Only one picture remained, maybe because he'd missed it or maybe because he simply hadn't been able to bring himself to get rid of it. Ronnie hadn't seen it on the first pass and he'd almost missed it on the second, perhaps because there were several people in the picture and his mum's face was only partially visible. She was sitting on a wall, swinging her legs and shielding her eyes from the sun. Three other people were in the picture, two other girls and a boy. Ronnie didn't recognise any of them. He barely recognised his mum, who must have only been about sixteen in the picture, but one thing he could clearly make out was the shadow across her eyes that came from the palm she was using to keep the sun from her face.

He stared at the photograph, thinking about how happy his mum looked in it and wondering if she was just as happy now. For years, he'd hoped she was miserable. There was even a period, in his early teens, when he had hoped for so much worse than that. But even though he couldn't say he'd truly forgiven her for what she'd done, he could, however, now say with all sincerity that he hoped she'd found whatever it was she was looking for. Yes, she had destroyed their family, but as Ronnie had grown older, he sometimes found himself feeling almost grateful that his mum had left, not because he hated her, not by then at least, but because he might have never had the same relationship with his dad if she'd stayed with the family. His dad was more of a background man until his mum disappeared, present enough to take up space in the house, yet not quite present enough to take up space in Ronnie's early memories. That might have been the sum total of Ronnie's recollections of his dad had things continued on the path they were on. It was only when his mum decided to forge a new path without them that his dad was left with little choice but to step into the foreground, take Ronnie's hand and try to figure out the smoothest route possible through the rocky terrain that awaited them.

Also, while his mum would never win any awards for the way she went about things (unless 'Most Unexpected Disappearance' was a category, in which case she would win), the older he became, the less Ronnie thought about the way she'd departed and the more he started thinking about the why.

He remembered the morning of his twenty-seventh birthday, sitting on the bus on his way to work. It was the same commute he'd done for the last ten years, on the same bus, with the same passengers, down the same roads in the same town. Resting his head against the window while the bus weaved through Bingham, knowing which shops and streets and parks would next roll into view without even having to think about it, he suddenly found himself wondering, 'Is this it? Is this all there is to life? Is this the best it's ever going to be?' It was only a fleeting thought, and by the time the bus pulled into the station he'd forgotten it completely, but later that evening, while lying in bed, it occurred to Ronnie that his mum was twenty-seven when she'd decided to make a new life for herself. Had she thought the same thing that he had on the bus to work that morning? As she'd looked around at the dishes in the sink and the laundry in the basket and the toys on the floor and the grass stains that needed scrubbing from Ronnie's clothes despite having told him countless times not to slide across the lawn in his school trousers, had she been gripped by a similar sense of despair? A feeling that this was all there was and this was all there was ever going to be unless she did something about it, no matter how drastic that something might be?

She wasn't even out of her teens when Ronnie was born, which wasn't particularly unusual for that time and that corner of the country, but just because it wasn't necessarily out of the ordinary, that didn't mean that some young mothers didn't quietly mourn the premature end of their own childhoods while simultaneously celebrating the start of another one. Perhaps that was why Ronnie's mum was never very motherly. Perhaps she never thought of herself as a mother at all, but as a kid who ended up stuck with a baby before she was ready to deal with one. Maybe Mr Higgins made her feel like that teenager again. Maybe he still felt like a kid himself. People grew up quickly back then, whether they wanted to or not, and before you knew what had happened, life had galloped along so fast that you were already old before you'd ever been young. Maybe that's what happened.

Or maybe not. Maybe Ronnie was giving his mum the benefit of the doubt because he liked this version of events much more than he liked the idea of his mum simply ditching him because she was a terrible person. He'd long since made peace with the idea of never getting the answers he wanted, and after close to thirty-five years having passed, it didn't really matter what the truth was anymore anyway. She'd done what she'd done and that was that. She had her reasons, and there was little point in trying to guess what those reasons were. After all, nobody could ever really know what went on inside somebody else's head, and sometimes the ones who were closest to you were the biggest mysteries of all.

'You're living proof of that,' said Ronnie to Hamlet, who, despite having no clue as to what he was living proof of, nevertheless proceeded to prove Ronnie's point by doing something he'd never done before. He stretched out, rolled onto his back and lay there with his legs in the air.

Had Hamlet been any other dog, then there would have been absolutely no doubt as to what this position expressed. It was universal canine sign language for 'belly rub', as any self-respecting dog owner would know, but even though Hamlet probably *would* have liked a belly rub – he was still a dog after all, despite all the evidence to the contrary – Ronnie was fairly certain that Hamlet didn't want *him* to be the rubber of said belly. And Ronnie didn't particularly want to be the rubber of said belly either. He knew that Hamlet didn't have fleas or mange or any other disease, but neither did tripe, yet he still didn't feel comfortable touching it with his bare hands.

'Is this a dare?' said Ronnie. 'Are you daring me?'

Hamlet lay there with his tongue lolling out and his paws in their air. He looked like he'd tried to stage-dive before checking whether there was anybody around to catch him. Ronnie wondered for a second if Hamlet was having some kind of episode, until he realised that he was staring at his dad's makeshift back-scratcher.

'Oh!' said Ronnie. 'I see. You want a bit of the old back-scratcher, do you?'

Holding the piece of wood as close to the end as possible, Ronnie cautiously extended it towards Hamlet until the gnarly end was resting on his equally gnarly belly. He left it there for a moment, waiting to see if Hamlet would try to attack it like he'd tried to attack Ronnie during the first and only time he'd ever attempted to invade his space, but Hamlet stretched out further until he looked like a sausage, although one you'd hope to never find lurking in the middle of your hot dog bun.

'I feel like we're bonding here, Hamlet,' said Ronnie as he gently scratched Hamlet's belly. 'Are we bonding? I feel like we're bonding.'

Whether or not Hamlet felt like they were bonding was open for debate. There was, however, little doubt that Hamlet was bonding with the carpet, if not in an emotional way, then, judging by the amount of drool emanating from the corner of his mouth, certainly in the adhesive sense of the word. Still, any bonding was better than nothing.

Chapter Twenty-One

Walking through the doors of the pub at exactly eight o'clock, Ronnie tried to exude a confidence he simply did not possess, namely the confidence of somebody who frequently meets up for drinks with friends, which, now that he thought about it, shouldn't really require any confidence at all, a realisation that only made him even more self-conscious.

He hadn't planned to be on time. He'd actually planned to turn up fashionably late – nothing too extravagant, maybe ten minutes or so, not late enough to seem rude, but late enough to give the impression that he had other things going on in his life – but he'd lost his nerve when it dawned on him that he wasn't sure if being late was even fashionable anymore. Perhaps being on time was *à la mode* these days. Or turning up early even. Perhaps being fashionably early was the new fashionably late. Ronnie had no idea, so he'd decided to play it safe and turn up right on time.

Noticing an empty table, he was just about to claim it with the old 'coat-on-the-back-of-the-chair' manoeuvre when he spotted Cate sitting on her own in the corner. She was sipping a pint and staring at her phone, seemingly oblivious to the world around her. Ronnie wondered if she was doing another maths quiz.

Relieved that he hadn't been the first person to arrive, he weaved his way through the pub towards her.

'Is this seat taken?' he asked, pointing to an empty chair.

'Yeah, sorry,' said Cate without looking up from her phone.

'Right,' said Ronnie, suddenly self-conscious again, especially as the people at the next table had overheard the exchange and were now laughing at what they must have thought was a sleazy old bloke having his advances rebuffed.

Perhaps aware that he was still standing there, Cate looked up from her phone and immediately clasped her hand over her mouth.

'I'm so sorry!' she said. 'I didn't know it was you! It's just, you know, some blokes see a woman on her own as an unspoken invitation, don't they? Like we're not alone because we want to be but because we're hoping for some hairy old creepster with fading tattoos to plonk themselves down at our table and start chatting us up.'

'I thought that only happened to me,' said Ronnie. Cate laughed. 'Don't worry, I don't have any tattoos.' Ronnie rolled up his sleeves to reveal the blank canvases of his pale forearms. 'Or much hair either, come to think of it.' He ran his hand across his head for emphasis.

'Then, in that case, pull up a seat,' said Cate. Ronnie sat down. 'Hamlet not with you tonight?'

Ronnie shook his head. 'He ate something that didn't agree with him, so I decided to leave him at home, just to be on the safe side.'

'Nothing serious, I hope?'

'He'll be fine. It's everybody else I was worried about. He ate a piece of green KFC he found during our evening walk and, well, let's just say that the smells coming out of him are probably making their very own hole in the ozone layer right now.'

'Oh yeah, I forgot to tell you, Hamlet's allergic to mouldy fried chicken, so, you know, don't let him eat it.'

'Thanks for the warning,' said Ronnie. He looked around. 'Where are the others?' he asked, half to himself.

'No idea,' said Cate. 'I don't know what they look like. They might already be here for all I know.'

Ronnie scanned the room for Brian and Harriet. He half-expected to find them both sitting at different tables, having also never met one another and therefore having no idea that they were in fact teammates, but neither of them were present.

It had never occurred to Ronnie that Brian might not turn up for the quiz. After all, who would go to the effort of inviting somebody to join their pub quiz team if they weren't intending to turn up? That just wouldn't make any sense. But, then again, from what little information Ronnie had gleaned from his brief encounters with Brian, sense didn't seem like something he was overflowing with.

What if he didn't turn up? What would Ronnie do then? He couldn't call Brian because he didn't know his telephone number. Nor did he know where he lived. He didn't even know his surname. Come to think of it, Ronnie didn't know very much about him at all. He was, to all intents and purposes, a complete and utter stranger. Why had he trusted a stranger? He'd actively tried to rid himself of his dad's inherent distrust of people, but sometimes, like now, he wondered if his dad had been right all along.

Still, not a problem, thought Ronnie. Worst-case scenario, they'd be a team of three instead of four. No big deal. But the more Ronnie thought about it, the more it dawned on him that this wasn't in fact the worst-case scenario. The worst-case scenario was if Brian *and* Harriet didn't turn up. What then? He had no doubt that their performance in the quiz would not be adversely affected by their absence. He was pretty sure Cate didn't even need *him* to be there, or at least he hoped she didn't, because if she did, then she was going to be gravely disappointed. But how they fared in the quiz was the least of his concerns. At the top of that list was the worry that Cate might start to think that he'd made up the other members of the team so that she'd agree to come out for a drink with him, and only him. She'd never met Brian or Harriet, so there was no actual proof they existed, and if she somehow found out that Ronnie didn't even have their telephone numbers, then her suspicions were likely to deepen. He felt his palms grow clammy at the idea that she might think he was one of those hairy old creepsters she'd just been telling him about, but even worse in a way because at least those hairy old creepsters did nothing to hide their creepiness. They hadn't tried to trick her into joining a pub quiz team by inventing other members to lull her into a false sense of security. And neither had he, he reminded himself, but the truth brought him surprisingly little comfort.

'I'm sure they'll be here soon,' said Ronnie, trying not to sound panicked. 'I'm just going to get a drink. Would you like another?' He pointed to her glass.

'Go on then,' she said, knocking back the remaining inch and handing him the glass. 'Dirty old perv.'

'What?' said Ronnie, his worst nightmare suddenly confirmed. 'No, really it's not like that. I know how this probably looks, but it's not, you know, how it looks. This wasn't a sneaky ploy to get you to come to the pub with me. I would never do a thing like that. I'm not a dirty old perv. I'm not even *that* old. But I'm also not dirty. Or a perv.'

Cate frowned at him like most people frown at a cryptic crossword. 'The beer,' she said, after what was quite possibly the longest and most painful silence of Ronnie's life. 'It's called Dirty Old Perv.'

Ronnie prayed for the wooden beam directly above him to suddenly and inexplicably dislodge itself from the ceiling and bonk him on the head, hopefully with sufficient force to either kill him outright or at least sometime before the paramedics arrived. Only when it became clear that the beam was not about to put him out of his misery did he point towards the bar.

'I'll be right back,' he muttered, before disappearing into the crowd.

Ronnie leaned on the bar and sighed before sighing again when he felt the sludgy puddle of countless spilled drinks slowly seeping into his sleeves. He wondered if Cate would still be there by the time he returned with the drinks. Probably not. Hopefully Brian and Harriet wouldn't turn up either so he could call it an early night. The evening was a catastrophe and it hadn't even started yet. He wondered what else could go wrong.

'You kept that one quiet!' came a voice from behind him at the same time that a fleshy hand slapped him on the back. Ronnie turned round to find Alan standing at the bar beside him. So *that's* what else could go wrong, he thought.

'Kept what quiet?' said Ronnie.

'Your girlfriend, of course!' Alan nodded in the direction of Cate. 'Right dark horse you are. I didn't think you were into that whole scene.' Alan wore jeans and a button-down shirt with a design that reminded Ronnie of a Magic Eye picture. He wondered what he'd see if he stared at it for long enough.

'What whole scene?' asked Ronnie.

'You know. Relationships. I thought you were more like, I don't know, an earthworm or something. No offence.'

'I'm not sure you can tell somebody not to take offence after calling them an earthworm.'

'I didn't call you an earthworm,' said Alan. 'I said you were *like* an earthworm.'

'Oh, that's OK then.'

'You know what I mean.'

'I really don't,' said Ronnie.

'Well, they don't need a mate, do they? They just, you know, reproduce with themselves.'

'That's the scene you thought I was into? The whole "reproducing with myself" scene?'

'Hey, I'm not judging.'

'Good, because there's nothing to judge,' said Ronnie. 'And anyway, she's not my girlfriend. She's just a friend.'

'With benefits?' said Alan with a wink.

'I don't know if she's on benefits,' said Ronnie, finding the question a little left-field. 'What's that got to do with anything?'

'No, I mean is it, you know, a purely physical arrangement.' Alan jiggled his eyebrows. 'Like an open relationship.'

'We're not in any sort of relationship. Like I said, we're just friends.'

'Right, right,' said Alan, clearly unconvinced.

'Is she still there?' asked Ronnie.

Alan peered over his shoulder. 'Yeah. Why?'

'No reason,' said Ronnie, quietly relieved.

The server appeared on the other side of the bar. He looked on the wrong end of a long shift.

'What can I get you?' he said to Alan.

'He was here first,' said Alan, pointing at Ronnie.

'Two pints of, er, that one, please,' said Ronnie, pointing to the pump with 'Dirty Old Perv' written on it so he didn't have to say it out loud. 'Thanks,' he said to Alan while the barman was pulling the pints. Giving way to whoever had arrived at the bar first was basic pub etiquette, but his boss had always struck him as the sort of person who would revel in getting served first. Ronnie had never been on the receiving end of courtesy from Alan before, and the experience was a little disorienting. 'What are you doing here anyway?' he asked. 'You here for the quiz?'

'Yep,' said Alan. 'Me and the lads.' He pointed to a table where 'the lads' were sitting, although 'lads' was a generous description for the motley crew of middle-aged men that Alan was referring to. Ronnie had never seen two of them before, but he recognised one of them immediately.

'I didn't know you and Carl were friends,' said Ronnie. He also didn't know that Carl was the pub quiz type. Not that Ronnie knew what the pub quiz type was exactly, or even if there *was* a pub quiz type, but if he'd been asked to stand behind a two-way mirror and pick one out of a line-up, and Carl was in said line-up, Ronnie would not have identified his colleague even if the other participants had been a garden gnome, an inflatable doll, a golden retriever and one of those tubular-shaped balloons that danced outside car dealerships. Had the purpose of the line-up been to identify a criminal, however, Ronnie would have pointed at Carl before he'd even been told what the crime was. Carl just gave off those kinds of vibes.

'Carl?' said Alan. 'Oh yeah. We go way back.'

'How way back is way back?' asked Ronnie, genuinely surprised by this revelation.

Alan shrugged. 'A year or so.'

'Since you started working at the bus station, you mean?'

'Something like that,' said Alan.

'Right,' said Ronnie. 'I guess that means we go way back as well.'

'Exactly!' said Alan, patting Ronnie on the shoulder.

Ronnie had never thought of Alan as a friend. He'd never even thought of him as an acquaintance. At most, he thought of him as a colleague, but mainly he tried not to think of him at all. But based on how sincerely Alan had responded to his joke about them going way back, Ronnie wondered for the very first time whether Alan thought of *him* as a friend.

The barman reappeared and placed two pints on the bar. Ronnie paid and grabbed the drinks.

'Well, good luck with the quiz,' he said.

'And good luck with your date,' said Alan, giving him a playful nudge in the ribs, which probably wasn't the best thing to do to a man holding two very full pints of beer.

Ronnie returned from the bar to find that Cate had inherited a cat in his absence. It was only when he saw Brian that he realised where the cat had come from. Ronnie was relieved that Brian hadn't abandoned them, although he was a little surprised to see them chatting as if they were old friends.

'I see you two already know each other,' said Ronnie, putting the drinks on the table.

'I don't know her,' said Brian, pointing to Cate.

'And I don't know him,' said Cate, pointing at Brian. 'I just saw this little bundle of cat-shaped loveliness and couldn't help myself.'

Brian looked disappointed, as if he'd hoped that he was the reason she'd singled him out and not Beethoven.

'This is Brian!' said Ronnie. 'Our glorious leader,' he added, eager to pass the baton of responsibility should the night be an unmitigated disaster.

'Oh! Hi, Brian, nice to meet you. I'm Cate,' she said, extending her hand, which Brian took but didn't shake so much as allow it to be shook, like a Labrador forced to play 'How do you do?'.

'Hi, Cate,' said Brian. 'I'm Brian. But you already know that. Because you just called me Brian. And Ronnie just told you I was called Brian. But still, I'm Brian. Hi.'

'Hi,' said Cate. 'Again.'

Ronnie smiled, reassured to know that he wasn't the only awkward person at the table.

'Room for one more?' asked Harriet, who suddenly appeared behind Ronnie.

'Harriet!' said Ronnie. 'Glad you could make it.' He looked at her clothes. 'Come to think of it, this is the first time I've seen you with clothes on!'

Everybody looked at Ronnie, and then at Harriet, and then at each other as an uncomfortable silence descended.

'Oh!' said Ronnie, belatedly realising what he'd said. 'No, I didn't . . . I mean . . .'

'Nice to meet you, Harriet,' said Cate, saving Ronnie from further embarrassment. 'I'm Cate and this is Brian.'

'And who is this handsome chap?' asked Harriet, pointing at Beethoven.

'That's Beethoven,' said Brian.

'Did you name him after the dog in *Beethoven*?' said Cate.

'I did actually,' said Brian.

'I love those films!' said Cate.

'Me too!' said Brian. He rolled his eyes at Ronnie. 'Ronnie thought I named him after the composer.'

'Why would you name a cat after a composer?' said Cate incredulously, as if naming a cat after a composer was akin to naming a cat after the head of the SS.

'Why would you name a cat after a dog?' asked Harriet.

'He's training him to be one,' said Ronnie.

'To be what?' said Harriet.

'A dog,' said Brian. 'I thought that giving him a dog's name might help him to get into the role.'

'Right,' said Harriet. She looked at Ronnie, or perhaps she was looking at the exit behind him.

'That makes sense,' said Cate. She looked at Ronnie and Harriet, who clearly didn't share her confidence. 'Well, it's like method acting, isn't it?' she continued. 'You know that film *Lincoln*? The one about Abraham Lincoln? Apparently, Daniel Day-Lewis insisted that everybody called him "Mr President" for the entire shoot, even Steven Spielberg! He said it helped him to get into the mind of the character.'

'Thank you,' said Brian. 'I'm glad that somebody understands. Everybody else just looks at me like I'm some kind of weirdo.'

'I can't imagine why,' said the look that Ronnie and Harriet shared between them.

A man with a ponytail appeared on the small stage in the corner. He tapped the microphone and everybody winced as a high-pitched squeal passed through the room.

'That got your attention, didn't it?' said the man. A murmur of contempt rose up from the crowd. 'Evening, everybody,' he continued. 'Just to let you know that the quiz will be starting in a few minutes, so anybody who doesn't already have a drink, now's the time to get one. Stacey will be doing the rounds with the pens and the quiz sheets shortly, so don't forget to put your name on the top. Also, don't forget to return the pens at the end of the night. I'm serious. You know who you are. You do it every week, and it's not funny. I mean, how many pens do you need, for Christ's sake? What are you doing, writing a novel?'

He paused here, as if he genuinely expected somebody to answer this question. Nobody did.

'Yeah, that's what I thought,' he said. 'Oh, and while we're on the subject of underhanded shenanigans, don't forget to either turn your phones off or put them on aeroplane mode, or, as I like to call it, "don't-be-a-cheating-bastard" mode. Anybody caught trying to google the answers will face a lifetime ban and a kicking in the alley outside. Isn't that right, John?' he said to the bouncer at the door.

John shrugged as if to say that he really wasn't getting paid enough to go above and beyond the call of duty, but that he probably would do anyway because he quite liked kicking people in the alley.

'You hear that, George?' said the man, staring at one man in particular. 'No cheating, or else.'

A collective 'ooh' rose up from the crowd, like the sort of sound kids make when the teacher tells one of them to go to the headmaster's office.

'Don't encourage him,' said the man. 'You wouldn't laugh if this were an Olympic event, like the high jump or the pole vault or that weird sport with the brooms. If you were all competing against each other, and you'd been training really hard and eating the right diet and you'd been really disciplined and everything, while George just sat on his arse eating Doritos and drinking beer in front of the TV all day, you wouldn't be laughing if George still won because he'd been pumping himself full of performance-enhancing drugs, would you? Well, this is like that. Googling is like the doping of the pub quiz world, so don't be a dope and just say no. To Google. But also to drugs. Both are going to land you in trouble, one way or another. Isn't that right, Stu?'

The man known as Stu nodded solemnly from the corner, although it wasn't clear which offence he was supposed to be a poster child for, drug use or a rampant googling addiction.

'Right, now that we've got that out the way, the only thing that's left to say is . . . let's get quizzical!'

Olivia Newton-John started playing over the speakers, while Stacey went around distributing quiz sheets and pens.

Everybody stared at the piece of paper in the middle of the table, but nobody made a move to grab it, perhaps because they were waiting for Brian, their captain, to take the initiative.

'OK then,' said Cate when it became clear that Brian had no intention of assuming responsibility for the quiz sheet. She slid it towards herself and picked up the pen. 'What's our name?'

'Brian,' said Brian. Everybody laughed.

'I think she means the *team* name,' said Harriet.

'Oh. Yeah. Sorry.' Brian looked around the table. 'What's our team name?' he asked.

'You don't know?' said Cate.

'Why would I know?'

'Because you're the captain,' said Ronnie.

'Am I?' said Brian. 'I thought *you* were the captain.'

'How can I be the captain? You asked *me* to join *your* team.'

'Yeah,' said Brian. 'As the captain.'

'Right,' said Ronnie. Brian's logic was iffy at best, but he didn't want to argue about it. After all, being the captain of a pub quiz team didn't actually mean anything. He wasn't required to lead his men into battle or negotiate the release of hostages or make life-changing decisions for any of them. He didn't have to *do* anything besides answer to the name of captain, which, come to think of it, was actually kind of cool. Still, he wasn't going to let Brian off that easily. 'I guess I'm the captain then,' he said. 'And as the captain, I would like to delegate team-naming responsibilities to Brian.'

'Oh,' said Brian. 'Right. Erm. I don't know, to be honest. I've never actually done a pub quiz before.'

'Another pub quiz virgin!' said Cate. 'Phew, I thought I was the only one.'

'I've never done a pub quiz either,' said Harriet.

'Or me,' added Ronnie.

'Then maybe we should call ourselves The Virgins!' said Cate.

'I don't think we should call ourselves The Virgins,' said Ronnie, who couldn't even begin to imagine the shit he'd get from Alan and Carl for the rest of his life.

'How about the Fourmidables,' said Harriet. 'You know, because there's four of us.'

'What does "midable" mean though?' said Brian.

'Nothing,' said Harriet. 'It's a pun.'

'Right,' said Brian, who clearly didn't get it.

'How about the Beethoven Quartet!' suggested Cate. 'You know, Beethoven because of Beethoven and Quartet because, well, there's four of us. The Beethoven Quartet is also the name of a Russian string quartet founded in the early 1920s. They collaborated closely with Dmitri Shostakovich. You know Dmitri Shostakovich?' She looked around the table at all the blank faces. 'One of the major composers of the twentieth century?' More blank stares, which most people would have taken as ample reason to stop talking, but Cate was not most people. 'Shostakovich actually premiered one of his symphonies – Symphony number seven – at the Grand Philharmonia Hall in Leningrad *while the city was in the middle of being bombed by the Germans*. Leningrad had been under siege for nearly a year by then, but even though the Bolshoi Theatre Orchestra kept collapsing during rehearsals because they were literally starving to death, they still went ahead and played the concert. Not only that, they did it on the ninth of August, the same day that Hitler had planned to have a massive banquet to celebrate the fall of the city. How's that for a two-fingered salute to the Führer? They put speakers all over the city so everybody could hear it, and they even played it across enemy lines to psych out the Germans. How amazing is that?'

Ronnie smiled. Harriet looked gobsmacked. Brian looked in love.

'Amazing,' said Brian, although it wasn't clear whether it was Cate's impressive knowledge of military history, the resilience of the Bolshoi Theatre Orchestra and the people of Leningrad, or Cate herself that he found amazing.

'Are you like a military historian or something?' said Harriet.

'No,' said Cate. 'I work at the dog shelter.'

'Then how on earth do you know all of that?' asked Harriet, a tone of genuine awe in her voice.

Cate shrugged. 'I read a lot,' she said matter-of-factly.

'Now you can see why I asked her to join the team,' said Ronnie.

'You shouldn't be on a pub quiz team, you should be on *University Challenge*!' said Harriet. Cate smiled at Ronnie.

'No, you should definitely be on our team,' said Brian. 'Please stay.'

Cate laughed, although Brian looked quite serious.

'So what do we think about the name, everybody?' said Ronnie.

'The Beethoven Quartet,' said Harriet. 'I like it.'

'Me too,' agreed Brian.

'That's settled then,' said Ronnie. 'Cate, would you do the honours?'

Cate wrote their name down on the top of the sheet just as the man with the ponytail reappeared on stage.

'Everybody ready?' he asked. A murmur of agreement rose up from the crowd. 'Great,' he said, adjusting his glasses and peering at the sheet of questions in his hand. 'Let's get started then, shall we?'

Chapter Twenty-Two

The quiz had six rounds in total, with each round focusing on a different category. The first round was popular culture, the second round was sport and the third round was history. There was then a short break so that people could go to the bathroom, nip outside for a cigarette or pop to the bar for a drink before the second half of the quiz commenced.

To stop people from phoning a friend, asking the audience or simply double-checking their answers on the internet and correcting any mistakes they'd made, the quiz sheets were handed to the quizmaster in exchange for a new sheet that teams could use to record their answers to the second round of questions. As an extra measure of security, the man with the ponytail folded each of the completed quiz sheets and sealed them with a wax stamp, as if the contents weren't hastily scribbled answers to pub trivia stained with beer and cheese and onion dust, but important notes to be sent to the king via a messenger waiting on his trusty steed outside.

Ronnie winced as he watched the quizmaster accidentally burn himself with a dribble of hot wax. He admired the man's commitment to his job, even if he wasn't sure that the wax was entirely necessary. Most of the teams didn't seem to be taking the quiz even half as seriously as the man with the ponytail was, perhaps because the grand prize wasn't exactly the sort of thing that people were willing to waste their energy getting overly competitive about. Aside from a free round of drinks (one alcoholic beverage per person, no double measures of whisky, vodka or gin, no single measures of anything remotely expensive, and no wine except for the stuff in the box), the winning team were also presented with The Trophy, which wasn't really a trophy at all but a gold-painted eggcup that passed from team to team on an ever-rotating basis. That was the idea, anyway, although Ronnie had overheard another team talking about how the eggcup hadn't changed hands for as long as they could remember. It seemed to have taken up permanent residence with a team called – somewhat aptly – The Egg Heads (which caused Ronnie to wonder what came first, the eggcup or The Egg Heads?).

They sat at the table closest to the stage like nerds at the front of assembly, no doubt because they wanted to hear the questions more clearly or, as Ronnie had noticed during the first, second and third rounds of the quiz, so they could ask for pointless clarifications ('When you say "What is the average speed of a common garden hedgehog," I assume you mean on land?') or constantly correct the quizmaster's pronunciation ('When you say "oto-*reeno*-laryngologist", I assume what you actually meant to say was "oto-*rhino*-laryngol-ogist"?'). The team was comprised solely of men, who all appeared to be in their mid-to-late sixties and all sported the same button-down-shirt-under-musty-old-moth-eaten-jumper combo. They reminded Ronnie of retired university professors, not because they looked clever, but because they all had furry ears and red noses and wild hair that had never seen a comb. That's what Ronnie imagined retired university professors to look like anyway, although he'd never actually met one before, retired or otherwise.

Professors or not, The Egg Heads obviously had a wealth of knowledge between them. Whenever the quizmaster read out a question about history or sport, they all smiled and nodded smugly at each other, as if to say 'Don't worry, fellow nerds, I was literally just listening to an audiobook about this very topic while simultaneously reading an actual book, also about this very same topic.' Only the questions about popular culture seemed to facilitate any sort of discussion, especially the question about twerking, which kicked off a hushed and rather angry debate, as if they were arguing about the finer points of The Battle of Waterloo and not the origins of bum jiggling.

In contrast, there were no hushed or angry debates among The Beethoven Quartet. Nor were there any smug or knowing nods at one another. There was, however, a lot of non-smug and non-knowing nodding, mainly from Brian, who, in an attempt to make Cate think that he too was something of a fellow savant, agreed with basically every answer she came up with while saying something about how he was just about to say something similar himself.

Not that Ronnie had any more to offer than Brian did. As expected, his contribution had been almost non-existent, but he convinced himself that this was OK because he was the captain and had therefore delegated all question-answering responsibilities to the rest of the table. Also, as expected, Cate seemed to have little need for anybody else's input, although she made a point of consulting her teammates anyway, keen to make everybody feel involved, even if a large part of their involvement amounted to shrugging and saying 'Sounds good to me' or 'If you say so.'

She didn't need to answer all of the questions on her own though. Brian had won them a point by correctly guessing which two teams had faced each other in the 1974 World Cup Final. He'd also earned himself about a bajillion points with Cate after effortlessly identifying a sample verse from 'Rubberband Girl' by Kate Bush. As for Harriet, she revealed herself to be quite the repository of sporting knowledge, something she attributed to years of being married to a man who would literally watch anything just as long as there was a competitive element to it. All in all, while The Beethoven Quartet were still very much a one-woman band, they were at least a one-woman band with three backing singers, or two backing singers and one useless manager named Ronnie.

'What can I get you?' asked the barman.

'A gin and tonic and three pints of that one please,' said Ronnie, pointing at the Perv pump.

'Make that four,' said Carl, draping his arm around Ronnie.

The barman looked at Ronnie for confirmation. Ronnie nodded, even though he knew from experience that buying a drink for Carl was like buying a drink for a wombat, a species that was not known for buying you a drink back.

'How's the quiz going so far?' said Ronnie.

'Fuck knows, mate, I'm just here to get pissed,' he said, slurring as if to demonstrate his commitment to this task.

Ronnie nodded towards the table where Alan was sitting with the two other men. All three of them were staring at their phones. 'I didn't know you and Alan were, you know, mates.'

'Mates?' said Carl. He couldn't have looked more offended if Ronnie had asked if he and Alan were lovers. 'We're not mates. You think I'd be mates with that giant testicle? No fucking chance. Why, is that what he told you?'

'No,' said Ronnie, surprised to hear himself covering for his boss. 'I just thought, you know, because you were on the same pub quiz team and all.'

'Only because he's buying my drinks.'

'That's very . . . generous?' said Ronnie, although 'strange' felt like a better choice of words.

'Desperate more like,' said Carl. 'You know your life's gone to shit when you're having to bribe people to come to the pub with you. He's buying *their* drinks as well,' he added, nodding towards the other two men. 'It must be costing him a fortune, especially 'cos I've been ordering doubles all night.'

'Who are they?'

'No idea. I don't even think Alan knows them. Think he found them on the internet or something. Anyway,' he said, taking one of the pints that the barman placed in front of them. 'Cheers!' He took a sip and pulled a face like he'd just drunk a mouthful of frogspawn. 'Christ, what's that?'

'What you asked for,' said Ronnie.

'I think I'll stick to the doubles,' said Carl, returning the pint to the bar. 'See you later,' he said, disappearing into the crowd, while Ronnie stared at the foamy crescent that Carl had left on the edge of the glass. He wasn't sure what annoyed him more, the fact that Carl had asked for a drink despite Alan already buying them for him, the fact that he'd sullied an otherwise perfect pint and then left it on the bar, or the fact that Ronnie had never realised until that moment just how much he and Alan had in common.

Ronnie returned to the table to find Harriet sitting on her own.

'What happened to the others?' he asked as he put the tray of drinks down.

'Cate popped out for a cigarette and then Brian suddenly developed a smoking habit,' said Harriet with a little chuckle. She took her gin and tonic. 'Cheers,' she said, knocking her glass against Ronnie's pint.

'Cheers,' said Ronnie. He took a sip and wiped the foam from his top lip. 'So, how do you think it's going so far?'

'Honestly?' she said. 'This is quite possibly the most fun I've had since, well, you know.' She patted Ronnie's hand. 'Thank you for inviting me. Getting drunk with other people is much more fun than getting drunk on your own.'

'Aye aye, captain,' said Cate as she returned to the table with Brian and Beethoven in tow. 'Cate and Brian, reporting for duty.' They both gave him mock salutes.

'At ease,' said Ronnie, playing along. 'So, what do you reckon, you think we're winning?'

Cate took a contemplative sip of her pint. 'There's a couple of questions I'm not absolutely one hundred per cent certain about, but otherwise I think we've got everything right so far. They're going to be the biggest problem,' she said, nodding towards The Egg Heads. 'It all depends on what the next three categories are. If the questions are about pipe tobacco, the monarchy and the history of the trouser press, then we might be in trouble. Otherwise I think we're in with a chance.'

'Thanks to you,' said Brian, gazing at Cate like a dog might gaze at a tennis-ball factory.

'Thanks to all of us!' said Cate, raising her glass. 'Let's hear it for The Beethoven Quartet!'

Everybody knocked their drinks together and cheered.

'Hey!' shouted Harriet, waving her hand at The Egg Heads' table. 'Better be careful with that trophy of yours. You never know when someone might "poach" it! Get it?'

One of The Egg Heads sighed as if somebody had just informed him that his subscription to *The Economist* was going to increase by a penny. 'Very funny,' he said in a tone designed to imply that he found the joke anything but.

'Yes, well done,' said another with such a condescending tone that Ronnie half expected him to get up, walk over and pat Harriet on the head.

'Obviously can't take a joke,' whispered Harriet, hiding behind her glass as she pretended to take a sip. She tried to laugh it off, but Ronnie could see that she was clearly a little embarrassed.

He cleared his throat and turned towards The Egg Heads. 'Careful you don't "crack" under pressure!' he shouted.

Harriet laughed into her glass, sending gin and tonic everywhere.

'Don't think we're going to go over-easy on you!' shouted Cate.

'We should leave them alone, they're starting to look a bit terri-fried!' said Harriet.

'Hope you have "un oeuf" points to beat us!' said Cate. Everybody stopped laughing and looked at her. '"Un oeuf" means "one egg" in French,' she explained.

'Oh!' said Harriet. 'Good one.'

'We're going to smash your heads open and scramble your brains!' said Brian, eager to show Cate that he too was capable of making egg-related puns. Everybody fell quiet. The Egg Heads shuffled uncomfortably in their seats.

'Bit much, Brian,' whispered Cate.

'Yeah, too far,' said Harriet.

'Sorry,' whispered Brian.

'We didn't mean that,' said Ronnie, raising an apologetic hand to The Egg Heads. 'Just got a bit carried away. Good luck with the quiz.'

'Yes, sorry about that,' said Harriet. 'May the best team win.'

The Egg Heads refused to look at them, perhaps out of spite or perhaps out of fear. Instead, they stared straight ahead, like drivers who had cut somebody up and now found themselves waiting parallel to them at the traffic lights.

'Okey-dokey,' said the quizmaster, returning to the stage and plucking the microphone from the mic stand. 'Let's get cracking on the next round, shall we?'

The Egg Heads sighed so loudly that the quizmaster's ponytail almost fluttered in the breeze. Ronnie, Harriet, Cate and Brian, who had just about managed to compose themselves, suddenly burst out laughing again.

'What's so funny?' said the quizmaster. 'What did I say?'

'Nothing,' said Cate, wiping the tears from her eyes. 'Sorry. Please, *crack* on.'

234

Geography, politics and general knowledge were the themes of the next three rounds. General knowledge came last, presumably to give anybody without a specialist subject a chance to snatch a few last-minute points before the quiz was over. It was the easiest round by far, so easy in fact that even Ronnie was able to contribute, although given that the questions were simple enough that Beethoven could probably have answered them, his contributions felt more symbolic than anything.

'Well, well, well,' said the quizmaster once he'd tallied up the scores. 'It looks like we've got ourselves a good old-fashioned tie! How exciting is that?'

Judging by the apathetic murmur that passed through the room, the collective answer appeared to be 'not very'. Harriet seemed excited though, as did Cate, and Brian looked excited because Cate looked excited, which only left Ronnie, who, despite his best efforts to maintain a decorum fitting of a captain, was also rather excited to see how The Beethoven Quartet had fared against the other teams.

'Coming in last, with a still respectable thirty-two points, please give a round of applause for Alan's Army!' said the quizmaster. A few ironic cheers rose up from Alan's table. Alan returned Ronnie's conciliatory nod with an encouraging thumbs-up.

'Well, at least we're not last!' said Cate.

'I'll drink to that!' said Harriet.

'In third place, we have . . . drum roll please . . . We Thought This Was Speed Dating! Well done, team, you finished with forty-one points.'

A group of men in the corner, who looked like they wouldn't have had much more luck had they actually been speed dating, cheered and raised their drinks in toast.

'Next up is . . . wait for it . . . wait for it . . . Monty's Python!' said the quizmaster, gesturing towards a table at the back of the room. 'Good job, gang, you managed to "snake" your way into second place with forty-five points.'

'Blimey!' said Harriet. 'You know what that means?' She looked around the table.

'We're in the tie!' said Brian.

'Which just leaves our last two teams, The Egg Heads and The Beethoven Quartet, who are neck and neck with a whopping fifty-eight points each!'

'Go team!' shouted Cate, although Ronnie could see that she was secretly trying to figure out which two questions they'd answered incorrectly. The Egg Heads looked at them with a mixture of amusement and surprise, like most people would look at a smoking marmoset.

'What happens now?' asked Ronnie, looking around the table. Everybody shrugged.

'This is actually the first time we've ever had a tie,' said the quizmaster, 'so I'm not exaggerating when I say that all of you lucky folks in this room are literally witnessing history in the making right now. Just like people ask, "Where were you on September eleventh?" and "Where were you when JFK was assassinated?" so too will future generations ask you fine people here tonight, "Where were you when the Pig in the Pond pub quiz had a tie?" And you'll be able to look them in the eye and proudly say, "I was right there."'

'Where were you when they invented haircuts?' shouted somebody from the crowd. Everybody laughed except for the quizmaster.

'Where were you when John kicked the shit out of the last heckler?' said the quizmaster, glancing at John the bouncer, who was eyeballing the crowd in search of the phantom disruptor. Everybody stopped laughing. 'Anyway, let's see who's going to be crowned tonight's champion! The winner will be decided by sudden death! Not actual sudden death, obviously. Although if one team did suddenly die, then, well, I suppose the other team would win by default. But that's not the sudden death I was talking about. I was talking about the non-violent version. This is a family pub after all. Basically, I'm going to pull out one random question from this here hat.' He held up a battered top hat for all to see. 'The winner will be the first person to answer the question correctly, so, without further ado, could the captains of each team please come up to the stage. Give them a round of applause, everybody!'

The captain of The Egg Heads slid his chair back and walked up to the stage with the confidence of somebody who had already won and was off to collect his prize.

Ronnie looked at Cate, suddenly panicked. 'Cate, you go!'

'I can't!' she said.

'Just say you're the captain! It could be anybody for all he knows!'

'I had to write it on the quiz sheet!' said Cate. 'I know I'm not the most feminine of women, but I'm pretty sure I don't look like a Ronald! At least I hope I don't. No offence.'

Ronnie looked at Brian, who was the only other person at the table who could feasibly pass as a Ronald. Given his contributions so far, Brian had proved that his pub quiz skills weren't much better than Ronnie's. But they *were* better, regardless of how *much* better, which meant that Brian would make a better Ronnie than Ronnie would in this case. Also, as Ronnie attempted to remind Brian via a combination of telepathy and accusatory facial expressions, Brian was supposed to be the captain, not him. Perhaps sensing what Ronnie was thinking, Brian began to pay a great deal of attention to a loose thread he'd just found on his sleeve. When he finally looked up and saw that Ronnie was still staring at him, he grabbed his phone, which wasn't even ringing, put it to his ear and scurried away through the crowd.

'Come on, Ronald!' said the quizmaster before Ronnie had a chance to chase down Brian and remind him that the team only had enough space for one coward and that position had already been filled. 'Get up here and show us what you're made of!'

'Don't worry,' said Cate. 'It's only a stupid pub quiz.'

'Yeah,' said Harriet. 'Who cares? It's just a bit of fun.'

Ronnie nodded. He knew they were right. It *was* just a bit of fun. He didn't care about the free drinks and he certainly didn't care about the golden egg cup. He just didn't want to let everybody down. He'd never been a part of a team before, not a proper team anyway, and he might never be part of another one after tonight, so he wanted to mark the occasion with a victory, something to look back on and smile about in the future. But then it occurred to him that he didn't need to win the quiz for the night to stick in his memory. The night felt like a win already, golden egg cup or not.

'OK,' he said. 'Let's do this!'

'Ronnie! Ronnie! Ronnie!' chanted The Beethoven Quartet as Ronnie made his way to the stage. Some of the other customers also chanted his name, not because they knew him or because they wanted his team to win, but because chanting things is fun, especially when you're drunk.

'All right, Ronnie. All right, Keith,' said the quizmaster, standing between Ronnie and the captain of The Egg Heads. 'I want a good clean fight, no punching below the waist, no punching above the waist, and no punching anywhere else either for that matter. Save that for the car park. Like I said already, the rules are very simple. I'm going to read out a question and the first person to answer it wins. And yes, you have to answer it correctly. If I say, "What's the capital of Paraguay?" and you say, "Giraffe", that will not make you the winner, even if you are technically the first person to answer. Got it?'

'Got it,' said the two captains.

'Right. Touch gloves. Can we dim the lights, please? Colin? Dim the lights would you, mate?'

'We ain't got a dimmer!' shouted Colin, whoever Colin was.

'What kind of pub doesn't have a dimmer?' said the quizmaster. He looked at Ronnie and Keith as if waiting for a response.

'This one?' said Ronnie.

'Correct,' said the quizmaster.

'Yes!' said Ronnie. Everybody laughed.

'That wasn't the question,' said the quizmaster. 'It was *a* question, but it wasn't *the* question.'

'Sorry,' said Ronnie, 'Bit nervous.'

'Don't be,' said the quizmaster. 'There's absolutely nothing to be worried about. I mean, yeah, the fate of your team is in your hands, and all of their hard work could be flushed down the toilet if you fail to answer the following question correctly, so from that perspective, then, yes, there's plenty to be worried about. But despite the fact that you might very well be about to throw away everything you've worked so hard for this evening, it's important to remember that this is all just a bit of fun.'

'Right,' said Ronnie, wondering how bad it would look if he suddenly leapt off the stage, burst through the door and didn't stop running until Bingham was a distant memory.

The quizmaster dipped his hand into the upturned top hat that was sitting on a table in front of him. He looked at the question, smiled to himself, folded it up and stuffed it into his back pocket.

'Right,' he said. 'Here we go. Fingers on buzzers. Are you both ready?'

'Ready,' said Keith. Ronnie said nothing.

'Which UK band had a hit record in 1997 with a song called "Tubthump— "'

'Chumbawamba!' shouted Ronnie, grabbing the quizmaster's arm and pulling the microphone towards him. 'Chumbawamba! It's Chumbawamba!'

'All right, mate, no need to pull my bloody arm off,' said the quizmaster, retrieving his arm from Ronnie. 'The correct answer is indeed Chumbawamba!' he shouted.

Cate and Harriet leapt from their seats and cheered while hugging each other. Brian, who had conveniently returned from his suspiciously well-timed disappearance a few minutes ago, also joined the celebrations.

'You said, "the first person to answer the question"!' said Keith, puffing out his bobbled chest and squaring up to the quizmaster.

'What about it?' said the quizmaster. 'He answered first, so he won.'

'But you didn't finish asking the question!' said Keith. 'You only asked *part* of the question. *He* cut you off before you finished the question!' He poked his finger into Ronnie's chest in the same way that Ronnie had seen old ladies poking their fingers into the freshly baked bread at the supermarket. 'You didn't say, "the first person to answer a partial question" or "the first person to answer the question regardless of whether I've finished asking the question or not", you said, "the winner is the first person to answer the question"! A question ends in a question mark! There was no question mark!'

'John!' shouted the quizmaster. 'Looks like we've got a troublemaker over here.'

'I'm not a troublemaker. *You're* the troublemaker! This is a fix! This whole thing is a fix!' Keith's voice receded through the pub as John the bouncer dragged him away. The rest of The Egg Heads glumly followed, no doubt deeming it bad form to stick around for another drink when their captain was getting beaten up outside.

Cate, Harriet, Brian and Beethoven joined Ronnie on the stage. Everybody hugged him and slapped him on the back as if he hadn't just answered the winning pub quiz question but had in fact just returned from a successful mission to destroy an asteroid that was going to end all civilisation.

'Well done, team,' said the quizmaster. 'That was a close one.'

'A little too close for my liking,' said Ronnie with a nervous laugh.

'Well, it's nice to see another team lifting the trophy for once. I think I speak for everybody when I say that we were all getting a little tired of seeing The Egg Heads winning all the time.'

'Too bloody right!' shouted somebody from the crowd.

'So what's the story behind your name? Are you all musicians or something?'

Everybody looked at Cate, fully expecting her to launch into her story about the siege of Leningrad and the triumph of the human spirit, but it was Brian who answered.

'Well, there was this big battle at Stalingrad, right? I think it was in World War One, and—'

'Brian's cat's called Beethoven and there's four of us,' said Cate before Brian could continue. She smiled at Brian as if to thank him for trying, and Brian smiled back as if to thank her for intervening before he made an even bigger fool of himself.

'Well, let's hear it for Beethoven and his Quartet, the newly crowned Pig in the Pond pub quiz champions!'

Chapter Twenty-Three

Everybody but Ronnie lived on the other side of town, but Ronnie wasn't ready to call it a night yet, the high of the evening having not yet worn off, so instead of bidding his team goodnight and making the short journey home on his own, he decided to take the scenic route by walking through town with the rest of them. It wasn't like he had much to get up for in the morning, tomorrow being a Saturday. Nor did he have much of a reason to rush home, unless he counted Hamlet, which he didn't. Despite feeling like the two of them were bonding, or if not bonding exactly, then at least learning to live with one another in a fragile state of existence, he had no doubt that Hamlet was enjoying whatever party he was currently throwing for his various invisible friends. Also, Ronnie had enjoyed not having to worry about accidentally getting into his personal space, just as much as he imagined that Hamlet had enjoyed not having to worry about having his personal space invaded.

There was an old wooden bench on the edge of town that offered a panoramic view of Bingham. By day, it was often occupied by an old man known locally as Drunk Derek, who spent his time either shouting 'Good morning!' at people (regardless of the time of day) or asking passers-by if they could spare ten pence for a cup of tea he had no intention of buying. The bench was usually empty at night though, even if the methylated odours of Derek still lingered, and tonight was no exception.

Everybody took a seat without even discussing it, as if this had been their end destination all along. Brian sat beside Cate, who sat beside Harriet, who sat beside Ronnie, who was perched on the end. Nobody said anything for a moment as they all stared out across Bingham, which actually looked rather quaint in the flattering light of night.

'Beautiful, isn't it?' said Cate finally. Everybody looked at Cate and then at each other.

'No,' they said in unison. They all burst out laughing, including Cate.

'Oh well, I tried,' she said.

'When are they going to tear that thing down?' asked Brian.

'What thing?' said Ronnie.

'The Bingham Eye,' said Brian, nodding towards the Ferris wheel.

'Bingham Eyesore more like,' said Cate. 'I always feel like it's watching over us like the Eye of Sauron.'

'I quite like it actually,' said Harriet. 'It reminds me of better times.'

'Bingham had better times?' joked Brian.

'Have you ever been on it?' asked Cate. She didn't say it to anybody in particular, but the wheel hadn't turned since Ronnie was a teenager so he knew she could only be talking to him or Harriet.

'I did once, a long time ago,' said Harriet. 'I was with my husband at the time. He wasn't my husband then though, he was just a lad who kept asking me to go out with him when I worked in the post office. We were too young for the pub, and the cinema was miles away, so we decided to go on the Ferris wheel. A lot of kids used the wheel for dates back then. Well, we didn't call it dating, we called it "courting", which sounds really old-fashioned now, like something from a Jane Austen novel. It didn't cost very much, and it took about ten minutes to go round, which meant ten minutes of privacy that you usually couldn't get anywhere else at the time.' Harriet smiled at the memory. 'You can do a lot in those ten minutes,' she said.

'Harriet!' said Cate. 'You saucy old so-and-so.'

'I should be so lucky,' said Harriet. 'As soon as the wheel started turning, Sidney decided he was terrified of heights and spent the next ten minutes clinging to the side and screaming for it to stop. That was the first and only time we ever went on a Ferris wheel.'

Cate laughed. 'I'm surprised it wasn't the first and only time you ever went on a date with him,' she said.

'You know what? It might sound strange, but it made me like him more. I didn't really fancy him very much before then. I only went out with him to shut

246

him up, to be honest. He thought he was a tough guy, you know the type, smoking and drinking and whistling at girls and whatnot. But then I saw him on the Ferris wheel and realised he was actually a big softie at heart, and he saw that I saw and so, well, I suppose he thought there was no point pretending to be anything else after that. He told me not to tell anybody and I didn't. It became our little secret. Well, until now, that is.' She looked around. 'Don't tell anybody, will you?'

'Your secret's safe with us,' said Ronnie.

'Yeah,' said Cate. 'I won't tell anybody.'

'Or me,' said Brian. 'Beethoven's also good at keeping secrets,' he added, stroking Beethoven, who was curled up in his lap.

Harriet smiled. They all sat in silence for a moment, perhaps thinking about Sidney clinging on to the Ferris wheel for dear life, or perhaps, like Ronnie, they were thinking about how everybody becomes an anecdote sooner or later, and the most you can hope for in life is to become an anecdote worth telling.

'I also have a deep dark secret about the Ferris wheel actually,' said Ronnie. 'I've never told anybody until now, but I feel it's time that I finally came clean.'

'What did you do, Ronnie?' said Cate, leaning forward and looking at Ronnie down the length of the bench.

'Did you push somebody off it?' asked Brian. 'I'm pretty sure I heard a story about somebody being pushed off it once.'

'I thought they jumped,' said Harriet. 'Didn't they jump?'

'No, they were definitely pushed,' said Cate. 'The police spoke to the bloke who was in the carriage with them, but they ended up letting him off because they couldn't prove it.' Everybody was looking at Ronnie now. 'Was that you, Ronnie?' asked Cate, her eyes wide with morbid fascination and maybe just a little bit of fear.

'It's a lot worse than that, I'm afraid,' said Ronnie. He felt the bench tremble slightly as his teammates leaned closer. 'When I was nine, I lied about my height so they'd let me on.'

Everybody let out a collective sigh, which could have been disappointment or could have been relief.

'How have you been able to live with yourself all this time?' said Cate, her tone mock serious.

'I wouldn't even be able to look at myself in the mirror,' said Harriet.

'I know, I know, I'm ashamed, believe me,' said Ronnie. 'But I feel a lot better for getting it off my chest.'

'Wait,' said Brian. 'How can you lie about your height? I mean, it's not like lying about your age or your weight, is it? Your height's right there, it's not like anybody has to take your word for it.'

'Good point,' said Cate. 'What's the story, Mr Liar? Are you lying to *us* right now?'

'OK, maybe "lying" is the wrong word,' said Ronnie. 'Basically, there was this bloke who used to run the Ferris wheel, Mr Fenton I think his name was. He was this miserable old bugger with an unlit cigarette permanently wedged in the corner of his mouth. Nobody ever saw him smile and nobody ever heard him talk. All he did was usher people in and out of the carriages, but only if you were the right height. See, the Ferris wheel had a height restriction, which I still don't quite understand why, but anyway, those were the rules and anybody who wasn't tall enough wouldn't be allowed on the ride. I didn't know this at the time, and neither did my dad, so when he asked what I wanted to do to celebrate my ninth birthday, I told him I wanted to ride the Ferris wheel. I'd overheard a bunch of other kids at school talking about how cool it was and how amazing the view looked from way up there, so I couldn't wait to see it for myself. But Mr Fenton wouldn't let me on. He shook his head as soon as he saw me and pointed to the wooden board with the height markings on it. I stood against it and tried to make myself as tall as possible without going onto my tiptoes. I even spat on my hand and ran it through my hair to make it stand on end.'

'You spat in your hair?' said Brian.

'Desperate times call for desperate measures,' said Ronnie. 'It didn't work though, I was still about a centimetre too short. Mr Fenton wouldn't budge, so we had no choice but to call it a day. Walking home through the fairground, my dad saw a news kiosk and ran off to get a paper. I thought he just wanted to read it, but he pulled out some pages, folded them up and told me to give him my shoes, which I did. He slid the folded pieces underneath my insoles and told me to put my shoes back on before he took me by the hand and led me back to the Ferris wheel. All of this happened in the space of about five minutes, so Mr Fenton recognised us immediately. He shook his head and pointed at the board, but when I stood against it again, this time I was tall enough. Mr Fenton didn't know what to say. He knew something wasn't right, but he couldn't for the life of him figure out what. "They grow up so fast, don't they?" said my dad. I'll never forget the look on Mr Fenton's face when he said that. Poor bloke must have thought he'd lost his marbles or something. Anyway, long story short, I got to ride the Ferris wheel for my birthday.'

'And was it as great as everybody at school said it was?' asked Cate.

'I don't know,' said Ronnie. 'I spent the ride puking into a pick 'n' mix bag.' Everybody laughed.

'Well, good on your dad for going the extra mile,' said Cate. 'My old man wouldn't have made that kind of effort, not in a million years.' She smiled, but Ronnie saw the sadness behind it.

'I heard they're going to make it turn again,' said Harriet.

'Really?' said Brian. Harriet nodded.

'To commemorate its seventy-fifth anniversary,' said Harriet. 'They're going to time it to coincide with the fair next week apparently. It might just fall over or roll into the sea, but either way, it'll be eventful.'

Bingham fair was an annual event that used to lure people from all across the country but now struggled to lure even the locals away from their televisions.

'We should go!' said Cate. 'All of us. It'll be fun.'

'I'm not sure throwing cricket balls at coconuts and hooking ducks in the rain counts as fun,' said Ronnie.

'Yeah, but it'll be fun in an ironic way!' said Cate. 'We can have ironic fun!'

'I don't think I've ever had ironic fun before,' said Harriet thoughtfully. 'I'm not sure I'd even know how to do it.'

'It's easy,' said Cate. 'You just have to pretend that crap things are actually good. People do it all the time. Just look at folks who wear bumbags. Or people in their twenties who say they like Rick Astley. Or people of any age who say they like Rick Astley. Or people who say they like fancy dress parties. Nobody likes fancy dress parties, they're rubbish.'

'I don't like fancy dress parties,' said Brian.

'I quite like Rick Astley, though,' said Harriet.

'See, now you're getting the hang of it!' said Cate.

'But I'm not being ironic.'

'Very convincing. You're a pro already!' said Cate.

'Right,' said Harriet, a little unsurely, as if she no longer knew if she was being ironic or not.

'So who's up for the fair?' asked Cate.

'I don't have anything planned,' said Ronnie, surprising himself. Usually, he would have waited to see what the general consensus was before committing himself to something, but the evening had left him feeling oddly uninhibited, so much so that he probably would have responded in exactly the same way had Cate suggested they all go skinny-dipping in Bingham pond. He had no doubt that alcohol had something to do with this.

'Me neither,' said Harriet.

'Great!' said Cate. 'How about it, Brian?'

'Er, yeah. Maybe,' he said. 'I'll have to check with my mum.'

Cate laughed. 'You need your mum's permission to go to the fair? How old are you, twelve?'

'No,' said Brian with a nervous laugh. 'It's just . . . she isn't very well, and she doesn't have anybody else, so . . .' he trailed off with a shrug.

'Shit, sorry, Brian,' said Cate. 'I was only having a laugh. I didn't mean to take the piss.' She put her arm around him and rubbed his shoulder.

'It's OK,' said Brian in a tone that implied that it wasn't completely OK but he would nevertheless find it in his heart to forgive her, just as long as she left her arm where it was.

'I thought we were pushing our luck,' said Harriet, holding out her hand and looking up at the sky. Ronnie held his own hand out and felt the first few drops of rain on his palm. 'We better make a move before it pours down.'

'I think it's going to pass,' said Brian, determined to stay on the bench with Cate for as long as humanly possible, but even as he said it, the distant sound of thunder rumbled across the sky towards them.

'I'm not sticking around to find out,' said Cate, standing and pulling her hood up. 'Come on, let's get going before we're all drenched.'

Chapter Twenty-Four

They walked a little further together before reaching the T-junction in the centre of town.

'I'm this way,' said Harriet, pointing left.

'Me too!' said Cate. She looked at Brian. 'Where do you live, Brian?'

Ronnie hoped that Brian would say that he also lived in that direction. That way, he could turn round and make his way home before the heavens opened.

'Down the hill,' said Brian, pointing in the opposite direction. 'How about you, Ronnie?'

Ronnie felt silly telling everybody that he actually lived two minutes round the corner from the pub they'd left half an hour ago, which meant that his only options were to go left with Cate and Harriet or right with Brian. Left would get him home slightly faster than right, but Ronnie felt bad about letting Brian walk home on his own, even though he technically wasn't on his own because he had Beethoven for company, and even though Ronnie would be able to offer close to zero assistance in the event of a dangerous encounter with one of Bingham's many unsavoury characters, or with one of the many foxes that prowled the streets at night and had been known to attack people who were too drunk to defend themselves or to identify their attacker in a police line-up.

'Same,' said Ronnie.

'Hey, let's all swap numbers,' said Cate, who seemed to have become the de facto leader of their group. 'You know, so we can coordinate and stuff.'

'Yes!' said Brian, whipping out his phone so quickly that he almost dropped it in the gutter.

'Good idea,' said Harriet.

Ronnie smiled, happy to know that everybody wanted to meet up again as much as he did. The ripping of Velcro tore through the empty streets as he took his phone from its holster. Everybody flinched.

'Sorry,' he said. 'It's new.' He pointed to the holster that he'd bought so long ago that he couldn't even remember where he'd purchased it from.

'I like your phone,' said Harriet.

'See, now you're getting it!' said Cate.

'Getting what?' said Harriet.

'Wait, I thought you were being ironic. Weren't you being ironic just then?'

'Why would that be ironic?' said Harriet, removing her phone from her pocket. It was even older than Ronnie's. Cate looked at it and shook her head.

'No reason,' she said.

They all swapped numbers and said goodnight before heading off in opposite directions.

'Thanks for coming tonight,' said Brian as they made their way down the hill. 'I wasn't sure you were going to turn up.'

'I wasn't sure *you* were going to turn up,' said Ronnie.

'I almost didn't, to be honest.'

'Thanks a lot,' said Ronnie sarcastically.

'Not because I didn't want to or anything. Mum just took a turn at the last minute and I didn't know if she'd be all right on her own.'

'It must be difficult,' said Ronnie. Brian looked at him. 'You know. Looking after someone.' Being an only child to a single parent, Ronnie had always just assumed that there would come a time when his role as son would slowly give way to the role of caregiver. Stupid as he felt when he thought about it now, it had never once occurred to him that such a time would never come, not because his dad would pop off at ninety-nine without so much as the need for a walking stick, but because he might never reach an age where Ronnie's help would be necessary. Ronnie had always imagined a period of steady decline, a period that would give him a chance to prepare himself for what was coming and make as much peace with it as anybody could make peace with the idea of saying goodbye to your only parent and your only friend. Having lost his mum so unexpectedly, he'd naively assumed that such a thing couldn't possibly happen again, that somewhere there existed a great big book of celestial regulations and within that book there was a rule which prohibited Ronnie from losing both of his parents without any warning. The hardest part about losing his dad wasn't saying goodbye. The hardest part was not getting the chance to.

'You get used to it,' said Brian. 'It was harder when I was a kid.' Ronnie smiled. Brian was still very much a kid to him, but he didn't want to tell him that for fear of sounding condescending. Still, Brian seemed to sense what he was thinking. 'Listen to me, I sound like an old man!' he said. 'But it does sort of make you feel like an old man sometimes. I've been looking after her ever since I was twelve, and you have to grow up pretty fast when you're somebody's only carer. Dad buggered off the moment she got ill, so I basically had to do everything myself. Cooking, cleaning, shopping, gardening. You name it. And I still had to go to school.'

'Doesn't sound like you had much chance to be a kid,' said Ronnie.

'I don't blame my mum or anything,' said Brian. 'She can't help it, it's not her fault. But yeah. It wasn't exactly the sort of childhood you see in the movies. Well, maybe the depressing ones. You try making friends when you can't play out because you need to stay home to look after your mum.'

'I didn't have any friends at school either,' said Ronnie.

'Rubbish, isn't it?'

'I didn't mind it at the time, to be honest. But then again, my situation was a bit different from yours. It was more, well, self-inflicted.'

Brian frowned. 'How do you mean?' he said.

'My mum left when I was a kid, and it made my dad stop trusting people. And then he convinced *me* to stop trusting people, so I did, and, well, that was that.'

'I'm not sure that's the best advice to give to a kid,' said Brian. 'Take it from somebody who would have killed to have a friend or two.'

Ronnie nodded. 'I know he was only trying to help me in his own messed-up way. He was just trying to protect me from life's disappointments, I suppose.' Ronnie couldn't help but smile when he said this. He was forty-two, he worked at the bus station and he didn't even know enough people to act as pallbearers at his own funeral. With that in mind, it was hard to say that his dad had completely succeeded in sparing Ronnie the full force of life's many disappointments. 'It wasn't so bad then. My dad was like my best friend. But then he died, and I suddenly realised that I was forty-one without a friend in the world.' Ronnie hadn't intended to share this much information about himself. Usually, he would have found such a confession embarrassing, but he felt oddly comfortable talking about this stuff with Brian, perhaps because Brian had been so open about his own struggles.

'Well, you seem to have friends now,' said Brian. 'I like them, they're nice.'

'You mean you like Cate,' said Ronnie.

'What?' said Brian. 'No.' He laughed dismissively. They walked a few steps in silence. 'Why, does she like me?' he asked, trying to sound casual and failing miserably.

Ronnie laughed. 'You'd have to ask her,' he said.

Brian sighed. 'It's a shame she's so clever.'

'Why is that a shame?'

'Because she's too smart to be interested in me.'

'Don't be so hard on yourself,' said Ronnie. 'You both looked like you were getting along pretty well to me.'

Brian smiled. 'You think so?'

'You got her number, didn't you?'

Brian rolled his eyes. '*Everybody* got her number.'

Ronnie laughed. 'True,' he said. 'Still, you have to start somewhere, I suppose.'

Brian paused outside a terraced house. Some of the tiles were missing from the roof, and the door looked like it could use a lick of paint or three. The two men said goodbye and Ronnie watched as Brian and Beethoven disappeared through the front door. Then, turning round, he made his way back up the hill and cut through an alley that took him onto the same road they'd walked down earlier.

Passing the bench they'd been sitting on, he noticed a scarf draped over the back of it. He wondered who it belonged to, until he remembered that Harriet had been wearing a scarf. Guessing it must be hers, he picked it up and slipped it into his pocket.

The downpour started just as Ronnie reached a stretch of road without any bus stops, shop awnings, bridges or doorways for shelter.

Throwing his hood over his head and zipping his jacket up to his neck, he picked up the pace in a futile attempt to make it home before he got drenched. The sound of the rain on his hood was so loud that he didn't hear the footsteps behind him. Only when the rain miraculously stopped did he look round to find Pearl walking beside him while she sheltered them both with the umbrella that Ronnie had given to her.

'Oh, hi, Pearl,' said Ronnie. 'What are you doing out on a night like this?'

'I'm homeless,' said Pearl matter-of-factly. Ronnie cringed at his own stupidity. 'What's your excuse?'

'I'm just on my way back from the pub quiz.'

'You really should have an umbrella in this weather,' she said without a hint of irony.

Ronnie smiled. 'You're right, I should.'

'How did you do?' asked Pearl. 'In the quiz?'

'We came first actually.'

'Win anything nice?'

Ronnie removed the golden egg cup from his pocket and sheepishly handed it to Pearl. 'It's not real gold,' he said, as if such a thing needed clarifying.

'No,' said Pearl as she turned it over in her hand,

'but it is a real egg cup.' Ronnie smiled. 'Know what I found the other day? An ostrich egg, right there at the bottom of the bin in the corner of the car park behind the high street.'

'What did you do with it?'

'I left it, of course,' said Pearl. 'You should never disturb a bird's nest.'

Ronnie thought about telling her that the chances of an actual ostrich laying an egg in a bin in Bingham were considerably more remote than the chances of somebody buying one and then discarding it for whatever reason (like being unable to open it), but remembering who he was talking to, he decided to keep his mouth shut.

'I've found all sorts of weird things over the years. Stuffed alligators, inflatable sheep, three entire box sets of *Mrs Brown's Boys*. You name it, I've found it.'

Ronnie cleared his throat. 'I don't suppose you've found . . . a shadow by any chance, have you?' He braced himself for the inevitable side-eye, but Pearl just shook her head.

'I usually go through the bins after dark. You don't see many shadows at that time of night.'

Ronnie smiled. 'I suppose not,' he said.

They walked in silence for a moment. The sound of a police siren wailed in the distance before fading into the night.

'Sorry about what happened the other day,' said Ronnie.

'What happened the other day?'

261

'You know. Alan putting you on that bus to Fingle Bridge. He shouldn't have done that.'

'Oh, yes,' said Pearl with a chuckle. 'It's OK. It was quite funny, to be honest.'

'Really?' said Ronnie, surprised by this. 'You're more forgiving than I am.'

'Alan told the driver to drop me off just round the corner. I didn't actually go all the way to Fingle Bridge.'

'I never knew he was a practical joker.'

'He isn't. He was just showing off, trying to act tough in front of you. I think he secretly likes it when I come to the station. It gives him a chance to flex his manager muscles.' A taxi drove past and ploughed through a giant puddle, displacing most of the water from the road onto the pavement in front of them. 'It's not his fault,' she said. 'He gets it from his dad.'

Ronnie frowned. 'You know his dad?'

'Unfortunately,' said Pearl with a sigh. 'I used to be Alan's babysitter, back in the day.'

Ronnie looked at Pearl, certain he must have misheard.

'I know what you're thinking. Hard to imagine anybody entrusting somebody like me with a child, right? Well, believe it or not, I didn't always look like I was going to eat them. I'll have you know that I used to be quite "respectable",' she said, making air quotes with her fingers.

It took Ronnie a moment to process this information. 'Alan never told me that you two knew each other.'

'I'm not surprised. Would you want people to know that the local lunatic used to be your babysitter?'

'I never had a babysitter,' said Ronnie in a feeble attempt at dodging the question.

'He's a good person at heart,' said Pearl. 'He might come across like an arse sometimes, but that's only because his dad's an arse. The man was about as affectionate as a barbed wire fence. He never had any time for Alan. He didn't like him very much, so Alan would try to make himself more likeable by being as unlikeable as his dad. It was quite sad really, watching him try to be somebody he wasn't, just so the miserable git would accept him. He never did though.'

'What about his mum?' asked Ronnie, wondering where she fit into all of this. 'What was she like?'

'I don't know,' said Pearl. 'She died when Alan was a toddler. That's why his dad hired me.'

While Ronnie had never taken his dad for granted, there were certain things he thought a child could reasonably expect their fathers to do – embarrassing their kids with their questionable dance moves at weddings, birthdays and any other gathering involving music and a free bar, for instance, or telling jokes of such poor quality that even a Christmas cracker manufacturer would reject them. Loving their children was another one of those things, or if not loving, then at the very least *liking* them. But even that much wasn't guaranteed, as Alan knew all too well, it seemed, and even though Ronnie had always known how lucky he'd been to have such a good relationship with his dad, it was only while listening to Pearl talk about Alan's relationship (or lack of) with his own father that he realised just *how* lucky he'd been.

'He sometimes brings me sandwiches, and we chat about this and that. I think he thinks he's doing it for my benefit, but I reckon he just likes the company, to be honest.'

'That explains a few things,' said Ronnie, remembering the conversation he'd had with Alan in the park, as well as what Carl had told him earlier about Alan buying his drinks all night in exchange for being part of his pub quiz team.

'Don't tell him I told you any of this though,' said Pearl. 'He'd be mortified if he found out.'

'Of course,' said Ronnie. 'I won't say anything.' They slowed as the junction loomed into view up ahead. One road led to town, the other back to Ronnie's house. 'This is me,' he said, pointing left.

'Then I'll bid you *adieu*,' said Pearl.

'Do you want to come back for, I don't know, a cup of coffee or something?' he said, knowing she had nowhere to go and feeling bad about leaving her out in the rain.

Pearl frowned. 'Are you trying to seduce me?' she asked.

'What? No! No. God no,' said Ronnie, tripping over his words while he tried to explain himself, until he saw Pearl smiling and realised she was joking. 'Very funny,' he said.

'Thanks for the invite. Maybe another time,' said Pearl.

'My door's always open,' said Ronnie. 'Although, come to think of it, I'm not sure how my dog feels about ferrets. Or, to be more precise, how ferrets might feel about him.'

'Ferrets?' said Pearl.

'Yeah. You know. The ones inside your coat.'

'Why would I have ferrets inside my coat?'

Ronnie laughed, certain that Pearl was pulling his leg again, but this time she looked deadly serious. He nervously cleared his throat. 'No reason,' he said.

Pearl looked at Ronnie for a long and awkward moment before turning and making her way down the road.

'And people think *I'm* crazy,' she muttered to herself.

Chapter Twenty-Five

Ronnie flinched as Dr Sterling grabbed his hand and poked it with all the delicacy of a drunk person jabbing the buttons on a fruit machine.

'Does it hurt when I do that?' he asked.

'Yes,' said Ronnie. 'It does.'

'What about if I do this?' he said, doing exactly the same thing.

'Yes. It hurts,' said Ronnie through his teeth.

'And how about this?' he said, jabbing it again, this time with the chewed end of a biro he'd removed from his top pocket.

'For the last time, yes, it hurts, so please can you stop poking it, especially with a chewed-up pen.' Ronnie nodded at the offending item. 'Is that sterilised?'

'Obviously not,' said Dr Sterling. 'It's a pen. Who sterilises a pen?'

'Isn't that a bit unhygienic?'

'It's OK, I'll clean it afterwards.'

'I'm not worried about you, I'm worried about me. I'm not comfortable with you poking my hand with a pen that's been in your mouth.'

'Don't worry, I have a very clean mouth. I take oral hygiene extremely seriously. In fact, I'd probably make a much better dentist than a doctor.'

'That's very reassuring,' said Ronnie, who was already starting to regret his decision to seek Dr Sterling's medical advice for the cut on his hand that he was now convinced was riddled with tetanus.

'Actually,' said Dr Sterling, staring at the pen. 'You know what? This isn't even my pen!'

Ronnie sighed. The worst thing about getting ill in Bingham wasn't the pain or the suffering that came with being ill, but the pain and suffering that came with having to deal with Dr Sterling.

'Where did you say this happened again?' asked the doctor, tilting Ronnie's hand towards the light.

'On the beach.'

'Which beach?'

'North Beach.'

'Whereabouts on North Beach?'

'What does it matter?' said Ronnie, still irritable about having his hand poked and prodded so roughly, especially with the chewed end of a stranger's pen.

'I can't solve a case without knowing where the crime scene is.'

'What case? What crime scene? You're a doctor, not a detective.'

'Doctors are a bit like detectives though, if you think about it.'

'How so?'

'Well, we both have to solve problems, don't we? And we both have to have strong stomachs because we sometimes have to look at really disgusting things that make us want to throw up.' Dr Sterling scanned the room while he struggled to identify more similarities. His gaze landed on his desk. 'And we both have desks,' he said, as if desks were prohibited from every other profession in the world besides doctors and detectives.

'Well, whatever, there's no crime scene because there's no crime. Nobody attacked me.'

'*Nature* attacked you,' said Dr Sterling.

Ronnie pinched the bridge of his nose and closed his eyes. When he opened them, he was disappointed to find that Dr Sterling was still there.

'You know what the number one biggest killer in the world is?' said Dr Sterling.

Ronnie shrugged. 'Nature?' he said with a sigh.

'No, heart disease.'

'Great. Why are you telling me this?'

'Because. Knowledge is power. Take care of your heart. That's all I'm saying.'

'But I'm not here about my heart! I'm here about my hand!'

'All right, all right, don't get your pants in a pickle,' said Dr Sterling. He grabbed the lollipop jar on his desk and was about to unscrew it, presumably to offer Ronnie a lollipop, but seeing the look on Ronnie's face, he removed his hand from the lid and gently put the jar back where he found it.

'It happened about halfway along North Beach,' said Ronnie, deciding to play along in the hope that it might bring his consultation to an end sooner. 'I grabbed a piece of wood with a nail sticking out of it and it stabbed me in the hand. That was about a week ago, and the pain's been getting worse ever since. I was worried it might be tetanus.'

'What makes you think that?'

'Well, I woke up this morning with a really bad headache, like somebody had mistaken my ear for a letterbox and spent the night trying to cram a copy of the Yellow Pages into my head. Also, my skin was pretty clammy and my heart was beating faster than usual. I checked online and apparently they're all symptoms of tetanus.'

'It's not tetanus.'

'How do you know?'

'Because you've had your tetanus jab. It's right here on the records,' said Dr Sterling, rapping the chewed-up pen against his monitor.

'Yeah, but it's not one hundred per cent though, is it?'

'It is. That's exactly what the tetanus jab is. It's one hundred per cent.'

'Right,' said Ronnie.

'You sound disappointed,' said Dr Sterling. 'Most people don't sound disappointed to learn that they don't have a potentially fatal bacterial infection.'

'I'm not disappointed, it's just . . . what is it if it's not tetanus?'

'It's a cut. Correction, it's a graze.'

'It's more than a graze.'

'It really isn't.'

'Then why does it hurt so much?'

'It doesn't. You just think it does.'

Ronnie sighed. 'Not this again.'

'Not what again?'

'This "it's all in your head" stuff. I told you already, I'm not a hypochondriac. I'm not pretending to be ill. I can't invent a headache, can I? I can't invent the sweats.'

Dr Sterling's eyes narrowed. He appeared to be thinking. It bothered Ronnie how unfamiliar he was with Dr Sterling's thinking face.

'You say you woke up with a headache, and that your heart was racing and your skin was clammy?'

Ronnie nodded. 'I also felt a bit nauseous, come to think of it.'

Dr Sterling stood up and placed his palms on his desk. 'May I?' he said, leaning across his desk until his face was about a foot from Ronnie. He sniffed the air a few times, nodded to himself and sat back down. 'Do you mind me asking where you were last night?'

'I was at the pub,' said Ronnie.

'You were there alone?'

'No, I was there with . . . friends,' said Ronnie. He wasn't sure that 'friends' was a totally accurate description of what Cate, Brian and Harriet were, but 'acquaintances' sounded a bit formal, and anyway, it felt good to say the word 'friends', so much so that he couldn't help but smile as he said it. Dr Sterling smiled as well.

'And how much did you drink with these friends?' he asked.

Ronnie shrugged. 'Not much. Three pints, I think.'

Dr Sterling nodded, still smiling. 'Then I think I know what the problem is.' Ronnie shuffled forward on his chair. 'You suffer from something called Lightweight Syndrome.'

'Lightweight Syndrome?' said Ronnie. 'I've never heard of it.'

'It's a fairly common problem, but most people don't talk about it because they're either embarrassed or they simply refuse to accept that they have it. There's a lot of stigma around the condition, especially among men of a certain age. They see it as an affront to their masculinity.'

'But what is it exactly?'

'It's an intolerance to alcohol. You're a lightweight. You get drunk easily. It's nothing to be ashamed of.'

Ronnie laughed incredulously. 'I'm not a lightweight,' he said.

'Then why do you have a hangover?'

'I *don't* have a hangover.'

'Are you sure about that?'

'Yes!' said Ronnie, but now that he thought about it, he realised that he actually *was* hung-over. Not *massively* hung-over. Not *never again* hung-over. Not so hung-over that he thought he must have food poisoning because nobody could be that sick just from alcohol and alcohol alone, but obviously hung-over enough that he thought he must have tetanus, which was, come to think of it, still pretty hung-over. Ronnie sighed. 'No. I'm not sure. Maybe you're right. Maybe I do have a hangover.'

'Well, luckily for you, I have a cure for that,' said Dr Sterling. His hand crept towards the lollipop jar while he waited to get the nod from Ronnie.

'Go on then,' he said.

'That's my boy!' said Dr Sterling as he unscrewed the lid and offered the jar to Ronnie.

'Thanks,' said Ronnie, taking a lollipop.

'Not the red ones,' said Dr Sterling. 'Take a yellow one. I hate the yellow ones.'

Ronnie took a yellow lollipop, even though he wanted a red one.

'It's been a while, hasn't it?' said Dr Sterling.

'Since I've had a lollipop?' said Ronnie.

'Since you've had a hangover.'

'Oh. Yeah, I guess so,' he said. The truth was that it had been so long that Ronnie had quite literally forgotten what a hangover felt like, and even though most people would be happy to forget what a hangover felt like, Ronnie suddenly felt oddly proud about his. He wasn't hung-over because he'd sat at home drinking alone in front of the television. Nor was he hung-over because he'd spent the day sipping from a paper bag on a park bench. He was hung-over because he'd spent the night at the pub, with friends, doing a pub quiz, with friends! He opened and closed his fingers while he looked at the cut on his hand. It suddenly felt much better.

'Well, don't make a habit of it,' said Dr Sterling. 'The "getting drunk" thing, I mean. Not the "spending time with friends" thing. You should definitely make a habit of spending more time with your friends. But, come to think of it, most people spend time with friends at the pub, don't they? And you can't just sit in the pub without a pint in your hand, can you? Well, I mean you *could,* but that'd be like going to a nudist beach with your underpants still on, wouldn't it?'

'I really wouldn't know,' said Ronnie.

'I'll tell you what. Keep on drinking, but only with friends, and only in moderation.'

'That's your medical advice? Keep on drinking?'

'With friends. The emphasis is supposed to be on the friends part. Not the drinking part.'

'Got it,' said Ronnie, standing to leave. 'Thanks, doctor.' He put his hand on the door handle and then paused. 'Can I ask you something?' he said, turning round.

'That's what I'm here for,' said Dr Sterling.

'What would you say if a patient came in and told you that their shadow had disappeared?' he asked.

'I had a patient who once lost their shadow,' Dr Sterling replied, matter-of-factly.

'Really?' said Ronnie, excited to hear that he might not be alone after all.

'Yeah,' said Dr Sterling, nodding. 'Oh. Wait. No, sorry, he'd lost his dog. His *dog* was called Shadow.'

Ronnie would have shaken his head had his head not hurt so much.

'What would I say if a patient told me they'd lost their shadow, you say? Their actual shadow?' Ronnie waited for Dr Sterling to tell him that the patient was probably mad or delusional or needed locking up, something along those lines. 'I'd tell them not to worry about it,' he said after what appeared to be a period of genuine reflection.

'You would?' said Ronnie.

Dr Sterling nodded. 'I'm sure it'll come back when it's good and ready.'

'What makes you say that?'

Dr Sterling shrugged. 'Because the dog did.'

Chapter Twenty-Six

Mrs Higgins wasn't at her usual spot by the window.

Up until recently, Ronnie would have considered this a good thing. The freedom to come and go without the constant fear of being interrogated about the whereabouts of his mother was a scenario he had found himself daydreaming about on countless occasions over the years, yet now that he was faced with that very scenario, instead of making the most of the situation by disappearing through his front door before she saw him, he found himself lingering on the pavement outside her house.

Ever since Hamlet had been foisted upon him (although he had no doubt whatsoever that Hamlet saw himself as being on the receiving end of the foisting and not the one actually being foisted), Mrs Higgins had revealed herself to be a surprisingly useful intermediary concerning his and Hamlet's ongoing interpersonal differences. But it wasn't just the fact that he needed her to remove Hamlet's lead that kept him from turning round and scurrying home. He also couldn't help but wonder if she was OK. After all, she lived alone, she had no family he knew of and she didn't seem to have any friends or visitors. In that respect, she and Ronnie were somewhat similar. The only difference was that Ronnie was still in that age bracket where people didn't automatically assume he'd fallen down the stairs or slipped in the shower if they hadn't seen or heard from him in a while.

'What do you think, mate?' he said to Hamlet. 'Should we go and investigate?'

Ronnie had never rung Mrs Higgins's doorbell before, and he knew that doing so now would only encourage her to talk to him more in the future (which Ronnie actually wouldn't have minded, just as long as Mrs Higgins talked about the weather, or Netflix, or the state of the government, or the decline of civilisation, or the ills of social media, or the teenagers who always hung about outside the off-licence with their hoods up when it wasn't even raining, or literally any other topic than the topic of his mum). Still, compared to what could happen if he didn't ring her doorbell – namely finding out at a later date that she had in fact taken a tumble, a tumble that had ended up being fatal because nobody had come to her aid in time – Ronnie knew that it was a relatively small price to pay.

'Come on,' said Ronnie, leading Hamlet through the gate. He pressed the doorbell and waited while he tried to listen for any sort of sound coming from inside. He was just about to peer through the front window when the door opened and Mrs Higgins appeared with an empty mug in her hand.

'Oh, hello, Ronnie,' she said. 'What a nice surprise. What can I do for you?'

'Hi, Mrs Higgins,' said Ronnie, relieved to see her alive and well. 'I was just wondering—'

'Oh, yes, of course,' she said, looking down at Hamlet. 'You probably need some help with this little chap, I assume.' She smiled, but Ronnie could see that she seemed a little disappointed.

'Actually,' said Ronnie, 'I just thought I'd pop by and say hello.'

'Really?' said Mrs Higgins, her face lighting up. 'Well how lovely. And perfect timing too,' she added, jiggling her empty cup. 'I've just made a pot of tea. Come in, both of you.'

Ronnie and Hamlet followed Mrs Higgins down the corridor and into the living room. It was the same room that Ronnie often saw Mrs Higgins spying on him from, although it was slightly less dark and dingy than it looked from the outside.

He peered through the window at his own house across the road. He'd never seen it from this angle before, and it looked strange, different somehow. He looked at each of his windows and wondered if Mrs Higgins ever watched him at night. He reassured himself that her eyesight probably wasn't that good, although he still scanned the windowsill for binoculars.

'Take a seat, and I'll go and get the tea,' she said, unclipping Hamlet's lead before disappearing into the kitchen.

Hamlet lingered in the doorway, clearly torn between the nice warm radiator on the far side of the living room and the journey through cat country that he had to take to get there. There wasn't actually a cat in the room, but it was obvious from the various paraphernalia that littered the floor that this was his main lair. Hamlet edged his way across the carpet like a soldier traversing a minefield, braced for the moment that Winston leapt out from behind the curtain or dropped on him from the ceiling light.

Ronnie took a seat on the couch and looked around the room. It seemed as if it hadn't been redecorated in quite some time. It wasn't rundown or unkempt. It was very neat and tidy in fact, but that only added to the feeling that Ronnie had stepped into a museum diorama celebrating the interior design of the 1980s. The carpet was brown and sported a pattern not dissimilar to the sorts of patterns often found on the seats of public transport, and the couch, which was so big and soft that Ronnie wondered if he'd ever be able to extract himself from it, was riddled with the sort of floral design that, on the plus side, probably masked stains and spillages very well, but, on the downside, also looked worse than whatever pattern the stains and spillages might have made. A big box television with a glass screen that was thicker than most actual modern televisions stood on a wooden cabinet in the corner, and beneath it sat what Ronnie thought for a second was a VHS player until he looked at it more clearly and realised that it actually *was* a VHS player.

In the corner was a bookshelf that ran from floor to ceiling. Ronnie couldn't make out the titles, but he noticed that a number of them had coloured stickers on the base of their spines. They looked familiar somehow, so he fought his way out of the chair before it digested him completely and went over for a closer look.

As he suspected, the ones with the stickers were old library books from Bingham library. There were about ten of them in total, all dog-eared thrillers by Sidney Sheldon and Sue Grafton and Robert Ludlum. He plucked one from the shelf and opened the front cover to reveal the old library card still attached to the first page. Ronnie smiled as he looked at the dates on the stamps. The book had mostly been borrowed in the 1980s and 1990s, with the last stamp dated 1999. Mrs Higgins had obviously bought them during one of the library's annual sales, back when Bingham still had a library, or at least a functioning one.

He absently flicked through the pages, releasing the musty smell of the library still trapped within them. As he did so, something fell out and fluttered to the floor by his foot. He guessed it was the library card until he picked it up and found himself holding the eight of clubs. Ronnie thought about that day all those years ago, when he'd walked around the library slipping playing cards into random books while waiting for his mum to finish talking to Mr Higgins, or whatever the two of them were doing in the military history section. He wondered what the chances were of the card belonging to that very same deck. It could just as well have been placed there by somebody else as a makeshift bookmark, one they'd forgotten to remove before returning the book to the library, but he knew deep down that if this card were sent off to forensics for testing, it would be his pudgy little seven-year-old fingerprints that they'd find all over it.

'I think these books might be a little overdue,' he said when Mrs Higgins walked in with a tray containing a tea set and a plate of Jammie Dodgers.

Mrs Higgins laughed. 'Yes, I dread to think what the fine might be,' she joked as she placed the tray on the coffee table. 'You're not going to grass me up, are you?'

'Your secret's safe with me,' said Ronnie, slipping the card back into the book and returning it to the shelf. 'But it'll cost you a Jammie Dodger.'

'Deal,' said Mrs Higgins as Ronnie took a seat on the couch, this time perching on the edge of it for fear of being enveloped again.

'Where's your cat?' he said, asking on behalf of Hamlet, who was clearly still on high alert.

'Winston? He'll be out until it's time for tea. He's no doubt prowling the neighbourhood in search of a grisly present for me. He generally alternates between headless mice and disembowelled squirrels. Today is a squirrel day, I think.'

Ronnie looked at Hamlet. 'You hear that?' he said. 'You can relax, Hamlet.'

Hamlet still seemed on edge, the news of Winston being out perhaps offset by the news about him being a violent disemboweller.

'How do you like your tea?' asked Mrs Higgins, picking up the teapot.

'You can let it stew for a little bit longer if you don't mind,' said Ronnie. 'I could do with the extra caffeine.'

'Heavy night last night?'

'You could say that,' said Ronnie, nodding and then wincing from the pain of nodding. 'Actually, that's a lie. It wasn't a heavy night at all. It was a very civilised night. I think I'm just a little out of practice when it comes to the whole "going out" thing.'

'That makes two of us,' said Mrs Higgins. 'Winston has more of a social life than I do. Although I suppose it's more of an antisocial life, if you count all the murders.'

'Are you sure you don't want to take Hamlet off my hands? If you don't want him full time, then maybe we could arrange some kind of joint custody agreement. I could take him every other bank holiday, for example.'

Mrs Higgins laughed. 'You love him really,' she said.

'I wouldn't go that far,' said Ronnie. Then, glancing at Hamlet, he lowered his voice to a whisper. 'It has been nice having him around, though. I didn't think it would be, but, well, he makes the house feel . . . I don't know . . .'

'Less empty?' said Mrs Higgins. Ronnie nodded. Mrs Higgins looked around the room. 'I know what you mean. I was never really much of an animal person, I didn't have pets growing up or anything like that. I didn't see the point of them, to be completely honest with you. But after my husband left, I noticed that I was, well, I was talking to myself a lot. Don't worry, I'm not mad. At least I don't think I am. But, then again, mad people never do, do they? Maybe I'll just let you be the judge of that one.'

'I talk to myself as well,' said Ronnie reassuringly. 'At home, at least. I try not to do it in public. People look at you strangely when you talk to yourself in public.'

'It's funny, isn't it?' said Mrs Higgins. 'If somebody hears you talking to yourself, then they think you're off your trolley, but nobody bats an eyelid if they hear you talking to an animal. That's why I like having Winston around. I know he doesn't understand me when I say, "I wonder what's on the telly tonight?" or "I really should vacuum the house" or "Does that leg belong to a squirrel or a rabbit?" but it's nice to fill the silence without worrying that I'm losing my marbles.' She took a sip of tea and chuckled to herself. 'What a pair we are,' she said. 'Talking to ourselves when we live right across the road from one another.'

Ronnie smiled and nodded. Then, hoping to change the subject, he pointed to a photograph on the mantelpiece. 'Is that your sister?' he said. The woman in the frame looked to be in her fifties. She didn't bear a striking resemblance to Mrs Higgins – she didn't even bear a passing resemblance – but Ronnie couldn't think of who else it might be.

'Who?' she said, turning to follow Ronnie's finger. 'Oh, no, that came with the frame. I bought it on sale the other day. I just haven't taken the picture out yet. I don't have any siblings.'

'Me neither,' said Ronnie pointlessly, knowing that Mrs Higgins already knew this.

Mrs Higgins took a bite of her biscuit and returned it to her saucer. 'It would have been nice to have a brother or a sister, come to think of it. I would have enjoyed being an aunty. Children bring so much joy, don't they?' Her eyes seemed to sparkle for a moment, perhaps with wonder, perhaps with tears.

'I'm not sure my mum would agree with you,' said Ronnie. He hadn't meant it to sound self-pitying. He'd meant it as a joke. Nor had he intended to mention his mum, and the moment he did so, he knew precisely what Mrs Higgins was going to say next.

'No,' said Mrs Higgins. 'I suppose not.' She absently stirred her tea while staring into her cup. 'Have you heard from her at all?' she asked, looking up.

Ronnie swallowed a sigh. 'No,' he said. 'I haven't.'

Mrs Higgins nodded sadly. 'Oh well,' she said. 'Maybe one day.'

'I don't think so, Mrs Higgins,' said Ronnie, surprising himself. Then, realising that now seemed as good a time as any to have this conversation, he continued, 'I don't think I'll ever hear from her, and that's OK. I barely even remember her. She's nothing but a distant memory to me now. I've had a long time to make peace with the fact that I'll never see her again. And I think, well, I think it's time that you also tried to make some peace with the situation.'

Mrs Higgins took a sip of her tea. 'What situation?' she said.

'Well, I don't mean to be rude, Mrs Higgins, and I'm sorry if this isn't what you want to hear, but, well, I really don't think your husband's coming back.'

Mrs Higgins frowned. And then she smiled. And then she laughed. 'I think you're probably right,' she said.

This time it was Ronnie's turn to frown. 'You mean . . . that doesn't bother you?' he asked.

'Not half as much as it would bother me if he *did* come back. He has been dead for about seven years, after all.'

'Wait, what?'

Mrs Higgins nodded. 'Lung cancer. I'm not surprised, he always did smoke like a chimney. It took years before the house stopped smelling like an ashtray. Years and a lot of Febreze.'

'Oh,' said Ronnie. 'I didn't know.' The news left him feeling oddly conflicted. There was a time when he would have rejoiced at such news. After all, what teenage boy wouldn't wish for the death of the man who ran off with his mum? But now, he didn't know what to feel. 'I'm . . . I'm sorry to hear that,' he said.

'Don't be,' Mrs Higgins said. 'I'm not. You don't get to ruin as many lives as he did and still expect sympathy when karma comes knocking on your door.'

Ronnie brushed an imaginary crumb from his trouser leg. 'Was he . . . Did he have a family or . . .' he trailed off.

Mrs Higgins shook her head. 'No, not that I'm aware of.'

Ronnie nodded while he quietly processed this information. He wasn't sure what sort of reaction he was supposed to have, but the one emotion he never would have expected to experience was anger, yet that's precisely what he felt. His mum had sacrificed so much, and for what? It felt like such a waste, and he found himself wondering if his mum had ever felt the same.

'What made you think that I thought he might come back?'

Ronnie shook his head, suddenly unsure. 'I don't know,' he said. 'It's just . . . whenever I see you, you always ask about my mum, and, well, I always thought you were asking because you thought that maybe, I don't know . . .'

'That maybe I could find out where my husband was?' said Mrs Higgins.

Ronnie nodded. Mrs Higgins chuckled. 'I'm sorry,' he said. 'It sounds quite silly now that I've said it out loud. I just couldn't think of another reason why you were so interested in knowing where my mum was.'

Mrs Higgins smiled. 'I don't think that's silly,' she said reassuringly. 'I mean, it's not like I didn't want to know where he was, at least in the early days. I hated the two-faced bastard, don't get me wrong, but I missed him as well, if that makes any sense.' Ronnie couldn't help but smile at her matter-of-fact tone. She didn't sound angry, simply like she was stating a fact. 'But no, that's not the reason I'm always asking about your mother. I stopped caring about my husband a long time ago, so long ago that I can't even remember what it felt like to care about him at all.' She took a sip of her tea and slowly returned it to the saucer before looking at Ronnie. 'It's you that I was worried about,' she said. 'Not him.'

Ronnie frowned, her words so unexpected that he had trouble processing them. 'Me?' he said with a nervous laugh.

'I wanted your mum to get in touch for your sake, not for mine,' she continued. 'I know what she did was wrong, but I always hoped she'd realise her mistake and try to make it right someday. You were such a lovely boy, and your dad was such a lovely man. Neither of you deserved to go through that, and it broke my heart whenever I saw the two of you without her.'

Ronnie opened his mouth to speak, but he didn't know what to say. It had never once occurred to him that the lady who had lived right across the road from him for his entire life – the lady who he had actively avoided whenever humanly possible, and would have continued to actively avoid were it not for the fact that he needed her help with Hamlet – might actually care about him more than his very own mother, and this sudden realisation left him temporarily lost for words.

'To be completely honest with you, I've always felt a little bit guilty about everything that happened,' said Mrs Higgins. 'I mean, I know it wasn't my fault. At least I hope it wasn't, although I remember some lovely people telling me shortly after my husband left that maybe he'd still be around if only I'd looked after him better, whatever that's supposed to mean. But over the years I've often wondered how different things might have been if only we'd lived on another street, or in another town, or if only I'd married somebody else. I know what's done is done, but it doesn't stop you from wondering what could have been done differently.'

Ronnie smiled, hoping it might chase away the tears he felt gathering in the corners of his eyes. 'I used to feel exactly the same way,' he said, his voice suddenly cracking. 'For years, I felt guilty about what my mum had done. It was like she'd left me with this awful debt that I could never repay. I spent a long time avoiding you because I thought that you might hate me.'

'Well, I'm glad that's no longer the case,' she said, patting the back of his hand. 'And if I hated you, then I wouldn't have given you my best biscuits,' she added, nodding at the plate of Jammie Dodgers.

Ronnie smiled and took one.

'How about we make a deal, right here and now,' she said. 'I'll forgive you if you'll forgive me.'

'Deal,' said Ronnie, shaking her outstretched hand.

'Wonderful,' said Mrs Higgins. 'Now that's settled, how's about that cup of tea?'

Ronnie was getting ready for bed when he saw it, or thought he saw it, whatever *it* was exactly. He was half asleep at the time, idly shunting his toothbrush back and forth across his teeth while staring at the mirror in front of him, not so much into it as through it. He was tired, but it wasn't the sort of tiredness he usually felt at the end of the day, or, come to think of it, at every other time of the day as well. That was a heavier sort of tiredness, the sort that you learned to live with because you knew it wasn't going anywhere, regardless of how many hours of sleep you got. That sort of tired was deep and embedded, burrowed in like an army of ticks that had sucked out all your bone marrow and set up home in the cavities.

This was a good tired, even if part of it was due to a hangover. The feeling was akin to the feeling you had when you finally put something heavy down after carrying it for a very long time, like when he missed the bus and had to carry several bags of shopping all the way back from the supermarket. Dropping the shopping in the hallway, he'd felt an almost delirious sensation of weightlessness, as if he might just float away now that he was no longer tethered to the earth by tins of beans and bags of very-much-defrosted oven chips. But he hadn't carried any shopping today. He'd only carried himself, yet the burden of doing so had felt much greater when he'd woken up that morning than it did right now. In fact, it didn't feel like a burden at all.

Cupping his hands beneath the tap, he rinsed his mouth with water and spat it into the sink. Then, splashing more water onto his face, he grabbed a towel and dried himself.

'Hi, mate,' he said when he saw Hamlet in the corner of his eye, but when he looked again a second later, Hamlet was nowhere to be seen.

Ronnie went out onto the landing and peered into his dad's bedroom. Hamlet was fast asleep on the bed, and looked as if he'd been fast asleep for quite some time. It only then occurred to Ronnie that what he'd seen in the mirror wasn't Hamlet. It was his shadow, he was sure of it. He looked down at his feet to see if it had finally returned. It hadn't, but the more he thought about it, the more certain he felt that it had at least just paid him a visit.

Chapter Twenty-Seven

Something felt different when Ronnie woke up the following day, although he couldn't quite put his finger on what. His face looked normal in the bathroom mirror, the house looked normal when he walked downstairs and the world looked normal when he peered through the window. Only Hamlet looked abnormal, but that was to be expected.

Deciding that he only felt odd because he was no longer hung-over, he thought no more about it and made himself a cup of tea.

'Fancy a trip to the beach?' he said when Hamlet appeared in the doorway of the kitchen.

Hearing the word 'beach' made Hamlet's tail start to wag like a wonky windscreen wiper. Or maybe it was the mention of the word 'trip'. Of all the animals that might be receptive to the idea of tripping, it was Hamlet.

Ronnie's reasons for wanting to go to the beach were twofold. The first reason was that he wanted to return Harriet's scarf. The second reason was that he wanted to try out his new gadget, which had arrived in the post the previous day.

'What do you think?' he said, brandishing the thinga-mabob at Hamlet. It was a long adjustable plastic pole about the length of a selfie stick. One end contained a rubber handle with a little trigger on it, and the other end sported a small plastic holster that you could feed the clipper of a dog lead into. The trigger was connected to a mechanism inside the pole that looped around the lever of the dog lead clip, thereby enabling the user to attach a dog leash from a distance (up to a metre away, according to the instructions). The device had been designed for dog owners with bad backs, reduced mobility or any other condition that might make it difficult for them to bend down far enough to manually attach a dog lead. The package didn't mention anything about it also being suitable for dogs who simply didn't trust their owners, but Ronnie hoped it was multipurpose.

Hamlet stared at the pole as Ronnie slowly extended it towards him. He seemed to be trying to make up his mind about something, as if trying to remember if this particular pole owed him money or if that was a completely different pole.

'It's OK, Hamlet. There's nothing to be scared of. Don't fear the weird stick thing.'

Hamlet sniffed the pole when it came into sniffing range. Ronnie looked around to make sure all exits were blocked, certain that Hamlet would try to make a run for it at any moment, but instead of attempting to escape, Hamlet did the complete opposite. He toppled over, rolled onto his back and stuck his legs in the air. He looked like a fly that had just flown into the window and knocked itself out.

Realising that Hamlet had clearly mistaken the pole for his dad's scratching stick, Ronnie quickly attached the lead before Hamlet wised up to what was actually going on.

'It works!' he said, looking at the pole in surprise. 'How cool is that?'

Hamlet remained where he was for a moment, perhaps in protest, perhaps in denial.

'Wait a minute,' said Ronnie, staring at the pole. 'How am I supposed to get your lead back off again?'

He searched the instructions while Hamlet, having grudgingly accepted that a belly scratch would not be forthcoming, got back onto his feet and stared at the lead that had magically attached itself to his collar.

'Well, that's just brilliant,' said Ronnie after reading the instructions and finding out that the pole he had purchased was only a pole for attaching leads and that there was an entirely different pole for removing leads. 'No wonder it only cost a quid.' He looked at Hamlet. 'Still, at least this solves half of our problem, right?'

Hamlet stared at Ronnie as if *he* were the other half of the problem.

Ronnie locked up the house, making sure to give extra-special attention to the window in his dad's room. It was only then that he understood what felt so different. He looked at the urn on the windowsill and smiled. Then, fetching a gift bag that had once held a bottle of wine that his dad had given him for his birthday, he carefully placed the urn inside and opened the front door.

'Today's the day,' he said to Hamlet as they both walked down the garden path. 'Hope you don't mind if we take a little detour.'

Ronnie and Hamlet fought their way through the undergrowth before emerging at the same obscure part of the river that he and his dad had found when they'd gone on their ill-fated fishing trip together. It was only when he and his dad were on their way home that they'd realised there was in fact an official, infinitely more accessible fishing spot further along the riverbank, by which time they were caked in mud and soaked through to the underpants. Ronnie smiled as he recalled the memory.

'This is the place,' he said to Hamlet, who was wrestling with a branch he'd found that was twice as big as he was. The branch appeared to be winning. 'I bet nobody's been here since we were here last. Not if they had any sense, anyway.'

Ronnie slid the urn from the bag and held it in both hands.

'What do you think, Dad? I know we never caught anything here, but I thought it might be a nice place to let something go.'

He stood there in silence for a moment, listening to the gentle trickle of the river and watching the ripple of raindrops on the surface. The air smelled fresh as he took a deep breath and slowly exhaled before removing the lid. Then, crouching down by the riverbank, he carefully emptied the urn into the water.

'Bye, Dad,' said Ronnie, blinking away the tears. 'See you down the river.'

He stood and watched the water as it slowly carried his dad downstream. Realising that Hamlet had gone suspiciously quiet, he looked down to find him quietly watching the river with him, as if paying his respects.

'Thanks for coming with me, mate,' he said. 'I don't think I could have done this alone. I know you didn't technically have a choice in the matter, but still. I'm really glad you're here.'

He returned the urn to the paper bag and looked at the river one last time.

'Come on,' he said, gently tugging on Hamlet's lead. 'Let's go to the beach.'

As the lifeguard tower loomed into view, Ronnie could see that it was empty. He looked up and down the beach, but Harriet was nowhere to be found.

'Hope nobody's planning on drowning today,' said Ronnie. 'Right, Hamlet?'

Hamlet wasn't listening. He was too busy inspecting what looked like a radioactive pebble half-submerged in the sand.

'What's that you've got there?' said Ronnie, crouching down beside Hamlet.

The item in question was a tennis ball, no doubt left behind by another dog walker. Ronnie dug it out and patted the sand off.

'OK,' he said, looking at Hamlet. 'Let's try this again, shall we? I'm going to throw this and you're going to retrieve it. That's how fetch works. There is literally no simpler way to explain this game. Everything you need to know is right there in the title. Fetch. So . . . fetch!'

He threw the ball a short distance, hoping that Hamlet might be more inclined to play along if he didn't have to make much effort, but Hamlet simply stood there, looking at the ball and then back at Ronnie, as if trying to figure out why his unelected master had taken such a dislike to this particular piece of tennis equipment.

'Oh well, it was worth a try,' said Ronnie, absently kicking the tennis ball along the beach. He didn't see it hit a rock and bounce into the crashing waves. Nor did he see Hamlet's eyes light up as he watched the ball disappear into the sea. He was too busy staring at Jumper's Rock, trying to make out what the shape on the cliff-edge was.

'Is that a person?' he said to himself. It was difficult to say for sure at that distance. It certainly *looked* like a person, which wasn't necessarily strange in itself. After all, not everybody who went up to the cliff jumped off. The vast majority took the same way down that they took up, namely the steep set of steps carved into the rock that could be dangerous when slippery, but still not half as dangerous as taking the faster route down. Some people went up there for the view. Others went up there for the exercise. But Ronnie had an awful feeling that whoever was up there – and it was a person, he could see that now – had no interest in the scenery and no desire to improve their cardiovascular fitness.

He was too distracted by the person on the cliff to notice that his grip on Hamlet's lead had loosened, not enough to drop it but enough for it to be whipped out of his hand when Hamlet, who had chosen this precise moment to finally comprehend the complex inner workings of the game known as fetch, went racing down the beach after the ball.

'Hamlet!' shouted Ronnie as Hamlet galloped towards the waves before leaping into them like a furry David Hasselhoff. Noticing the lead trailing behind him, Ronnie chased after it and tried to stop it with his foot, but the current dragged Hamlet out so fast that the lead disappeared into the sea before Ronnie could get to it.

He kept on running towards the waves, mainly because it was slightly downhill and his momentum was carrying him towards them whether he liked it or not.

Splashing into the shallows, the cold dark water made him gasp as it soaked into his shoes and jeans, but still he ploughed forward, wading into the waves without stopping to think about whether he'd be wading back out again with Hamlet or whether he'd end up washing ashore weeks later like so many others who had looked at that awful sea and still seen something in it that was preferable to their own lives.

The seafloor suddenly vanished beneath him as a vicious current picked him up and dragged him down the coast. He couldn't see Hamlet, so he called out for him, but water filled his mouth the moment he opened it. Ronnie felt himself being pushed and pulled, shoved and shunted, like a kid in a playground fight being thrown back into the ring whenever he tried to escape. It seemed like the sea was making a point of letting him know just how little control he had over the situation, of how out of his depth he now was, both literally and figuratively.

Another wave crashed over him and plunged him under the surface, twisting him and turning him like the blind man in blind man's bluff so that he no longer knew which way was up and which way was death. In his desperation to find some air, his arms and legs stopped working together and seemed to be trying to save themselves. He'd never been a good swimmer – he'd never even been a mediocre swimmer – but even a strong swimmer had little control over their fate out here. If they survived, then it wasn't because they'd fought the waves and won. It was because the sea hadn't felt like fighting that day.

The sky was as grey as the murky water, so Ronnie struggled to orient himself. He thought he might be upside down, so he was surprised when his head suddenly broke the surface. He grabbed a small gulp of air, but another wave punched it out of his lungs as it crashed down on top of him and drove him underwater again.

While he tossed and turned beneath the surface like a goldfish in a bag being carried home from the fair, his lungs empty of air and soon to be filled with water, it suddenly occurred to Ronnie that he was in all likelihood about to die. Until then he'd assumed that the waves would let him go at some point, either pushing him out of the deadly current into less turbulent waters or throwing him back onto the shore, where he hoped that Hamlet would be waiting for him, soggy and utterly unremorseful but otherwise unscathed. He'd read and heard so many stories about people dying while trying to rescue their dogs from fast-flowing rivers and icy ponds – dogs that, as it turned out, were perfectly capable of rescuing themselves – that he really should have just waited on the beach for Hamlet to find his own way out of the surf. And he probably would have done, had Hamlet not been Hamlet but basically any other animal, because any other animal would have the biological advantage of a self-preservation instinct. But Hamlet was not equipped with such an instinct. He'd fallen off the production line at the precise moment that such instincts were being inserted. If anything, his tendency was geared towards self-destruction, not self-preservation. He couldn't even be trusted not to eat his own leg, never mind take active care of his physical and emotional well-being, which was why Ronnie was now about five seconds away from death by saltwater.

Still, hopefully Hamlet would make it out of this OK, thought Ronnie, if not because he'd somehow manage to miraculously save himself, perhaps by clinging to a piece of driftwood or flagging down a rescue helicopter, then because the sea, not wanting to touch him any more than it had to, would spit him back out like a python expelling a garden gnome when it realised that it didn't taste anything like a little bearded old man.

And anyway, he thought, one of them had to live to tell the tale, and it certainly wasn't going to be him. The thought hit him like the biggest plot twist ever, even though it wasn't really much of a plot twist at all. Drowning was very much the likely outcome of leaping into choppy seas without so much as a pair of water wings, especially when those choppy seas were rumoured to have once dragged a cargo ship off course. But just like when you get trapped in a lift for hours, or have to evacuate a building when you're in the middle of having a shower, you never believe it's going to happen to you until it actually does.

As his lungs trembled with the urge to refill them-selves with air that wasn't available, Ronnie's mind began to empty itself, throwing out all non-vital thoughts like a leaking boat throwing out cargo, until his head was void of everything except for five simple words and five simple syllables.

I don't want to die.

I don't want to die.

I don't want to die.

This thought should not have come as a surprise to Ronnie. It was, after all, a thought that would go through the mind of anybody who found themselves in the unfortunate position of staring death in the face at the moment they least expected it. But he *was* surprised, and this fact only surprised him more.

It was only then, at the end of his life, that the life that had led him up to this moment finally made sense to him.

Ronnie didn't want to die. Not here. Not now. Not like this. But he *had* wanted to die, up until a couple of weeks ago. He hadn't been consciously aware of it then, but it was suddenly crystal clear to him now, even in the murky waters that surrounded him.

He hadn't wanted to kill himself. Nor had he felt suicidal. Not in the traditional sense of the word anyway. He hadn't wanted to hang himself or overdose or asphyxiate himself with exhaust fumes. That all took a measure of courage he simply did not possess. Instead, Ronnie had been hoping for an easier way out. Not easy in the sense that his death should be a quick and painless one (although he certainly wouldn't have complained if it had been), but easy because he hoped that fate might intervene to relieve him of having to make a decision about the whole thing. He wanted to be zapped by lightning or squashed by a bus or taken out by a terminal illness. He didn't have the guts to jump to his death from the top of a multi-storey car park, but he would have been more than happy for the multi-storey car park to jump on top of him. His frequent visits to Dr Sterling hadn't been because he needed to know that everything was OK. He wasn't looking for reassurance. He went because he wanted to hear the opposite, that everything *wasn't* OK and that whatever ailment he'd come in with was going to be the ailment that finished him off.

But there weren't any ailments. Lumps in his armpit. Bumps on his bum. Tetanus in his thumb. It was all just wishful thinking, albeit a rather antithetical sort of wishful thinking. He couldn't blame Dr Sterling for thinking he was a hypochondriac, but whereas hypochondriacs went through life worrying that they might have an undiagnosed and potentially fatal medical condition, Ronnie went through life worrying that he might be perfectly healthy because as long as he was, then he had no choice but to see out life to its natural conclusion. That's why he'd been disappointed when Dr Sterling told him that he didn't have tetanus, just like he'd been so disappointed when Dr Sterling had given him the all-clear on everything else he'd come in to see him about. He didn't want to hear that all was clear. He wanted to hear that all was lost, that nothing more could be done, that his time on earth was rapidly running out and that he needed to start making preparations for the end, even though he'd been making such preparations unknowingly for the last twelve months.

But things were different now. Suddenly, he felt like his life had a purpose. Not a *massive* purpose, but a purpose nonetheless. He hadn't figured out a way of restoring the eyesight of blind people and he wasn't even close to discovering a cure for cancer. Nor did he have a wife or children or another human being who depended on his continued survival. What he *did* have, however, was a neighbour who cared about him more than his own mother did, a group of friends who genuinely seemed to enjoy his company, and a dog that he loved, even if he hadn't realised that until the moment he ran into the sea to save the daft bugger. And that was enough. That was all he needed. Friends. Companionship. Love. Those were the things that made a life worth living because those were the things that made a life.

This is not how I imagined it would be, thought Ronnie as he started to lose consciousness. He didn't just mean the drowning part, although for a man who hated swimming and hadn't even set foot in a swimming pool since the age of nine, death by drowning did seem like a rather cruel irony. He meant that he hadn't imagined dying when he finally had something to live for again. It just didn't seem right, but before he had time to dwell on the utter injustice of it all, the hand of fate that he'd waited so long for, yet now desperately tried to squirm away from, rose up from the gloom, grabbed him by the ankle and pulled him down into the darkness.

Chapter Twenty-Eight

Ronnie woke to the sight of foam ceiling tiles, which he took as a sign that he'd either survived his near-drowning and was now in hospital or he had in fact drowned and was now in hell. He couldn't imagine heaven had foam ceiling tiles.

Had he lived a life worthy of eternal damnation? He admitted that some of his life choices had been questionable. He'd once owned a Tamagotchi, for instance, which was bad enough in itself, but he'd also let it die after forgetting to feed it for several days (although he wondered if this somehow cancelled out the crime of owning one in the first place).

He'd also gone through a phase of keeping bubble gum after he'd chewed all the flavour out of it. Instead of throwing it in the bin like any normal person, or spitting it out and volleying it like a lot of other boys were doing back then (before they grew up and realised that there were other, less disgusting ways to try to win a girl's heart), he chose instead to add it to an ever-growing saliva-infested monstrosity that lived in the drawer beneath his bed before his dad found it and made him throw it out.

And now that he was repenting, he also remembered that he had, for a very brief period of time between the ages of fifteen and fifteen and a half, taken to wearing a beret. He wasn't sure why, but his best guess was that he wanted to look like either an artist, a revolutionary, a member of the Guardian Angels or perhaps a combination of all three. To everyone else in town, however, he simply looked like an arse, an opinion that was frequently shared with him whenever he'd walk down the street.

Still, that was pretty much the extent of his sins. He'd never robbed anybody or stolen anything. He'd never maimed or killed anybody. He'd never verbally abused somebody on social media, he'd never jumped a queue, he'd never dropped litter or put his feet on a seat while riding public transport, he'd never used his phone to play loud music on a bus, he'd never used a public toilet without flushing it afterwards and he'd never owned a personalised number plate. He had, however, once let his dog poop on the pavement and then tried to walk away without clearing it up. Was that enough to warrant an eternity of being poked and prodded with pitchforks and whatever else went on in a Hieronymus Bosch painting? He hoped not. Hamlet had caused him enough trouble in life, but he drew the line at having his afterlife buggered up by him as well.

'Hell?' he muttered, partly to himself and partly to anybody who might be in earshot and therefore able to confirm or deny whether or not he was in fact currently staring at Satan's ceiling tiles.

'What was that?' came a familiar voice from somewhere to his right.

'Did he say something?' said somebody else, their voice a whisper.

'I think he said "help",' said a third person.

'Or was he trying to say "hello"?' said the second person.

It took Ronnie a moment to put faces to the voices, and when he did so, he felt an overwhelming sense of relief. If Cate, Harriet and Brian were there, then it meant he must have survived, and for the first time in a long time, it felt good to be alive.

'I think he just said "hell" actually,' said Cate.

'Hell?' said Brian.

'Yeah. You know. The place where bad people go,' clarified Cate.

'Why would he say "hell"?' asked Harriet.

Ronnie wanted to laugh as he listened to his friends trying to decode what he'd just said. But then he remembered Hamlet and suddenly a great sadness washed over him. The last time he'd seen him, Hamlet had been paddling out to sea, not towards the land but towards the horizon, with his tongue lolling out and his eyes wide with what should have been fear but very much resembled excitement. Far from looking like he was fighting for his life, Hamlet looked like he was fighting to win a freestyle swimming competition. In many ways, it would have been a fitting end for a dog whose entire life seemed defined by misunderstanding. Then again, perhaps he was still out there, halfway to Norway, confusing every fishing boat he passed in the North Sea. Ronnie liked to think that he was, even if he knew deep down that he wasn't.

'Ham . . .' he said, his throat too raw and painful to finish saying 'Hamlet'.

'Ham?' said Cate.

'Why's he talking about ham now?' Harriet asked.

'Maybe he wants some ham,' suggested Brian.

'Why would he want some ham?' said Harriet.

'Maybe he's hungry,' said Brian.

'Yeah, but why specifically ham?' said Harriet. 'It's a bit random, isn't it?'

'Maybe he was saying "hall", not "hell",' said Cate. 'And now he's saying ham. Maybe he's trying to say "Hallam".'

'What's a hallam?' said Harriet.

'A place in South Yorkshire,' said Cate. 'Maybe that's where he thinks he is.'

'That's where Robin Hood comes from,' said Brian.

'I thought Robin Hood came from Nottingham,' said Harriet. 'Isn't that where Sherwood Forest is?'

'Yeah, but he was called Robin of Loxley, and Loxley is a place in South Yorkshire. They think that's where he was born.'

'How do you know all that?' said Cate.

'Just, you know, general knowledge,' said Brian, trying to act nonchalant.

'I'm impressed,' said Cate.

Brian beamed, his nonchalance obliterated.

'Hamlet,' said Ronnie, coughing as he forced the word out. 'Where's Hamlet?'

'Oh, Hamlet!' said Harriet.

'Yeah, that makes more sense, come to think of it,' said Cate.

'He's fine, Ronnie,' said Brian as Ronnie managed to roll himself onto his side. 'Don't worry. He wanted to come in, but the doctors said he might scare the patients.'

'The last thing you want to see when you're in hospital is a black dog lurking in the corner of the ward,' said Cate.

Ronnie didn't realise he was crying until he felt the tears roll down his face. It wasn't just the news that Hamlet was OK but the sight of his friends at his bedside that made him suddenly emotional. They weren't doctors or nurses, they didn't work at the hospital and they weren't being paid to be there, yet there they were, watching over him.

'What happened?' he asked.

'We were going to ask you the same thing!' said Harriet. 'What on earth were you thinking of, going into the sea like that. You could have died.'

'You almost *did* die,' said Cate.

'I think you actually were dead for a little while,' said Brian. 'Which is kind of cool, if you think about it.'

'I was trying to save Hamlet,' explained Ronnie. 'He chased a tennis ball into the sea.'

'That'll explain why he came back with a tennis ball in his mouth,' said Cate.

'He dropped it right beside you while you were being resuscitated,' said Brian. 'I think he wanted you to throw it again.'

'It seems that Hamlet has finally figured out how fetch works,' said Harriet.

'I think we're done playing fetch,' said Ronnie. 'It's a lot more dangerous than I thought.'

'Well, you're lucky that somebody fetched *you*,' said Cate. 'Otherwise you'd have been a goner.'

'Who?' asked Ronnie. 'Who saved me?'

Cate and Brian looked at Harriet, who instantly turned red.

'Anybody would have done the same thing,' she said dismissively.

'I wouldn't,' said Brian. 'No offence, Ronnie.'

'Me neither,' said Cate. 'That sea is well scary.'

'You saved my life,' said Ronnie.

'Well, sort of,' said Harriet, clearly uncomfortable with her newfound status as local hero. 'Somebody else saved your life. Or tried to, at least.'

'Yeah, and then you saved *their* life!' said Brian.

'Harriet basically saved two people's lives today,' said Cate. 'She's just being modest.'

'I don't understand,' said Ronnie.

'Somebody saw you drowning, and they dived in to save you, but then *they* almost drowned, so Harriet had to save both of you,' explained Cate.

'But there was nobody else around,' said Ronnie, struggling to comprehend what they were saying. 'I was the only person on the beach.'

'Not quite,' said Harriet, nodding towards the far end of the room.

It hadn't occurred to Ronnie that there was anybody else on the ward, but rolling over and following Harriet's gaze, he saw a man asleep in the bed next to him. Something about him looked familiar, but it was hard to make out who it was from that angle.

'Who is that?'

'Your mate from the pub,' said Cate.

'What mate?' said Ronnie, but even as he said it, he knew who he was looking at. 'Wait . . . Alan? Alan Stamp tried to save my life?'

Harriet nodded. 'I'd just popped to my car for a quick cup of coffee, and when I came back, I saw your friend there running into the sea. I didn't know what was happening at first, I thought he'd lost his mind to be perfectly honest with you, but then I saw you out there and I understood what was going on. He managed to get all the way out to you,' she said. 'He just, well, couldn't quite make it back.'

'Is he going to be OK?' asked Ronnie, surprised by the level of panic in his voice.

'The doctor said he'll be fine,' said Cate.

'And you're going to be OK as well,' said Harriet. 'They said you can leave tomorrow if you're feeling up to it.'

'Great,' said Ronnie.

'You're telling me,' said Cate. 'I don't know what we would have done if you'd drowned.'

Ronnie was touched by her concern. 'I'm sure you would have gotten over it eventually,' he said.

'No, I'm talking about the pub quiz team,' she said. 'We'd have to come up with a whole new name and everything!'

'Yeah, we wouldn't be a quartet anymore,' said Brian. 'We'd be a threesome.'

'Trio,' said Harriet. 'We'd be a trio.'

'That's what I meant.'

'And we'd have to find a new captain. Do you know how hard captains are to come by these days? They don't exactly grow on trees, you know. And what would I have done with Hamlet? Do you have any idea how hard I worked to force you into adopting him?'

Ronnie had to laugh at her honesty. 'I do, actually,' he said. 'And I haven't adopted him, just so you know.'

'Well, you should. It's the least you can do for almost ruining our pub quiz team,' said Cate. She paused before adding, somewhat sheepishly, 'Was it really that obvious?'

'I was willing to give you the benefit of the doubt until the whole static fire thing,' said Ronnie.

'What static fire thing?' asked Brian.

'I'll explain at the shelter,' said Cate. Ronnie frowned. 'Brian's helping out with the dogs for a bit,' she added.

'That's very charitable of you, Brian,' said Ronnie, trying to keep a straight face.

'Well, you know,' said Brian with a shrug. 'I'm just doing my bit.'

'Speaking of which, we should probably do *our* bit and let you get some rest,' said Harriet.

'I got your scarf by the way,' said Ronnie.

'What scarf?' asked Harriet.

'The one you were wearing the other night. You left it on the bench.'

Harriet looked at Cate and Brian. 'I didn't leave a scarf on the bench.'

'You weren't wearing a blue scarf?'

'Yes, but I took it home with me.'

'Oh,' said Ronnie. 'Right.'

'Is that why you came to the beach today?' said Harriet. 'To bring back my scarf?'

Ronnie shrugged, suddenly feeling a bit silly. Harriet smiled and patted his hand.

'The world needs more people like you,' she said.

'I agree,' said Cate.

'And me,' said Brian.

'And your officially adopted dog Hamlet agrees as well,' said Cate.

'I'm suddenly feeling very sleepy,' said Ronnie, faking a yawn.

'Come on,' said Harriet, ushering the other two out like the mother of the group. 'We'll see you tomorrow, Ronnie.'

'Thanks again,' said Ronnie. 'You know, for saving my life. I don't really know what to say.'

'Say you won't go running into the sea like a lunatic ever again.'

'My running-into-the-sea-like-a-lunatic days are most definitely over,' he said.

'I'm very glad to hear that. Now, get some rest.'

Cate grabbed Brian's hand and led him out of the room. Brian looked at Ronnie with an expression that was half excitement and half terror. Ronnie gave him an encouraging thumbs-up.

'If you wanted some time off work, then you should have just asked,' said Alan. 'You didn't need to drown yourself.'

Ronnie rolled over towards Alan, who was now awake and staring at him groggily.

'I couldn't be bothered filling out the holiday form,' he said, referring to the seven-page document that everybody had to complete when requesting time off.

'If you think that's bad, then you should try input-ting it all into the computer system,' said Alan. 'System error. Incomplete field. Incorrect item in the bagging area. It's a nightmare.'

Ronnie smiled. He'd always thought of Alan as the person who took pleasure in making everybody else do the crap jobs. It had never occurred to him that Alan had plenty of his own crap jobs to do.

'My friends just told me you tried to save my life,' said Ronnie. 'Thank you.'

'I didn't know it was you,' said Alan. 'I was hoping it might be Scarlett Johansson.'

'I heard she has a holiday home up here somewhere,' said Ronnie.

'I thought it was a caravan actually,' said Alan. They both laughed.

'All joking aside, though, thank you,' said Ronnie.

'Don't mention it,' said Alan. 'Seriously. Don't mention it. To anybody. Especially people at work.'

'Why not?'

'Because they'll only take the piss, that's why.'

'What are you talking about? You tried to save my life.'

'Yeah, and then somebody had to save mine. How embarrassing is that?'

'Not at all. Most people wouldn't have had the guts to do what you did.'

'Stupidity more like,' said Alan.

'Forgive me if I don't think trying to save my life is stupid,' said Ronnie. 'But still, if you really don't want me to say anything, then I won't.'

'Good. Thank you.'

'On one condition.'

Alan frowned. 'Go on,' he said.

'I want my old job back. Let me swap with Carl.'

Alan sighed. 'Fair enough.'

'Why'd you do it anyway?' asked Ronnie.

'Do what?'

'Give me the crap job.'

'I didn't give it to you because it was crap,' said Alan. 'I gave it to you because it was hard.'

'Isn't that pretty much the same thing?'

'No,' said Alan, 'what I mean is that Carl can't even tie his own shoelaces without falling over. That's not a joke either. He literally fell on his face while trying to tie his shoelaces the other day. I watched it happen.'

Ronnie nodded. 'I've seen him do that,' he said.

'He can't be trusted to do even the simplest things, never mind the difficult stuff. I needed somebody I could rely on, somebody who I knew would do a good job. That's why I gave it to you.'

Ronnie tried and failed to hold back a smile. 'Was that a compliment?' he asked. 'It almost sounded like a compliment.'

Alan smiled. 'Almost.' He coughed and rubbed his chest.

Ronnie had always assumed that Alan had given him Carl's job because he didn't like Ronnie for some reason. It had never occurred to him that the truth might be something closer to the opposite.

'What sort of person tries to bargain with the person who just tried to save their life anyway?' said Alan.

'The sort of person who won't go to the press to spread terrible stories about what a hero you are.'

'Let me know the next time you're planning on drowning yourself,' said Alan. 'So I know to avoid the beach that day.'

Ronnie smiled. 'Where were you anyway?' he asked. 'You know, when you saw me.'

'Just walking down the beach,' said Alan.

'The beach was empty though.'

'Well, it obviously wasn't because I was there,' said Alan.

'Right,' said Ronnie, unconvinced. He was certain that the beach had been empty. The only person he'd seen was whoever was standing on Jumper's Rock. He'd forgotten about them in all the excitement, but he thought about them now. He wondered what had happened to them and hoped they'd taken the safe route down. Then, turning to look at Alan, it occurred to him that the person on the cliff might very well be the person in the bed beside his. 'Were you on the cliff?' he asked.

'What?'

'Jumper's Rock,' said Ronnie. 'Is that where you were when you saw me?'

'What would I be doing on Jumper's Rock?'

Ronnie shrugged. 'Admiring the view?'

Alan laughed dismissively. 'Good one,' he said. 'If I was going to make the effort to climb all the way up there, then, believe me, it wouldn't be for the view.'

It was supposed to be a joke, and perhaps it was, but as Ronnie watched Alan suddenly start to fidget with his blanket and his pillow and anything else he could find, he couldn't help but think that his boss felt like he'd said too much.

Ronnie thought about what Carl had told him in the pub, what Pearl had told him in the rain and what Alan himself had told him in the park. As he did so, it dawned on him that the Alan he thought he knew and the Alan he was currently sharing a hospital ward with were two very different people. One was the sort of person who didn't seem to care about anybody else but himself, but the other one – the real one – wouldn't think twice about putting his life at risk to save what he thought was a total stranger from drowning.

It occurred to Ronnie that he and Alan were really quite similar in many respects. Not only had they both lost their mothers at a young age, they were also both lonely in their own ways, Alan even more so perhaps, because while Ronnie had at least grown up with a friend in his dad, Alan didn't even have that much, it seemed. The fact that there was nobody at Alan's bedside, nor were there any cards, flowers or any other signs that anybody had come to visit him, only deepened Ronnie's belief that Alan was the figure he'd seen on the cliff, and the thought of what might have happened had Hamlet not chosen that very moment to gallop into the sea brought an unexpected lump to Ronnie's throat.

'What?' said Alan, jolting Ronnie out of his thoughts.

'What?' said Ronnie, confused.

'Why are you looking at me like that?'

'Like what?'

'Like *that*.'

'I don't know what you're talking about,' said Ronnie, although he did really. He waited a few seconds for the weirdness to clear. 'Alan?'

'Yeah?'

'No man is an island, you know.'

Alan frowned. 'Have they got you on morphine or something?'

'I wish.' Ronnie readjusted himself in bed. 'Hey, when are we going to start that dog-walking club by the way?'

Chapter Twenty-Nine

Harriet looked up and squinted against the glare of the sun.

'I thought I'd got the wrong day when I woke up this morning,' she said over the trundle of a rollercoaster car and the screams of children whose excitement had soon turned to terror when they'd realised just how rickety the ride was.

'I know what you mean,' said Cate. 'It doesn't feel right, having the fair without the rain. How are we supposed to have ironic fun when the weather's so bloody nice?'

'Maybe we'll just have to have normal fun instead,' said Ronnie, looking down at Hamlet, who was having his own kind of fun by eating the wrapper of a Cornetto.

Cate looked unsure about this idea.

'What are we waiting for again?' asked Brian, who had chosen to leave Beethoven at home.

'I invited a friend of mine,' said Ronnie. 'I'm sure she'll be . . . Ah, there she is.' He raised his arm and waved until Mrs Higgins saw him and made her way over. 'Everybody, this is Mrs Higgins,' said Ronnie.

'Please, call me Janet,' she said as they all introduced themselves.

'How do you two know each other?' asked Cate.

'Mrs Higgins — sorry, Janet — lives across the road from me,' said Ronnie.

'And my husband ran off with his mum,' said Mrs Higgins matter-of-factly.

Nobody quite knew what to say to that.

'Right then,' said Cate, clapping her hands together. 'Who's ready to have some pretend fun?'

Mrs Higgins looked at Ronnie, clearly confused.

'I'll explain later,' he said.

They edged their way through the crowds as they slowly wandered around the fair. Concerned he might get trampled, Cate picked up Hamlet and cradled him in her arms.

Ronnie hadn't expected the fair to be so busy. The last time he'd seen such a large gathering in Bingham was back in 1987, when everybody raced to the beach after news had spread even quicker than the fire they had gathered to witness tearing along the pier. By the time the fire engine had arrived, the pier was beyond saving, just like Bingham in many ways, or so Ronnie had thought until that day at the fair with Cate, Brian, Harriet and Mrs Higgins. Much like that fateful Friday in 1987, there was still something ominous in the air, as if a ride might collapse at any minute or a bolt of lightning might hit the carousel and frazzle everybody and their gaudily painted ponies, but there was also something hopeful as well. It wasn't just the weather, although that certainly helped. To be able to walk around in the open air without the hood from a plastic poncho slapping you in the face while you desperately tried to nibble candyfloss off a stick before it dissolved in the rain was definitely a major plus. Nor was it the sight of the Bingham Eye finally turning again after all these years, a sight that made Ronnie unexpectedly emotional as he recalled the last time he'd ridden it and his dad's determination to give him the birthday he wanted.

It was only when he walked past the wall of funny mirrors (which, having not been replaced since long before Ronnie was born, were even more warped than they should have been) and paused to look at himself that he finally understood what was going on. It wasn't something in the air that made him feel hopeful. Nor was it the sight of his absurdly elongated legs or his freakishly bulbous waist. As he looked at his own face in a part of the mirror that was comparatively undistorted, he realised that it was something in *him*. *He* felt hopeful, about life, about the future – about everything. It was an odd feeling, but unlike the odd feeling of Hamlet staring at you while you slept, this feeling was one that he could get used to.

'Guess your age for a quid?' came a voice from nearby. Ronnie looked round to find a boy of about fourteen standing beside a hand-drawn sign scribbled on a piece of corrugated cardboard. His thumbs were looped through a pair of braces that held his trousers up, and above his floppy fringe was a tweed flat cap that made him look like some kind of street urchin from the Victorian era.

'I like your costume,' said Harriet.

The boy frowned. 'What costume?' he said, looking down.

'I think those are his normal clothes,' whispered Cate.

'Oh,' said Harriet, clearly embarrassed.

'Aren't you supposed to guess my weight?' said Ronnie.

'My mum wouldn't let me borrow the bathroom scales so I had to improvise,' said the boy with a shrug.

'Go on, Ronnie,' said Cate.

'How does it work exactly?' asked Ronnie.

'You give me a quid, and if I guess your age correctly, then I keep your money. If I guess wrong, then I'll give you a fiver.'

'But how can you prove I'm not lying?' said Ronnie.

'I can't,' said the boy. 'But what sort of person would lie to a fourteen-year-old boy just to save themselves a quid?'

'Good point,' said Ronnie, suddenly feeling ashamed for bringing up the question.

'Watch, I'll give you a freebie,' said the boy. He looked at Brian, Cate, Harriet and Mrs Higgins before his eyes returned to Cate. He stared at her for an awkward few seconds before nodding to himself. 'You're twenty-three,' he said. 'And four months.'

Cate frowned as she quickly did the maths. 'You're right!' she said, her eyes widening. She turned to the others. 'He's right!'

The boy took a bow and then looked at Ronnie as if to say, 'Your move, old man.'

'Do it, Ronnie,' said Brian.

'OK, OK,' said Ronnie, fishing around in his pocket. 'Here,' he said to the boy, handing him a pound.

'Thank you kindly,' said the boy, slipping the coin into his top pocket. His eyes narrowed and his eyebrows did a little jig beneath his fringe as he stared at Ronnie, who stood there laughing nervously, a little uneasy about being scrutinised so intensely.

'Got it,' said the boy, snapping his fingers and pointing at Ronnie. 'You're forty-two and four months old.'

Ronnie counted out the months on his fingers.

'Is he right?' asked Harriet.

Ronnie frowned and counted again before a smile crept across his face.

'Well?' said Brian.

The boy was right about the years, but he'd miscalculated the months. Ronnie was forty-two and *seven* months old, which meant that the boy technically owed him a fiver, but that wasn't why he was smiling. He was smiling because he couldn't remember the last time that anybody had even guessed his age correctly, never mind underestimated it. Alan thought he was fifty, Cate had unreassuringly placed him as being younger than seventy-three and Brian seemed to think that he and

Beethoven (the composer, not the cat) hailed from the same generation, yet this kid, who had already proved himself to be a freakishly accurate guesser of ages, had looked at Ronnie and seen a man a whopping twelve-ish weeks younger than he actually was. That was worth a lot more to Ronnie than a fiver.

'He's right,' said Ronnie. Everybody clapped. He looked at the boy. 'Well done.'

The boy took another little bow. 'Anybody else?' he said.

'I don't think I want to be reminded of my age,' said Mrs Higgins with a laugh, 'but thank you all the same.'

'And I can't even remember how old I am!' said Harriet. She and Mrs Higgins had a good chuckle about that.

'Who wants to go on the Ferris wheel?' said Brian, who'd clearly changed his mind about wanting to see it torn down and sold for scrap now that it was actually turning again.

'Me!' said Cate. She looked at the others. 'Anybody else?'

'Why not,' said Harriet. 'For old times' sake. Janet?'

'Go on then,' she said. 'Ronnie?'

'No thanks,' he said. 'I've thrown up on that thing enough already, thanks. I'll take Hamlet for a walk on the beach instead.'

'Suit yourself,' said Cate, putting Hamlet down and handing Ronnie the lead. Hamlet looked genuinely disappointed to have missed out on the Ferris wheel.

'Come on,' she said, grabbing Brian's hand and leading him away through the crowd.

Ronnie watched the four of them head towards the Ferris wheel, Brian with a big goofy grin on his face and Harriet and Mrs Higgins chatting like old friends. He waved at them as the wheel started to turn, Cate and Brian in one car and the two ladies in another, but Mrs Higgins was the only one who saw him. She waved back, smiling as she did so, and even at that distance, Ronnie could see how happy she looked.

The sun was high in the sky as he led Hamlet towards the beach.

'Blimey,' said Ronnie, running his palm across his forehead. 'I think the sun got lost on its way to Spain. What do you think, Hamlet?' Hamlet looked at him as if to say that the sun getting lost on its way to Spain was an entirely plausible scenario.

They walked along the beach for a while, Ronnie watching the waves while Hamlet scurried around sniffing things and licking sea junk. Picking something up in his mouth, he galloped over to Ronnie and dumped his find on the sand. It looked like a broken piece of fence post washed smooth by the sea.

'What am I supposed to do with this?' said Ronnie, picking it up after checking there were no nails laced with tetanus protruding from it. Hamlet's eyes remained fixed on the piece of wood, his tongue lolling out and his tail wagging furiously. It took Ronnie a moment to understand that Hamlet wanted to play fetch. 'I don't know,' he said. 'I almost died the last time we tried that. We both did.'

Seemingly unperturbed by this memory, Hamlet bounded down the beach and back again. He did this several times, perhaps in an attempt to convince Ronnie that he well and truly now understood how fetch worked.

Ronnie sighed. 'OK,' he said. 'But if you end up in the sea again, then this time you're on your own.'

Making sure he had a firm hold of the lead, Ronnie threw the makeshift stick with a light underarm throw. It landed a few metres away and Hamlet immediately set upon it. Clamping his jaws around the wood, he proudly returned it to Ronnie, or as close to Ronnie as he wanted to get.

'Good boy!' said Ronnie, picking up the stick. 'It looks like you're finally getting the hang of it!'

He threw the piece of wood again, this time with more force. Hamlet raced off after it and returned a moment later with the stick between his teeth. He plonked it down and waited for Ronnie to throw it again. They did this several more times, Ronnie growing increasingly hotter and Hamlet growing increasingly slower until he was no longer galloping, but trudging after his quarry.

'Congratulations, Hamlet,' said Ronnie as Hamlet returned with the stick for the umpteenth time, not so much carrying it as dragging it along the beach. 'You are officially a dog.' Ronnie winced as a bead of sweat trickled into his eye. 'I think that's enough fetch for today,' he said. 'Let's go and find the others.'

He looked down at the spot where Hamlet had been standing just a few seconds earlier, but Hamlet was no longer there. Remembering how their last disastrous trip to the beach had panned out, his heart did a little somersault before he realised that Hamlet was not once again attempting to doggy paddle to Norway. He was, if anything, doing something much more bizarre than that. He was standing next to Ronnie, not just near him, but right beside him, inches from his shoes.

'Well, this is interesting,' said Ronnie quietly to himself. He stood as still as he could, not wanting to scare Hamlet away with any sudden movements. 'Have I passed the test? Is that what this means? Have I been approved? Or do you just have heatstroke?'

Deciding that it was now or never, Ronnie slowly lowered his hand until his fingers grazed the tips of Hamlet's fur. He remained like that for a moment so that Hamlet had ample time to express his disapproval in whichever way he saw fit, whether it be by barking, biting or spontaneously combusting. When Hamlet did none of those things, Ronnie lowered his hand further until his palm lay flat on Hamlet's back. Hamlet watched him but didn't protest.

'Wow,' said Ronnie, surprised by how smooth and silky Hamlet's coat was. He might have looked like a toilet brush, but his fur was as soft as a watercolour brush. 'Have you been using conditioner? You've got hair like a Vidal Sassoon advert.'

It was only then that Ronnie realised what was going on. Hamlet wasn't trying to make friends. Or perhaps he was, albeit indirectly. That wasn't his primary motivation for wanting to be close to Ronnie, though. His primary motivation for wanting to be close to Ronnie was so he could use Ronnie's shadow to shelter himself from the sun.

Ronnie stared at his silhouette on the beach, the sight of it both oddly strange and oddly familiar.

'Hello darkness, my old mate,' he said with a smile. 'Nice of you to join us.'

Ronnie knew that his shadow might not be there when he woke up tomorrow. He knew that it might never come back again after today. But it was there now. They all were, and that was all that mattered.

Acknowledgements

A big thanks to the following people:

Joanna Swainson, the best agent a writer could have; the entire team at Hardman & Swainson for being so bloody brilliant; Lucy Brem, Sam Eades and everybody at Orion; Phillip and Linda Gould-Bourn and Bill and Stella Valentino, for your love, support and encouragement during a very crappy couple of years; Jarrod Gould-Bourn and Sarra Szmit, for the comic relief; Greg Lovell, for reading an early draft of this novel and for letting me grumble about the writing process; and finally, thank you to my wife, Vanessa Valentino. The first draft of *Lost & Found* was written during lockdown, and if there's one thing worse than being stuck indoors for months on end, it's being stuck indoors for months on end with a writer. Thanks for putting up with me, and thanks for always making me laugh, intentionally or otherwise.

Credits

James Gould-Bourn and Orion Fiction would like to thank everyone at Orion who worked on the publication of *Lost & Found* in the UK.

Editorial
Lucy Brem
Sam Eades
Suzanne Clarke

Copyeditor
Francine Brody

Proofreader
Jade Craddock

Audio
Paul Stark
Jake Alderson

Contracts
Anne Goddard
Dan Herron
Ellie Bowker

Design
Rachael Lancaster
Joanna Ridley
Nick May

Editorial Management
Charlie Panayiotou
Jane Hughes
Bartley Shaw
Tamara Morriss

Finance
Jasdip Nandra
Nick Gibson
Sue Baker

Comms
Alainna Hadjigeorgiou

Operations
Jo Jacobs
Sharon Willis

Production
Ruth Sharvell

Sales
Jen Wilson
Esther Waters
Victoria Laws
Toluwalope Ayo-Ajala
Rachael Hum
Anna Egelstaff
Sinead White
Georgina Cutler

If you loved *Lost & Found*, don't miss
James Gould-Bourn's hilarious and uplifting
debut novel . . .

KEEPING MUM

Danny Malooley's life is falling apart.

He's a single parent with an eleven-year-old son,
Will, who hasn't spoken since the death of his
mother in a car crash fourteen months ago. Struggling
to find work, and desperate for money, Danny
decides to do what anyone in his position would do.

He becomes a dancing panda.

He spends his last fiver on a costume, but the humil-
iation is worth it when Will finally speaks to him for
the first time since his mother's death. The problem
is Will doesn't know that the panda is his father, and
Danny doesn't want to reveal his true identity in case
Will stops talking again.

But Danny can't keep up the ruse forever . . .

AVAILABLE TO BUY NOW